THE AMNESIAC'S GUIDE TO ESPIONAGE

DAVE SINCLAIR

EVA DESTRUCTION IS BACK!

Eva is an MI6 agent who wakes to find armed men in her apartment hell-bent on revenge. The only problem is, she has no idea what they're talking about. Someone has stolen the last sixth months' worth of her memories and the fate of the world rides on getting them back.

On the eve of the G8 summit, Eva is thrown headlong into globe-trotting assassinations and gun battles on the trail of the mysterious plan known only as Halcyon. Together with a besotted CIA agent and a misogynistic MI6 operative, Eva races across the world to retrace her steps in the hopes of finding answers.

With the clock ticking, Eva must track down those behind her memory loss, as well as battle a foe she can't remember. The globetrotting takes her from London, to exotic Macau casinos, to Hong Kong hydrofoils, to French castles, to English mansions, to a car chase between an ice-cream van containing a nuclear weapon and black SUVs through the streets of London.

With betrayal at every turn, Eva discovers she can't trust anyone, including her own organisation. Eva must face down nuclear annihilation alone and she hasn't even had her coffee yet.

For the G-Mob

CHAPTER ONE

Eva was a spy with a problem. Two problems, actually. First, she'd just woken up in desperate need of a coffee. Second, there were four armed men in her bedroom. The former was more concerning than the latter.

The black-clad soldiers armed with short-barrelled Heckler & Koch UMPs and Kevlar vests weren't helping her headache. These boys weren't here to steal her TV.

Dappled light supplied just enough illumination to show crouched figures invading her bedroom. Weapons swept her apartment for threats. They needn't have bothered. There was only one, and she had a hangover.

Eva sat up in bed and her head throbbed in protest. What the hell had she drunk the night before?

Focus, she told herself. There were more pressing matters.

She stretched under her Aerosmith tank top. All four submachine guns retargeted at her. Eva rolled her tongue in an attempt to lubricate her parched mouth.

"Hey. Either you blokes have the wrong apartment or Mormons are getting way too aggressive," she croaked.

The lead assailant stepped forward, his weapon pointed very

clearly between her eyes. His close-cropped grey haircut was so sharp it looked military issued. He must have been in his late fifties, but fit – his muscles bulged under his armour. Eva dubbed him Captain Flat-top. The other men appeared slightly older, but all acted like they'd just marched off a parade ground somewhere.

"No, Ms Destruction. We have the right apartment, and you'll be meeting whatever god you like very shortly."

The accent was English with a slight Manchester twang. So, not from Utah then.

He was talking, that was a good sign. Eva needed answers. She directed her question to Captain Flat-top.

"So if you're not here to spread the word of God, what's this all about?"

Eva thought she was rather calm, given the circumstances. This wasn't the first time she'd had armed men burst into her bedroom. It was probably the third. Fourth? *How depressing is that?* She really needed to re-evaluate her life choices.

Captain Flat-top sneered at her like she was week-old milk. "You know why we're here."

Eva racked her foggy brain. She really didn't. Should she? She'd done a lot of bad things in her life but had always managed to remember them. Man, had she drunk tequila last night? It had always been her downfall. She hadn't had the fortitude for the stuff since a particularly drunken night in Playa del Carmen with an ex whose name she no longer mentioned; partially because he was the one who used to send armed goons into her bedroom. But he'd been locked away in a very deep hole for a year now, so who'd sent these guys?

Eva shook her head to dislodge thoughts of exes past. Bad idea. The headache doubled down. She breathed out slowly, righting herself.

"Alright then, if I'm to be executed in my underwear can you at least let me know why you're going to shoot a lowly coffee-shop owner?"

Captain Flat-top actually scoffed. "Ms Destruction, we both

know you're much more than that. I would have thought working for MI6 would warrant a mention before coffee-shop girl."

So, they were well-informed pushy Mormon terrorists, then.

"Don't be so quick to judge, you haven't tasted my coffee." Her attempt at levity had zero effect. She folded her arms. "I'm more of a barista than Jane Bond."

Captain Flat-top sighed, seeming bored with the conversation. "You know why we're here."

"I really don't."

His jaw tightened, as did the grip on his weapon. "You have to pay for screwing us over like this. You had to know this was coming."

"Look, in the immortal words of many inept boyfriends, I had no idea it was coming." Her reply was met with blank stares, also reminiscent of early boyfriends. "I really have no idea what you're on about, fellas."

"We'll make it quick if you tell us where you sent the shipment."

"Shipment of what?"

"This is your last chance. Tell us where you sent it and this will be over in a second. You don't, we'll be here for hours, and believe me, you'll be begging for the sweet release of death."

Eva sniffed indifferently. She had nothing to add. Especially for anyone who used the cliché "sweet release of death". Playing dumb went against every instinct she had—she never downplayed her intelligence. Unfortunately, in this instance she didn't even have the option.

Despite their adamance, Eva didn't have the foggiest idea what they were on about. What had gone so wildly wrong to send this shit tornado into her home? Whatever the answer was, that was a question for another time. Eva had already moved on to Plan B.

A grunt from Captain Flat-top. "Fine". He cocked his weapon.

What sort of twat enters a hostile arena with an unready weapon? Maybe these guys were more show than she thought.

She cracked her neck. "Whatever. I have a splitting headache, you'll be doing me a favour. Can I at least put on some pants before you shoot me?"

A glance at Captain Flat-top's compatriots didn't prompt an answer.

Eva let out an exasperated sigh. "Dudes. Grant a girl a dying wish that she doesn't cark it in her undies. It's undignified."

"Cark it?"

"It means to die." Eva pushed herself up. "I can pop out and grab an Australian–English dictionary if you like." She gestured at the door with her thumb.

Captain Flat-top pushed her roughly back onto the bed. "I don't think so." His face hardened like six-week-old playdough.

"Last chance." Captain Flat-top took a step closer. "Tell us what you know and we'll make this quick."

"Sweetie, what I know would make your hair curl."

Captain Flat-top didn't seem to find this amusing.

Her stalling tactics were working, though. Eva had the basis of a plan in her murky brain. Well, more of a plan-ette. Plan-lite.

They hadn't fired on her; that meant she was valuable alive, at least in the short term. That gave her an advantage. A very slight one.

"So, can I put on some pants or what?"

An indifferent motion to the end of the bed was her only reply. Taking this as confirmation, she slid along the bed towards the significant pile of clothes on the floor. Or, as Eva preferred to call it, the floordrobe. She wasn't what you would call a domestic goddess.

From this new vantage point Eva was better able to assess the four men. Her foggy mind was finally starting to become clear, as was her Plan B. She pointed directly at Captain Flat-top.

"One."

"One what?"

She smiled dismissively. "Oh, nothing." Eva turned to the man behind him, did some mental arithmetic, then under her breath muttered, "Two."

The men shifted on their feet uncertainly. Eva continued to do calculations in her head. Her bedroom became a chessboard, the assailants oblivious chess pieces.

A redheaded guy at the back, built like an overstuffed He-Man, moved cautiously to his left. Eva clicked her fingers and pointed to where he had been standing. With a puzzled expression he obediently wandered back to his original position.

"What are you doing?" Captain Flat-top tilted his head.

"Planning." She pointed at the redhead. "Karate, I assume, from your stance?"

He shook his head slightly. "Taekwondo."

"Okay, cool. Three."

She turned to the last of the four, a nasty piece of work with a nose so flat he was either a bungling rugby player or someone who'd had an exceptionally hard life. With a slanted grin he stared at her tats. Or something with a similar spelling.

Eva managed to deliver the first syllable of "Four" before Flat Face interrupted.

"I ain't going fourth in anything." He extracted a combat knife from his vest. "Like he said," he motioned to Captain Flat-top, "you don't give us what we need, we'll be taking our sweet time." He made a slow slicing motion aimed at her torso. "And I won't be getting no sloppy seconds."

Eva was horrified at the threat, but didn't react. She wouldn't give him the satisfaction. No man was allowed to see her vulnerable, especially this one.

Eva pointed at Flat Face and with a determined, unwavering voice said, "And four, you strap-on wearing shitgibbon."

Flat Face's face filled with rage but before he could take a step forward, Captain Flat-top yelled, "Stay where you are!" In a calmer voice, he added, "Don't complicate this."

Eva leaned down to retrieve her jeans. Captain Flat-top inched forward, within striking distance.

"No more chances, darlin'. Where did the shipment go?"

"No, this is your last chance to get the fuck out of my apartment unless you want to wind up with a face like him," she said.

"You really are a stupid cow, aren't you?" Flat Face spat.

5

"Halcyon can't happen unless she tells us," Captain Flat-top countered. "Let me handle this."

Flat Face tucked his knife away. "We're wasting time here. We need to get on with it."

"I know, idiot." Captain Flat-top shook his head. "I'm using threats to speed things up."

Flat Face shook his head. "Yeah, they're working brilliantly. The bitch looks terrified."

"Could you just..." Captain Flat-top used a hand to point to Eva.

She wrapped her hands around the cuff of her jeans. "Hate to interrupt this witty repartee, but it seems we're at an impasse. We may as well get the show started."

"What show?"

"This one."

Eva looped her jeans over Captain Flat-top's head and yanked hard. His head thrust forward, directly into Eva's waiting knee. Nose met kneecap with a nauseating pop, and his skull bounced back, spurting blood in an arc. He collapsed motionless on the floor.

Eva exhaled. "One."

The rest of them were momentarily stunned.

Eva wasn't. Using the first assailant's body as a vault, she leapt up and connected the ball of her foot with number two's nasal cavity. A second sickening crunch told her those hours of Krav Maga had paid off.

"Two."

She rolled towards her third target, the redheaded taekwondo expert. As her hand hit the ground, she picked up the nearest object. She threw the bra in the air, and while his eyes focused on the frilly black item, she picked up her hefty metal jewellery case and launched it at his head. By the time she heard the cry of pain and the thud of his fallen body she was already on to her next victim.

"Three."

That was where her plan fell apart. The last assailant, Flat Face, was out of position and ready for her. He didn't seem too pleased she'd taken out all three of his comrades in as many seconds.

Up to this point she'd been spared because they needed information. Having taken out the majority of the squad, Eva had to accept that all bets were now off.

In the corner of her eye, she spotted what appeared to be a samurai sword sitting on her bookshelf. She didn't own a samurai sword. Never had. Yet there it was, sitting on a stand. Had the armed goons brought it with them? To paraphrase *The Untouchables*, who the hell brings a sword to a gun fight?

In the split second she had, Eva realised she was facing off against an angry, armed, muscled thug – any weapon would do. The sword was likely ornamental, and duller than an accountant's Christmas party, but she didn't have a lot of options. She grabbed the hilt and flicked her arm straight. The scabbard flung off the end of the sword and flew across the room, aimed directly at the last remaining threat. He ducked, but too late. The scabbard glanced off his skull. It was far from a mortal blow, but it was enough.

The distraction bought Eva enough time to leap into the air, the ornamental sword held high above her head. As her feet landed before the hulking assailant, Eva brought the sword down with every ounce of strength she possessed. The blade sliced through his left hand like it was warm butter.

Flat Face collapsed, dropping his weapon, and clutched his now severed limb as it spurted blood into the air. His scream was the most pitiful Eva had ever heard.

So, the sword wasn't ornamental, then.

Eva sucked in gasps of air as agonising moans swelled about the room.

That wasn't the worst thing though.

She still didn't have a coffee.

Eva watched as the last stretcher was carried out her front door. It had been quite the morning. Police, MI5 and MI6 agents had been crammed into her tiny apartment. It hadn't been this crowded since her last New Year's Eve party. Probably the same number of cops had turned up to both.

As soon as she'd taken out the last assailant, she'd called Paul. He'd been one of her closest friends for ages, and about a year ago had become her MI6 handler. Paul had arrived within minutes, along with Bishop, an MI6 operative Eva had worked with before. He was also a friend. Of sorts. In the rare times he wasn't spouting innuendo-laden jibes, Bishop could actually be quite pleasant. Unfortunately, those times were few and far between.

The cops had wanted to take her jeans as evidence, but she'd talked them out of it. They were her only clean pair. She'd given her statement several times over. Once to Paul and Bishop, then to the local cops, then again to MI5's Security Service in case the incident was terrorist related. She was getting sick of her own voice. Thankfully, Bishop had corralled the various agencies and given Eva some time to collect her thoughts. Of which she had many.

By the time the last ambulance left, MI5 had already been and gone. The majority of the police had left once they'd bagged up all the weapons. Only Paul, Bishop, Eva and a couple of cops remained.

"Should I have put it in milk?" Eva asked, sipping her third cup of coffee. "I read that somewhere, I think."

"Put what in milk?" Paul asked.

"The hand. Aren't you meant to put it in milk to preserve it?"

"Pretty sure that's only for teeth, Evie."

"Oh, right." Eva glanced at Bishop. "Hey, if it's not too much trouble, could you put my bra down, please?"

Bishop scowled. "It's all evidence, Eva."

"Evidence of what?"

"Evidently I had misjudged your cup size."

"You really are a sexist pig, aren't you?"

Bishop tutted. "Darling, not in front of the children."

The two cops shook their heads, gave Eva their cards and left. Suddenly her place seemed huge.

Retrieving her phone from the nightstand, Eva saw that she

had a text message. When she opened it, she saw that the message was addressed to someone called "Chérie" and seemed to convey a series of sex acts, depicted in emoticons. Huh. And people said romance was dead.

Paul put his hand on her shoulder. "If you're up to it, we can go to headquarters. You were due to give us the briefing anyway, so we may as well keep that appointment, and you can give the department a rundown of this instead."

"What briefing?"

"Are you sure you didn't take a blow to the head?"

"Pretty sure." Eva rummaged around in her floordrobe for her thickest coat and put it on. "I'm fine, really. Just a bit of a sore head. Woke up with a cracker of a headache. I'll be fine."

She wrapped a scarf around her neck. Finding one glove but not the other, she tossed the lone glove on the floor.

Bishop frowned. "Why are you dressed like that?"

"Oi, that's quite enough," she said heading out in to the hall. "Not all of us can dress like we just walked off a catwalk in Milan. Some of us have mortgages."

"No, I mean—"

"Let's get on with it," Eva interrupted, and headed for the front door.

She glanced behind her. Paul and Bishop had followed her into the hall and were staring at her, their faces etched with concern.

"I'm fine, guys, really."

She yanked open the door. Instead of the icy blast she had expected, she was hit by what seemed like a wave of mid-summer heat. Across the street, children ran around the park in t-shirts. A woman wearing a sundress strolled along, holding hands with a man dressed in shorts.

Eva felt nauseous. She grabbed the door handle to steady herself. This wasn't December weather. Well, it would be, back home in Melbourne, but definitely not in London. *What is going on?*

"Evie, are you alright?"

She shook her head, dread seeping into her skin. "I was… it's not winter, is it?"

Paul shook his head. "What's the last thing you remember?"

"Um, last night, you, me and Nancy coming home from that shitty little club in Soho. Your wife needs to accept she doesn't have the metabolism for hard liquor anymore. No matter how hard she tries, she's not Patti LaBelle."

Paul stared at her with concern.

Eva didn't like that look. At all. "What?"

"That wasn't last night."

"It wasn't? It bloody well seems like it."

"Evie," Paul took a deep breath, "that was six months ago."

CHAPTER TWO

Eva stared out the window of the chauffer-driven government car, but couldn't tell what suburb she was in. Everything was a blur.

How could she have lost months of memories? Was it somehow tied to the goons breaking into her bedroom? What couldn't she remember?

One thing was for sure, she wanted those memories back.

"Anything?" Paul asked hopefully.

"Still donuts." Eva gave him a sad smile. "Which is quite apt, seeing as I appear to have a big hole in the middle of my mind."

Paul and Bishop had tried to jog her memory about briefings, missions, training, personal memories. As far as she could tell, she had all her memories up until mid-December. Eva never really liked Christmas.

"You can't just slice out six months from someone's head, surely? The human brain is far more complex than that."

"It's not really," Bishop mumbled to himself.

Eva poked him with her foot. "What was that?"

"Oh, ah, nothing. I mean, well, it is something, obviously."

"You're babbling. That means you're hiding something, Bishop."

"Marvellous observation, Ms Destruction. You really should look into espionage."

"And there goes the evasion. Alright, Pretty Boy, spill."

"Alright, fine. It's something the boffins on the fifth floor have been toying with for some time. Based on a study at Johns Hopkins, I believe. By removing a particular protein in a specific part of the brain, they think they can remove memories at a molecular level." When Paul and Eva gawked at him blankly, he added, "Apparently. Not sure they've actually tested it in the field."

"So it's possible people have been fiddling with my brain?"

"Either that or someone hit you with a frying pan," Bishop deadpanned. "But if they did interfere, it was done quite recently."

"What makes you say that?"

"Roll up your sleeve."

Eva did. On the inside of her elbow was a slight yellow mark, and a small scab where a needle had punctured her skin.

"Unless you've given blood recently, I'd say someone's cracked open your skull—metaphorically—and done some messing about."

Eva gave an approving frown. "Good observation, Bishop."

"Why, thank you. I noticed it while you were changing."

"See, now it's good but also creepy."

"That's me all over."

"If you two could stop flirting for a moment," Paul interjected, "this is serious, Evie. The Foreign Secretary will need to know about this."

"Freddie's gonna fucking love this."

Eva noticed Paul wince. Apparently it was disrespectful to refer to His Majesty's Principal Secretary of State for Foreign and Commonwealth Affairs, responsible for matters pertaining to ministerial oversight for the intelligence arms of the United Kingdom government, as "Freddie". Australians, never having had a class system, always had a hard time adhering to anyone else's. Eva decided not to tell Paul she also occasionally referred to Lady Kensington, an ex-Royal Navy woman, as Rear Admiral Fuckchop—to her face.

The car slowed and the din of shouting pierced even the heavily fortified Range Rover. About 50 metres ahead, the tops of placards could be seen above the cars. A large number of people were clearly angry about something.

Paul shifted in his seat. "Damn, I was hoping we'd have missed this."

"What is it?" Eva asked.

"They're protesting China," Paul said, squinting off into the distance.

"Why are they protesting China? They make all our stuff. It's like protesting Tesco."

"Where have you been?"

Eva issued an incredulous face.

"Sorry." Paul's features crumpled into a conciliatory arrangement. "They're protesting the proposed amendment to include China in the G8. Mostly because of human rights abuses, the recent aggression in the South China Sea and, well, basically, their failure to accord with the democratic principles enshrined in the original statement at Rambouillet on the founding of the G6 in 1975." Paul stopped when he saw Eva tilt her head with a smirk. "Sorry. I've prepared a few briefs."

Paul went up front to confer with the driver. Eva's phone vibrated, so she took it out of her pocket. Another message for "Chérie".

"What's that?" Bishop asked. "A secret admirer?"

"He's an admirer, alright, just not mine. And he's obviously an old-fashioned romantic, given his apparent yearning for the reverse cowgirl. And they say the young kids don't know how to woo anymore."

Bishop leaned over to examine her phone. "Are you sure it's not for you, given…" he pointed to his head.

"Not unless I changed my name to Chérie recently. I'm guessing some chick gave this guy a dud number at a club."

"The crowd's thinning," Paul advised, sitting back down. "We'll be through in a few minutes."

"As reluctant as I am to steer the conversation away from reverse cowgirls," Bishop began.

"What now?" Paul asked.

"… there's still the matter of your memory loss," Bishop continued. "Is this something we wish to advise all and sundry of, or should we keep it under our bowlers until we know what caused it?"

"Good question." Paul scratched his ever-increasing bald spot. "It might be worth keeping the memory loss to ourselves until we've had you assessed by our lead physician. We don't know who or what we're dealing with here; best to keep a few cards in reserve." Paul checked his watch. "The briefing is set for ten. You ready, Evie?"

"Not even in the slightest."

∿

The room was packed. Every meeting room at MI6 had a small plaque advising the room's capacity. This room's maximum occupancy was twenty. Eva counted thirty-six people in there. Not including herself.

For the past hour she'd recounted the events of the morning. She'd stuck to the facts as she knew them. Furious notes were taken, but thankfully interruptions were kept to a minimum. Much to her horror, photos were shown of her apartment. She hoped most people assumed the mess was due to the scuffle, not her lack of aptitude for the domestic sciences.

After the third time she'd gone through her story, Paul thanked her and opened the room to questions. Eva slumped in a chair next to Bishop. He took a sip from his glass and gave her a reassuring nod.

A dark-haired man at the back of the room coughed to get Paul's attention, then raised his hand. He wore a well-fitted suit, exuded confidence and reeked of bad decisions. Just Eva's type.

"Firstly, I want to thank Agent Destruction for her time today. I know the events of this morning could not have been easy, and I think her stoicism and fortitude deserve to be recognised before we move on."

He was American, too.

"And you are?" Eva asked, cringing inwardly as she did so. For all she knew they'd worked together for months.

"Hopeless at croquet," he said. "Loch Davenport, CIA liaison."

"Thank you, Mr Loch Davenport CIA. And what is your question?"

"Has Scotland Yard identified the perpetrators yet?"

Paul fielded that one. "We'll circulate an updated briefing pack, but the latest from the Yard as of an hour ago was that the assailants have not been forthcoming with their names, nor was there anything identifying on their person. The investigation is obviously continuing."

Eva still had a hard time getting used to her goofy friend being all official. This Paul was a million miles away from the vague, lovable oaf who'd married her friend Nancy years before. It was only recently that she found out he worked for MI6, and not the Treasury as he'd always claimed. She trusted Paul with her life—literally—and had done so several times over.

"If I may, a question," came a posh voice from the back of the room. The man sounded less like he had a plum in his mouth and more like he'd swallowed the whole orchard.

"Yes, Burlington?" Paul said, his tone indicating that Burlington wasn't one of his favourite people.

Eva thought Burlington seemed like the poster boy for private school twats. MI6 had once been the playground of the privileged few, but after some astute observers pointed out that inbreeding was perhaps not the most effective way to propagate success, the organisation had opened its hiring practices. Regardless, some traditions still prevailed, as evidenced by Mr Foppish Hair.

"Thank you. If I may, Miss Destruction, can you take us back to your methodology for taking down the armed intruders?"

Paul sighed heavily. "She has already covered that in detail, Nigel."

"Yes, but I'd like her to repeat it. I have some doubts."

"Doubts?" Eva asked, not trying to hide her resentment. "What doubts?"

"Well, look at you. You're a mere slip of a girl..."

"She is a highly trained operative of His Majesty's Secret Service, Mr Burlington," Paul said, again making little effort to hide his disdain. "Agent Destruction has shown her aptitude multiple times in the field, unlike some others in this room, which prompts me to ask if you actually have a point?"

Burlington wasn't thrown by the challenge. In fact, it appeared to have buoyed him. "Thank you, Mr Cavendish, but what I want to know is—and I mean this with the utmost respect to Miss Destruction—is it possible the kung-fu fest we've just been regaled with, which would have been a hard ask for an experienced SAS soldier, let alone some Johnny-come-lately girl, was somewhat misrepresented? I mean to say, this isn't a movie, and women spies have their place, but we're not running a honey pot here." There was silence. "Oh come on, it was a joke. Just some banter."

Instead of launching into a full-scale counter-attack, Eva took a moment to process what had just happened. This was MI6, not a pub meeting for some men's rights movement. That sort of attitude should have been flushed out long ago. Bishop's constant comments, while thoroughly sexist, came from a good place and was more smartarse than outright chauvinism. Eva and Bishop were friends, had been in harrowing situations together, and he respected her. In short, he was all talk and they both knew it.

Burlington's comments were nothing of the sort. He'd essentially accused her of being a prostitute.

"Banter, yes. It's a good word, isn't it, 'banter'? Or to put it another way, 'I'm gender-based bullying you, but don't you dare call me on it because we're only having fun, right?'"

Eva thought it was a well-made point. Only, she hadn't made it. She gawped at the beardy Loch Davenport, who wasn't quite finished.

"It's basically code for 'I'm a man and obviously more important than you, so I'm entitled to make you feel uncomfortable, being a man and all. And as a man, I make the rules about language and your place, and don't you dare question it. I determine what's funny because that's what us chaps do. So I'm going to call it banter and you'll live with it, because I'm a man and I hold the power.'"

Burlington certainly got the point. His face had dropped down a few notches on the smug scale. Davenport sipped his coffee, evidently pleased at his eloquent take-down. Eva noted that the coffee was from Kanga Brew—her café.

Keen to move on, Paul asked, "Are there any intelligent questions?"

Nobody answered, and people began shutting folders and laptops. Chairs were pushed out, mild chatter started up.

From the back of the room, in a loud whisper, Burlington said, "He probably wants to wind it up so he can examine her in private."

There were a few snickers. Eva had heard the rumours about her and Paul. She understood them; they were so close, and no one knew of their previous relationship. The talk had never bothered Eva, but she hated that a twat like Burlington would use it as some sort of snide weapon against her friend.

Paul was Head Spec Ops, a senior member of SIS, second-generation MI6. His father had put his life on the line, and was executed as a spy in Warsaw in 1982. Against all logic, Paul had followed in his footsteps and joined MI6, far exceeding the achievements of his father. A sexist jab at her was one thing, but for that snivelling toad to question Paul's professionalism flicked Eva's switch.

She stood, knocking over her chair in the process.

"Mr Burlington, I believe you made a remark?"

There was no missing the smug expression on his prattish face. "Who, me? Just a bit of banter." He virtually spat the last word.

Both Bishop and Davenport rose from their chairs, but Eva didn't need any white knights.

"That's your game, isn't it? If anyone disagrees with your lordship, you mock them or belittle them."

"Seems like everyone wants to psychoanalyse me today. I must truly be fascinating."

"Oh, you are fascinating alright—like a fungus or a poisonous spore—but don't think for one second that makes you a valuable human being. And later, when you're cry-wanking about how girls won't talk to you, know that I'll be here dismantling the patriarchy, you incomprehensible jizz-trumpet."

The room was deathly silent. For a moment Eva thought they were staring at her, mouths open, mesmerised by her razor sharp verbal joust. But then she realised their gaze was directed slightly to her right. She glanced behind her to see an extremely well-dressed woman with a bouncy bob wearing a conservative pantsuit. Of course the appearance of the Foreign Secretary would have that effect on people.

Eva was sure nobody in the room was breathing. She certainly wasn't.

"I was worried about you Eva, but it seems I needn't have been. Same as always, then?"

Eva gave her a wink. "Nothing I can't handle."

"I'm assured that goes for most things."

Eva and Lady Winifred Kensington, or Freddie, had a history. It dated back to when Eva first started at MI6. She'd been outside a meeting room, waiting to take another test on counter-terrorism theory, when a phalanx of blue-suited white men ambled past, the Foreign Secretary at its centre. Freddie had just made a wildly incorrect remark about Russian troop numbers in the Baltic. Completely against protocol, Eva had corrected her. Seeing the reactions of the men around her, Eva had half expected her fledgling spy career to end right then and there. Thankfully, Lady Winifred Kensington was not as stuffy as her name suggested. She stopped and asked Eva to clarify and she'd done just that, tactfully and articulately.

The answer had impressed Freddie so much she'd invited Eva to lunch, much to the horror of every man in the hallway. In her private dining room in the MI6 building, the minister and Eva had covered many topics, ranging from the current administration's

Asian diplomatic policy to 1980s Australian rock bands. Freddie had told Eva she reminded her of her late daughter, who had been killed in a terrorist attack while attending school in France. From then on, whenever possible, Freddie looked Eva up when she visited MI6, and followed her career with great interest. Perhaps Eva could ask her what she'd been up to lately, given that Eva herself had no idea.

Most attendees at the meeting quietly shuffled out, with only a handful remaining. Eva gave the minister a condensed version of the morning's events, and she responded with a hearty laugh.

"They picked the wrong Australian this time, didn't they?"

"Not really, you'd get the same response from most Aussies. That's why we continually kick your arse at cricket."

"Dream on, Eva, dream on. We'll wipe the floor with you come the Ashes."

"Wiping our floors, you mean."

Freddie shook Eva's hand. "I'm glad you're alright. Please let me know if there is anything I can do."

"Thanks, I appreciate it, Rear Admiral F... Rear, uh, Freddie, ah, Foreign Minister."

With a curt bob of the head, she was gone. Paul said he was late for a meeting dashed off, suggesting Eva could come by his office after lunch to see 'the gentleman we spoke of earlier'. Eva assumed he meant the physician.

Bishop had a 'thing' and disappeared just as quickly, leaving Eva alone in the room with Davenport. He sat, arms folded, on the edge of the conference table, a sly grin playing on his lips.

He pushed himself up and shut one door before crossing the room and closing the other. Then, with the prowl of a particularly self-assured leopard, he approached Eva, stopping mere centimetres from her face. Eva could feel his sweet breath.

"You're awfully close, Mr Davenport."

"I suppose I am. Do you know what else I am, Agent Destruction?"

"No, what?"

"Ravenous."

One hand slid slowly around her waist while the other glided gently along her face. In an instant, his lips were on hers. She should have punched him. That, after all, would be her first reaction to an uninitiated advance. But for all Eva knew, she had initiated this advance. He kissed her with all the passion of a lover. Eva pushed him away slowly, almost reluctantly.

He seemed not to notice the rebuff, and gazed into her eyes. "I've missed you, Chérie."

"What now?"

She was Chérie? Why Chérie? So many questions. Mainly to do with what salacious acts had performed with this stunning American man. And whether there were pictures of those encounters that she could peruse at her leisure.

She had to commend Past Eva's taste. He was bloody gorgeous, and willing to stand up for feminist ideals in a public forum, too. That was a lethal combination for her. Eva eyed the boardroom table. It certainly appeared sturdy. She wondered how long the meeting room was booked for.

But wiser heads prevailed. She didn't have the foggiest idea who he was. Which was a shame. After that kiss, she'd really like to find out. When she'd agreed to keep her memory loss a secret she hadn't realised that meant potential lovers.

"Sorry, I just had to kiss you," he said. "All I could think about during that meeting was holding you in my arms. Are you sure you're okay?"

"I'm fine, thank you... Loch."

"Jesus, I don't think you've ever called me that. Do you need a lie down?"

"Me? Ah, no. All good." Eva played with her hair. "I'm just tired, you know? Punching blokes is harder than it looks on the telly."

"Hmmm, about that..."

"Yes?"

"Just between you and me, that briefing wasn't one hundred per cent accurate."

"The bit about Burlington being a jizz-trumpet totally was."

"Oh, completely. No, I mean the part about not knowing the identities of your attackers."

"What?"

"Eva, you need to be careful. Those men in your apartment today weren't random thugs or extremists or anything they're likely to throw your way. They were all ex-British Special Forces."

"How do you know that?"

He held up his security pass and pointed to the part that said CIA.

"What do British ex-special forces have against one little Australian? I mean, sure, we gave them Jason Donovan and Rolf Harris, but come on. AC/DC and Hugh Jackman more than made up for it."

"That's not all."

"It's not enough?"

"Scotland Yard no longer have them. Actually, as far as we can ascertain, no arm of the British government has them. They've all disappeared."

"Even Lefty?"

"Lefty?"

Eva made a sword cutting move to her wrist.

"Even Lefty, I believe."

"Bloody hell. Wait, you knew who they were, but still asked in the briefing?"

"In my line of work it's always advisable to know more than everyone else in the room."

"Including me?"

"Oh darlin', every time we get together I learn something new."

This time she didn't resist the kiss.

CHAPTER THREE

"Nothing?"

"Nothing."

Eva leaned back and folded her arms. "Can I just say how offensive it is that the two of you keep saying you detected nothing in a scan of my brain?"

In the confines of the small doctor's office, nobody smiled. Not Paul, and not the mysterious Dr Geiger, who had conducted three hours of tests on Eva. She didn't consider herself all that funny, but had at least expected a sympathetic smile.

When Paul introduced her, Dr Geiger was referred to simply as a "doctor". When she'd asked what kind of doctor, he had simply said, "One with several qualifications." What had followed were hours of cognitive tests, scans, blood tests, probing and prodding and a general sense that Eva was more medical cadaver than human being.

Apparently the MRI scan had proven "inconclusive". As had the physical examinations, bar the marks on her arm. According to the doctor, there had been several clumsy attempts to find a vein, indicating a general lack of clinical experience. That still didn't bring them any closer to why Eva had a hole in her mind.

"If this memory loss actually occurred as stated—" the doctor started.

Screw you, Eva thought.

"— then it was not an invasive procedure. There are no incisions near the cranium, nor anywhere else." He paused and directed a rare glance in Eva's direction. "Although the patient's, er, decorations, made the examination somewhat more laborious."

Poor widdle doctor had to work slightly harder to get past her countless tattoos to look for cuts or needle marks. *Diddums*. Dr Geiger was not going on her Christmas card list. Not that Eva had one. Although she might create one now, purely for the express purpose of not including the snooty doctor.

The doctor moved on to the blood tests. He held up a colourful chart with a myriad of chemical names that meant nothing to Eva. Paul let out a low whistle and wheeled his chair closer to examine it.

Doctor Geiger went on. "However, as you can see, Decamethonium was detected in your blood, indicating you were anaesthetised. And the fact that we were able to detect it within your bloodstream means it was administered recently—within the last forty-eight hours. The toxicity results also showed smaller traces of drugs consistent with anaesthesiology, as well as a myriad of others that, well, to be frank, reads like the floor of a chemistry lab after an earthquake."

Eva wasn't sure the analogy worked, but she got the gist. She had more drugs in her than the second night of Glastonbury. No wonder she woke up with the headache from hell.

The doctor continued. "Besides the chemical cocktail there are also extremely elevated levels of GluA1 protein, as well as calcium-permeable AMPAR proteins."

"Which means?" Eva asked.

"Someone's been tinkering with your noggin, Evie," Paul said with the sympathetic smile she'd been looking for.

Eva groaned. "Next time maybe you guys could lead with the bit where you say I'm not crazy."

~

Eva munched on her salad but was so distracted she didn't even know what kind it was. It probably had kale and quinoa and god knows what other crap. The MI6 cafeteria was big on healthy living. All Eva wanted was a greasy hamburger and chips. She munched away, feeling more cow than human, while she tried to remember anything from the last six months. Unfortunately, her mind kept returning to the near present—specifically, to that kiss. Despite her best efforts, her thoughts kept circling back to Loch Davenport. She absentmindedly ran her thumb over her lips.

What the hell was Past Eva thinking, getting involved with someone from the CIA? Well, Eva didn't know for sure, but she could make a reasonable guess. It most likely involved weekends away. And wine. Definitely wine. And most probably restraints of some sort.

Loch Davenport was unknown to her, but Eva was good at reading people and she could read him like metre-high brail. She couldn't believe she'd done it again: fallen for another mysterious, self-centred man. After her last disaster she'd promised herself she'd do better next time. There had even been a ritual involving letters, a fire and two bottles of vodka. The fire department wasn't officially part of the ceremony, but did lend a sense of drama to the event.

Apparently it had not been enough. So what made Loch Davenport so special? It wasn't like she'd been short on options. Eva was constantly being asked on dates by all sorts of men, from band members to button-up types wanting to unleash their inner bad boy. She could have fallen for Bishop's charms, and almost had, once—the two of them standing before each other, completely starkers, was indelibly etched in her memory. But she hadn't. So why Davenport? Hadn't she learned she deserved better?

Eva's thoughts were interrupted as a tailored silhouette crossed her field of vision and took a seat before her.

"You okay, Eva?" Bishop asked. "You look a million miles away."

"Me? No, all good." She sat straighter in her chair and pulled at her hair.

Her thoughts weren't a million miles away. More like three floors up.

Bishop smirked, making it clear he didn't believe a word of it but was willing to let it slide. He really was a handsome bastard. Trouble was, he knew it.

"Paul briefed me on the results. Seems you've had an interesting twenty-four hours."

"Or six months, for all I know."

"True. I can't believe you don't remember us sleeping together."

"We haven't slept together, Bishop."

"How do you know?" he asked, one eyebrow cocked.

"You're still talking to me."

Bishop grunted. "You do know Pepé Le Pew is a cartoon character, and not someone I've modelled my life on?"

She shovelled a forkful of green into her mouth. "You're like the gritty 21st century reboot. All attitude, action with a new origin story, but at your heart, you're still a womanising little skunk."

"If I'm Pepé Le Pew, can you be Jessica Rabbit?" Bishop tilted his head sideways and rolled his gaze over her body lasciviously.

With a click of Eva's fingers Bishop snapped out of it, and took a bite out of his salad wrap. It was quite decadent by Bishop's standards—he usually kept his carb intake to a minimum. The man treated his body like a temple. As did his many admirers.

"Do you need somewhere to stay?" he asked the table.

"Why would I?"

"Well, for one thing, a lot of your possessions are coated in blood. And for another, the whole place looks like a bomb site—"

Eva pursed her lips.

"— and finally, there's the possibility that visit wasn't the last."

The thought hadn't even occurred to her. She loved her apartment, it was part of her identity. The idea that it could be violated again, that it was no longer her sanctuary, made her feel ill. Although that might have been the quinoa.

"I'll just stay at Nancy and Paul's," she decided.

Nancy had been her best friend for years. They had gone through so much. While Eva had bounced from one terrible relationship to the next, Nancy had been her rock. Most people have one or two 3 am friends—those people you can call at any hour who won't think twice about picking up the phone and helping. Nancy was the kind who would jump in the car and pick up three bottles of wine on the way.

Bishop stared at her for the longest time. "I don't think... I don't think that's possible."

"Why not?"

He hesitated. "She's been busy. Ah, with work."

"It doesn't matter. That woman would give up her own bed for me, but the couch is just as comfy."

"Paul will be working late on the looming G8 summit, so..."

"That doesn't matter. I'll be fine at Nancy's." She eyed him with a smirk. "I have to say, that was a lot less subtle than your usual seduction techniques. You'll do anything to get me into your bed, won't you?"

Bishop's pretty face moulded into mock umbrage and he held up his hands like a preacher. Not an innocent one—more like a televangelist from the Deep South who embezzles funds and has five illegitimate children.

"Yes, I will. Although this time, it was never going to be *my* bed. I have a spare. On another floor. With a lock. You can use the leopard as protection."

"With you, leopard could mean an actual leopard or some kind of condom."

"Or both." His eyes twinkled. He glanced at his watch. "But in all seriousness, we better head up to Paul's office."

Eva happily tossed the rest of her salad in the rubbish and they headed for the lifts.

Also waiting for the lift was a young office worker who appeared too young for high school, but was apparently old enough for MI6. He beamed at Eva in a familiar way. She vaguely remembered him helping her to manipulate the computer system so she could submit timesheets after the deadline, among other computer issues. For the life of her, she couldn't remember his name.

He seemed constructed from parts of other, unrelated, human beings. Unwanted parts. His ears were too big, his arms too long for his slight fame, and his head seemed to have had an unfortunate run-in with a tribe of headshrinkers. She politely returned his smile, wondering if her confusion was due to her memory loss or the prevalence of pimply office workers.

"I've been listening to Jebediah."

Eva nodded, suspecting this was a continuation of a conversation she couldn't remember. She didn't know who Jebediah was. She vaguely recalled someone in Accounts with an old-school name.

"They're good, I like them. Mind you, half the time I can't understand a word the lead singer is saying."

Oh, the band Jebediah, Eva realised. She must have put this kid onto the indie Aussie band.

"Yeah, me either, but it doesn't matter. They're great live."

"We should go."

Bless your little cotton socks. "Don't think they tour much these days." Using an old technique from parties, where she frequently forgot people's names, she said, "This is Bishop."

The lift pinged and the doors opened. All three got in and Bishop gave her an odd expression as he extended his hand. The kid took it.

"Trevor." He dropped Bishop's hand quickly and turned his attention back to Eva. "How was Japan?" he asked eagerly.

"Japan? I've never be—" She stopped. Maybe she had been to Japan. That would explain the sword in her apartment. Was that the mission she was on? Eva forged on, "—een happier than with that... thing... in Japan. So yes. Good. It was good."

Trevor seemed happy with the response. He got out on the next floor, giving Eva a wave, like a lovesick schoolboy, as the doors closed.

Bishop leaned his head against the wall of the elevator and gazed up. "Smooth. You should be in MI6. Very surreptitious."

"Shut it, you."

The doors opened on Paul's floor and they entered his office without ceremony. He gave them a cup of tea without asking and told them to sit.

The room was exactly like Eva had always expected MI6 to be. Wood panelling, wet bar, large mahogany desk. All that was missing was a few flags and a picture of the king.

They engaged in a quick round of small talk, which Eva suspected was for her benefit. It was almost sweet. But mostly patronising.

Bishop poured milk into his tea. "Well, on the plus side, at least she doesn't remember Vienna."

"The thing with the midget?" Paul asked.

"Wait, what?" Eva was confused. Again.

"Can you still say midget?" Bishop asked.

"What's Vienna?"

"I'm pretty sure you can." Paul scratched his neck. "I think. Can't you?"

"I don't think so," Bishop replied.

"Guys, what happened in Vienna?"

Paul and Bishop replied in unison, "You don't want to know."

"No, I do. See, whenever anyone says you don't want to know, you definitely want to know. Guys, I want to know."

Paul harrumphed and sat at the end of his desk. "Another time, Evie." He stirred his tea. "We have our work cut out, people. We need to get to the bottom of this memory thing ASAP. The team is working on identifying the men who attacked you—"

"You mean finding them after they skipped out?" Eva interjected.

"How on God's bright pink Earth did you know that?" Paul asked in astonishment. "I was only informed five minutes ago."

Eva pointed to her face. "Spy."

"Yes, well, be that as it may, I want to keep this memory loss between us for the time being. There are only a few organisations in the world who've been playing around with memory wiping, and that includes us, so I'm not willing to take any chances." Paul took a sip of tea and went on. "We need to try and jog that memory of yours, see if there are any holes. We'll start tomorrow by going through your mission dossiers, see if that shakes anything loose."

"Like my mission to Japan?" Eva asked innocently.

"How do you know about that? Is your memory coming back?"

"No, but I work at MI6, I'm expected to find things out surreptitiously," Eva said with a grin.

She proceeded to scratch the back of her head and simultaneously gave Bishop the finger. Smirking, Bishop took a sip of his drink and shook his head. She drank her tea in quiet repugnance. It was no coffee substitute.

Paul put his cup down and asked, "Is there anything you failed to mention in the briefing? Anything at all? Especially in light of the memory loss. It doesn't matter how inconsequential you think it might be."

In spite of the tea, this was the most relaxed Eva had been all day. With her eyes closed, she went through the attack step by step. Then it hit her.

"There was a word they used."

"Yes?"

"Something about it can't happen without me telling them about the shipment."

"What couldn't happen?"

"I think the word they used was Halcyon."

The cup in Paul's hand stopped halfway to his mouth and stayed there for the longest time. His face was as expressionless as pure marble. He walked over to the tea set and topped up his cup, even though it didn't need a refill. He filled it almost to the brim, then took his seat.

Calmly, he said, "I'll need you to repeat that, and be as accurate as possible. What exactly did they say?"

"They said Halcyon couldn't happen without me telling them where the shipment, whatever that is, was. Did any of my missions involve shipping anything?"

Paul shook his head. "No. Which makes it even more baffling."

"So what is this Halcyon thing?" Bishop asked. "I've never heard of it."

"Oh, nothing of importance," Paul said, trying to appear innocent but failing miserably. That was why he was never a field agent —and a completely rubbish poker player. "Just ensure it doesn't leave this room. No one is to mention it or investigate it in any way, is that clear?"

"Yes, boss," chimed Eva and Bishop.

"It is vital that you keep Eva's memory loss and especially Halcyon to yourselves." Paul peered into his tea then pushed it away. His gaze drifted to the window and he seemed lost in thought. He glanced at the ornate clock on his desk, then at Eva. "You better get a move on, you've got a shift at the café."

She shook her head, about to ask why she should look in on her business when it clicked. "So that's still happening then?"

Paul dipped his head in confirmation.

"Bet you're glad I kept the café, huh?"

This was an obvious attempt at baiting. Even though she knew perfectly well Paul wouldn't bite, it was fun nonetheless. Anything for a moment of normalcy.

Eva eyed Bishop. "You coming?"

"No, just breathing heavy thinking about Jessica Rabbit." He eyed Eva up and down, then shook his head as if to dislodge the thought. "But alas, I have an appointment."

"Appointment?" When she saw his self-assured expression she asked, "I'm sure it's a very important business meeting?"

Straight-faced, Bishop responded, "Absolutely."

"Blonde or brunette?"

Opening his mouth in mock indignance, Bishop said, "I find the very thought of what you imply offensive, vulgar and a transgression on my very character."

"So a redhead, then?"

"And apparently an ex-gymnast at that."

"Bully for you."

Paul sighed. "Please leave my office." As Bishop and Eva stood, Paul added, "And Bishop, don't you owe me an expense report?"

Eva thought Bishop appeared sheepish when he replied, "I have nothing to claim but the love of my country."

Paul scoffed and bid them farewell. They left his office and stepped into the lift.

Bishop asked, "You sure you want to stay at Nancy's?"

"I'll be fine. Don't worry your pretty little head."

The elevator pinged at Bishop's floor. "Okay. Have fun. Send me nudes when you're there so I know you're safe."

"You're a bad boy, Bishop."

"And you're a bad girl, Ms Destruction. We make a good pair."

"I'm not bad, I'm just drawn that way." Eva shoved Bishop out of the elevator. "Say goodbye, Bishop."

"Goodbye, Bishop."

Alone in the lift Eva rolled the meeting with Paul around in her head. There were several things that didn't sit well with her. Despite Paul's best efforts to pretend otherwise, Halcyon was clearly important. Something big.

The sweet smell of freshly brewed coffee invigorated her like nothing else. Her café wasn't the busiest in London. It wasn't the biggest, either. But it was hers, and that was the most important thing. When she'd started at MI6 Paul had wanted Eva to give up the café, but he may as well have asked her to lop off a limb. Coffee was in her blood. Probably literally.

Paul's opinion changed when he realised Eva's café could serve another purpose. A clandestine one. Eva's café was close to the diplomatic quarter, and once MI6 discovered there was a large amount of traffic coming from various embassies, their attitude shifted. Kanga Brew was no longer a distraction from her duties, it was an essential part of her role. The café became an asset.

The place was busy, as usual. Behind the counter was the big lumbering hulk of a man called Anchor. He was a melange of a Goth, a laid-back skateboarder and the Swedish chef from the Muppets. Eva loved him to bits.

In recognition of her long absences and his dedication, Eva had invited him to be a partner in the café, an offer he had enthusiastically embraced. The man had always worked diligently, but now worked even harder. She had given him the opportunity, and in return he had shown a knack for business. They made a good team.

"Eva! I am very pleased to be seeing you!"

"I missed you too, you big lug." Eva gave him a hug. It felt like she hadn't seen him in weeks, but for all she knew it could have been more recent.

"Yes, that also too, but more important I have to take the wiz."

"You're sweet."

Anchor didn't answer but slipped out of his once-white apron and dashed towards the rear of the café so fast he could have made the Swedish Olympic team. In no time Eva was back in the swing, serving coffees and interacting with customers like she'd never left. It was exactly what she needed. For the next hour she was in her element, blissfully forgetting the events of the day.

Then Li Wei walked in.

Li Wei's official title was Cultural Attaché Sub-Supervisor Office of Cultural Affairs for the People's Republic of China. But that wasn't his role. He actually worked for the Ministry of State Security, the Chinese equivalent of MI6. Eva didn't know how he'd come to be sharing state secrets with the British government, that was well beyond her pay grade. What she did know was that if she wasn't present when he turned up, His Majesty's government could very well miss a vital piece of intelligence. She had never missed an intelligence drop yet. That she knew of.

Li Wei's suit wasn't flashy, nor was his haircut. There was nothing special about his features or his presence. He was the perfect spy. There was no show of recognition, nor any act of familiarity. He simply approached the counter and ordered his coffee, like every other customer. He handed over his reusable coffee cup, like many other customers. But unlike many other customers, there was a hidden compartment at the base of the cup. Inside the compartment was a tiny USB stick containing state secrets that would most likely result in Li Wei's execution if his treason was discovered by the Chinese government.

In a well-practised move, she appeared to lose her grip on the cup then catch it before it hit the ground. In reality, she swapped the cup for another. Replacing a full USB with a blank one. Eva wrote his order on a piece of paper and slipped it into his cup. And then she made him a coffee, just like she did for every customer. That is, she made him a kickarse coffee. She believed it was vitally important that anyone betraying their country should at least get a great coffee for their trouble.

When Li Wei collected his coffee, there was no thank you, no tip, no fanfare. Just an ordinary man buying a coffee, rather than a spy selling out his own country and risking his life. Not for the first time, Eva wondered what made him do it. Was it greed? Was it ideological? Did he hope to save someone in his home country? The romantic in her hoped it was for love. She doubted she'd ever find out.

And then it was time to close up for the day. In a well-practised ballet, Anchor and Eva floated around the café, closing doors, stacking tables, cleaning and preparing for the next day.

Locking the front door, Eva gave Anchor a kiss goodbye and headed south towards the River Thames, just a regular café worker having a coffee as she walked home. In reality, Eva was headed for MI6 carrying a USB containing information that could change the course of history.

Or a recipe for Kung Pao Chicken.

Or seven seasons of The West Wing.

Or a sex tape of the Canadian Prime Minister and a well-endowed donkey called Sebastian.

She didn't know. And never would. That was one thing she did remember. Field agents were rarely privy to the context of missions —they were tiny cogs in the larger machine. Only a handful of senior staff members ever comprehended the full story, or at least pretended to. Eva hoped her perseverance and brains would propel her up the ranks, but it was a hard slog, and a single slip-up would cost her the career she craved, or possibly even her life.

Before she could continue down that morose line of thinking, her phone vibrated. She read the message:

My dear Chérie, are you on your way back in? We need to talk. LD

A grin crept across her face, and lower down, other parts of her anatomy also made their presence felt. Apparently her body was far more on board with Loch than her mind was. Maybe it knew things she didn't. Either way, one thing was certain: she was in trouble.

CHAPTER FOUR

Nothing good ever comes of the words *we need to talk*.

"We need to talk" is never followed by "we should buy a dirt bike", or "let's turn the second bedroom into a rockin' home theatre" or "let's have a threesome with Juan the hot Peruvian masseuse".

In Eva's experience those words were usually uttered by her. Nobody had ever said them *to* her. Which made the situation with Loch Davenport all the more intriguing. That, and she had no idea who he really was to her.

After dropping off the USB stick on the third floor, Eva found Loch's office and headed up. The door was open and he stood at the window with his hands behind his back, gazing at the Thames. Eva wondered if he'd been waiting there the whole time.

"Uh, hi," Eva said in a faltering voice she didn't recognise. Eva didn't do weak. Eva didn't do feeble. Why would she be like that around Loch?

He turned. "Chérie!"

Loch quickly crossed the room to embrace her. Eva held up her hand before his arms enveloped her. She was momentarily distracted by the way they bulged under his fitted shirt. *Stop it,* Eva chastised herself.

"Are you okay?" he asked, with such sincerity Eva felt all mooshy.

Mooshy? *Who the fuck are you?*

"Fine, fine," she said, waving her hand in the air. "After this morning, I, uh, I'm not entirely sure who I am right now." Never a truer statement had been made.

Loch considered her, his face remaining expressionless, for the longest time. Then he stepped forward and carefully reached behind her head. His fingers slid through her hair and he pulled her gently towards him. Then he ran his fingernail down her neck, sending shivers along her spine. God, he knows the spot. He probably knew where all her most interesting tats were, too. *Be strong, Eva, be strong!*

He leant in for a kiss but Eva put a finger on his lips. He reeled slightly, surprised.

"Is it my breath? I did have pasta for lunch."

"No, it's not that…"

"Then what is it?"

Oh boy. Eva wasn't prepared for this. Did keeping her memory loss a secret extend to lovers? Was he even a lover? If she didn't tell him, how could she ever find out? If they were lovers, would that mean they could do all the things lovers did?

She was screwed either way.

Literally and figuratively.

"I, uh, don't know who you are."

"I thought it took about ten years before we were meant to have the 'I don't know who you are anymore' conversation."

"No, I mean literally. I don't know who you are. Well, since this morning, anyway. I'm not explaining this well. Wait." She took a seat and motioned for Loch to do the same. "So since this morning I seem to have lost the last six months. Can't remember a thing. So… as far as I'm concerned the first time I met you, you stuck your tongue down my throat."

"Now that's what I call a proper introduction." His expression became less jovial. "You're serious? I thought you didn't take any blows to the head?" He felt around her skull. "Should you be in hospital?"

"Look, I'm fine, I'm… it's fine." She paused. "Fine."

A smirk creased his pretty features. "Are you saying you're fine?"

"Are you saying I'm not fine?"

"Oh, you've always been *fine*." Damn those twinkling peepers.

Eva gave him a condensed version of her memory loss. She kept the details to a minimum, but still felt like she was divulging too much.

"So, if it's alright with you," she sucked in a lungful of air, "I think you and I should, you know, keep a lid on this," she pointed between them, "for now, until I know where I'm at."

There. Reasonable, consistent and mostly true. You couldn't get fairer than that.

"But of course, don't be silly. I didn't know Eva, I'm sorry. I'll adjust, obviously. It will take some getting used to. I'm used to grabbing you and ravishing you—"

Meep.

"— so this little reset will be a slight adjustment."

Eva was silent, which was unusual in itself.

Loch's gaze extended far beyond the window. "So, nothing? You don't remember me at all?"

"Sorry."

A wicked grin spread across his features. "Not even Brighton?"

"Nope," Eva replied.

"Not the thing with the naked lemon meringue pie wrestling?"

"Nuh uh. Although that sounds… interesting."

"Don't tell me you don't remember getting kicked out of The Savoy for, and I quote, 'inappropriate behaviour and unnatural vibrations'."

She shook her head. He was certainly charming. It was obvious he was trying to cheer her up, and those events certainly sounded appealing. There was genuine concern in his deep green, expressive eyes. With long lashes. If Eva didn't know better she would have used the word smouldering. A word she was pretty sure she'd never used in her life. Eva had to leave before this turned into a Regency Romance.

"I should go." The words escaped her lips before she'd even considered them.

Loch nodded. "Before you do." He walked to his desk. "The reason I messaged you. The men, the ones from this morning?"

"I have a vague recollection."

He held up a series of multi-coloured folders. "Here are the dossiers for the two we've identified."

She considered them curiously. "MI6 will have this, there's no need to give them to me."

"But then I wouldn't have had an excuse to see you so soon." A cheeky expression spread across his face, which Eva couldn't help returning. "Plus, this information may not have filtered down to you. At least this way you can review the complete files."

Eva took the folders. Loch held onto them for a fraction of a second longer than necessary. "Thanks. Again."

As she passed through the door Davenport called out, "Remember, Chérie, don't trust anyone."

"Does that include you?"

"Especially me."

Man, he had a killer smile.

~

Eva didn't knock. She hadn't knocked on Nancy and Paul's door in years. There was no need. When you were so close to someone, knocking actually seemed ruder. Using her key, she unlocked the front door and let herself in. The sound of a sewing machine and colourful Irish swearing could be heard coming from the spare room.

Nancy had determined she needed a creative hobby some time ago, and in a fit of madness decided that sewing was the answer. She spent a small fortune on a hideously expensive sewing machine and all the peripherals, miles of cloth and mountains of thread. Then she discovered she hated sewing. With a passion. But she stuck with it. Because that's who she was.

Given the day she'd had, Eva really needed Nancy's company. She didn't need a shoulder to cry on, but craved normalcy. If that involved a night of wine and making fun of celebrity house swap shows, or whatever rubbish was passing for television these days, so be it. A night of laughs on the couch was exactly what Eva needed to feel like her life was at least slightly under control.

A smirk crossed her lips when the sewing machine was referred to as a "bog mutten gobshite". Good to see some things hadn't changed.

Nancy didn't know Eva was a spy. She didn't officially know Paul was a spook either, but Eva knew her friend well enough to suspect she'd pieced it together. The cover story of him working at Treasury was an unacknowledged lie in their relationship. Nancy and Paul were so strong that it wasn't an issue.

Eva dropped her bag on the floor, grabbed a beer from the fridge and plonked on the couch.

"I'm borrowing a beer!" she shouted towards the spare room.

And by borrow, Eva meant drink and never replace. She put her feet up on the coffee table and opened the beer.

The sound of the sewing machine ceased, as did the creative swearing. Glancing around the lounge for the remote, Eva rummaged behind cushions until Nancy's short figure materialised in the doorway.

"What the actual fuck do you think you're doing?" she asked in her Irish twang.

"Who lit the fuse on your tampon? There's one beer left, chill your knickers. I'm going to crash for a few days, my place is being, er, remodelled. Now, I'm thinking a really offensive curry for dinner, what do you say? Sanjay's?"

Nancy stood rigid on the spot, her fists clenched by her side.

"What the caffler balls are you doing in my house?"

The amusement washed from Eva's demeanour. Was Nancy actually serious? Eva knew her bestie well enough to know when she was taking the piss. Right now her piss wasn't being taken. It was staying exactly where it was.

"What do you mean? Is it the beer?" Eva asked, highly doubting it was the beer.

"It's not the beer."

Well, at least she was right about something.

"I repeat, what the actual fuck are you doing in my house?"

"Nance, I… what's going on? Why are you mad?"

Nancy's jaw clenched like a steel trap, as if she was fighting back a barrage of abuse. "Why… am… I… mad? Are you fecking kidding me? You waltz in here pretending everything is tickety-boo after what you did and you ask why I'm fucking mad?"

So it was something Eva had done. There was no use racking her brain. That only led to headaches and despair. It had to be major—the two of them had been through so much.

Like the time Nancy had set her up on a date with a man who had not one, but several body odour issues, as well as being the most boring man in the world. That Nancy had sent them off on a rowboat, from which there was no escape for several hours, had apparently resulted in Nancy laughing so hard she "weed meself". Eva's revenge came several weeks later when she abandoned Nancy in Roquetas de Mar in Spain and took the last bus out of town. She could still picture the red-headed firebrand at the bus stop casting creative profanities her way. It was hysterically funny at the time. Their love survived pretty much everything. So what had gone so wrong?

Eva would never have slept with Paul. Or worn Nancy's favourite jumper. Those things were sacred. Especially the latter.

So what could Eva have done? She wanted to discuss it, but Nancy had other ideas. She marched over to the kitchen bench and placed her hand on the knife block.

"You have five seconds to get out of my fecking house."

"Nancy, please. I don't know what's going on."

"Five."

"Nance, please, can we just talk?"

"Four."

"You're my best friend. I don't understand what's happened."

"Two."

"Wait, what happened to three?"

"You don't deserve a three. One."

"You were always shit at maths."

The slightest smirk made a fleeting appearance at the corner of her mouth, then disappeared just as quickly.

Nancy pulled out a small paring knife. "Get out."

Eva grabbed her bag and left. What had happened? What had she done to alienate her best friend in the world?

She pulled out her phone and called a man she could rely on.

She met him in the foyer and Eva was immediately blinded by the smug. It was brighter than the sun. Brighter than a nuclear blast. Brighter even than his usual smile. The trip up in the lift was conducted in silence. His stance and his stupid smile both screamed *I told you so*. Eva was thankful he hadn't said it.

The lift door chimed and they stepped out onto his floor. Bishop pulled out his keys. "I tried to tell you."

"You did nothing of the sort. All you said was she was busy with work. That does not translate to she hates my guts. You could have warned me, dude. I'm flying blind here. There's stuff I need to know. Number one, I would have assumed, was your best mate hates you so much she'll probably pull a knife on you."

"She actually pulled a knife?" Bishop was surprised.

"Yes. It wasn't a big one, but it was a bloody knife."

"I'm glad you didn't say, 'That's not a noyfe'."

"Your Aussie accent sucks. So, do you know what I did?"

"I have no idea. Nor does Paul. But apparently it was bad."

"I got that impression."

As Bishop turned the key in the lock, Eva was reasonably sure what to expect.

White.

There was sure to be a lot of white. Minimal furniture. Polished concrete, probably. A single wooden chair from Scandinavia or Norway or somewhere cold and dour. And a sex swing. There had to be a sex swing. That was a given.

Not that she'd spent a lot of time thinking about Bishop's apartment. Well, not much. A bit. A reasonable amount, if there was such a thing. There probably wasn't.

Bishop's front door swung open and Eva didn't know if she should laugh or gasp. This wasn't the minimalist wankfest she had expected. As Bishop ushered her through the front door, she took it all in. Various travel posters from the early twentieth century adorned the walls. Leather bound books filled every conceivable space. Not a stick of furniture was less than seventy years old. Everything was dark wood and blood-red wallpaper. If she was forced to name the style, Eva would call it 'gentlemanly bordello'. It was, she hated to admit, very cool.

"Not what you expected?" Bishop asked, oozing self-confidence.

Eva chose not to answer, and threw her hastily packed bag on the floor. Bishop walked over to an art deco drinks cabinet that Eva would have killed for and started mixing. After a minute he handed her a drink.

"Old-Fashioned. Put hairs on your chest."

Without anything to say, she tried the drink. It was good, damn good, and perfectly in keeping with her host's apartment. Earthy, strong with a hint of spice and exceptionally masculine. Or perhaps that was the host.

Bishop smirked. "What were you expecting? A sex dungeon?"

"As if." Eva sipped her drink.

"You seem surprised."

"That you have a cool place, or that I've been here for two minutes and I still have my pants on?"

Bishop ignored the jibe and showed her the spare room. It actually did have a lock. After a few minutes acquainting herself with her temporary abode they reconvened in the lounge and sprawled on an amazingly comfortable soft leather couch.

"Heard from Loch?" Bishop asked in a less-than-casual manner.

Eva scratched the back of her neck. "We've, uh, made contact."

"I bet."

"Not like that." She considered her words. "Well, not today."

"So you two have been hanging out before now? And when I say hanging out, I obviously mean conducting copious coitus."

"Been practising your alliteration, I see. If I didn't know any better I'd say that was slight hint of jealousy I detected, Mr Bishop."

"I don't do jealousy. Or children. Or Brussel sprouts, Phil Collins or relationships that last longer than this sentence."

Eva wasn't convinced by his flippancy. Was Bishop envious of Loch? That would definitely be a first. She'd always assumed his insatiable flirting was just part of his persona, that anyone with breasts was subjected to the same unending innuendo.

Once she realised Bishop knew their boundaries and would never act on anything without her unmitigated consent, she enjoyed their repartee. Had she misjudged him? Did his insinuations have an underlying honesty to them?

Eva shook her head. It wasn't worth contemplating, for all sorts of reasons. Firstly, he was an insatiable Lothario. Not that Eva was particularly chaste, but a womaniser wasn't her thing. Nor were medieval re-enactors, or anyone who clipped their toenails in the lounge room.

The other reason Bishop wasn't an option was that she seemed to have feelings for Loch. At least, her body did.

And besides, she could never be interested in the men's magazine comments section that was Charles Bishop. *Could she?*

Eva traced the rim of her glass. "Loch seems to think we have some, ah, history."

"And you believe him?"

"He was very convincing. He does know which buttons of mine to push."

"You have buttons? Where are these buttons? Can I see?"

Eva paused. "I kind of told him. About the memory thing."

Bishop's demeanour quickly changed. "You what?" He folded his arms. "You told Loch the cock?"

"That's what we're calling him now?"

"I don't think that was a good idea, Eva. We don't know if we can trust him."

"My gut says we can."

"That's all good and fine, but your gut doesn't have a security clearance." The statement hung in the air for a moment. "But I suppose it's done now." Bishop took a sip from his glass. "So, what should we do tonight?"

Eva grinned.

"When would you ever need teeth made of steel?"

Bishop was indignant, and, if Eva was not mistaken, a little inebriated. She would have expected a spy to have a higher alcohol tolerance. She certainly did, though those skills had been honed long before she joined MI6.

Jaws bit through a cable and glowered menacingly at Roger Moore. Eva gestured towards the TV screen, as if to say, "see?"

"Alright, besides that one thing, when else would it be useful?"

From the opposite couch, Eva glared at Bishop. She still found it inconceivable that an MI6 spy had never seen a James Bond film, and had taken it upon herself to educate him. There was probably merit in starting with one of the newer ones, *Skyfall* or *Casino Royale*, but Eva thought it would be fun to jump in boots and all and go the full Moore in all its insanity. *Moonraker* was the perfect place to start.

Bishop folded his arms. "So, if I am to get this straight, the plot of this film is this Nazi Disco Face fellow—"

"Drax," Eva offered.

"I prefer Nazi Disco Face. So Nazi Disco Face has built space shuttles so his Arian master race in disco pants can commit genocide with a flower. Do I understand this nuanced piece of high culture correctly?"

"I can't help but think you're being a smidge sarcastic. This is a classic."

"The plot is wildly absurd."

"Dude. Really? *Really?*"

"What am I missing?"

"Bishop, a year ago we were on an island fighting a private army to stop a madman—"

"Your boyfriend."

"*Ex*. From ransoming the world. He had a secret base! Christ, he even had an evil henchman. Sure, he was no Oddjob, but still."

"Odd job?" Bishop asked, confused.

Eva sighed in exasperation. "The point is that while the plot of this thing is nuts, we've seen similar, we've *lived* similar. Take away the pretty girls in bikinis and it's not a million miles from what we do for a living." She pointed at the scantily clad woman on the screen. "That was me, albeit temporarily. I was a fucking Bond girl."

Bishop shook his head. "That's absurd."

"Is it?"

"Yes, it most patently is. You look far better in a bikini."

Eva rolled her eyes good-naturedly. "There will come a day when you won't say something that has sexual overtones."

"And on that day you will be wearing a slinky black number and weeping over my coffin, lamenting all the rumpy, and dare I say pumpy, we never had."

"So you've accepted the fact that we'll never have sex?"

"Well, I'm sure Mr Davenport would prefer that to be the case."

"And we're back to him." Eva raised an eyebrow. "It bothers you that much we are, I mean were, an item?"

"My dear, you seem to be under an impression that is unequivocally not the case."

"Right. Because you don't do brussels sprouts or jealousy?"

"Or Phil Collins. Especially Phil Collins."

"Sure. So how was the redhead today?"

"Bendy." Bishop's eyebrows seemed to dance on his forehead.

"You're incorrigible."

"I do try."

Not wanting to further explore the possibility of Bishop being jealous, Eva walked over to the well-stocked bar and mixed two Negronis. When she returned, she checked her phone. Again. No messages.

Nancy still hadn't returned her calls and texts. That was no way for a best friend to act. Until today Eva would have thought that no matter what she did or said, Nancy would have her back. It seemed she was wrong, or that she had done something so hideous it was beyond even their friendship. Not knowing what had happened burned her insides.

Her phone vibrated and she leapt at it. But it wasn't Nancy. It was a message for Chérie. In spite of her disappointment, Eva was overcome with a sense of warmth. The message contained a picture attachment. There was the well-groomed Loch Davenport, standing next to what appeared to be a Christmas tree. He was holding an expensive brandy glass while wearing the ugliest knitted Christmas jumper she had ever seen. It was gloriously hideous. It had snowflakes, Christmas trees, candy canes and reindeers. The text read like a meme: "Admit it, you'd mistletotally hit this."

Eva laughed out loud. Well, at least Loch got her warped sense of humour. It was a welcome relief, but not from the person she'd hoped.

Maybe what she needed to do was get away, clear her head. She knew the place.

"Maybe I should take some time off and go to my other place, you know? Take some kick-back time."

Technically it was her place. It was in her name and all. That it had been bought for her as a Hail Mary pass for a relationship with a megalomaniac ex was neither here nor there. When most people break up they're lucky to come away with a pot plant and all their CDs. Eva was not most people. Out of her last relationship she took away a castle in the Rhone Valley in France. An actual castle. With a moat. And a drawbridge.

Bishop shot her a sideways glance and shifted on the couch. He suddenly became intensely interested in his drink.

"Don't tell me I sold the castle? Past Eva's not that much of an arsehole, is she?"

"No, it's not that, you still own it. It's, ah. I guess you'll find out."

"Dude, I've had enough of this mystery crap. Loch, Vienna, the last mission, Nancy—I have no flaming idea what's going on in my life. Can you just tell me *something* I should know?"

"Alright. So, you know how you're a bit of a bleeding-heart liberal?"

"You mean that in the most positive way, yeah?"

Bishop frowned. "Sure. Well, against my better advice of turning the castle into a casino slash gentleman's club slash stripper discothèque, you went and did the opposite."

A blank stare was his only reply.

Bishop continued. "You turned your castle over to a refugee relocation association, partly because you said it was the right thing to do and partly to piss off the current French administration. There are seven refugee families currently residing in your castle."

"That's actually pretty cool. Yay me. Well, if there's one positive out of this memory loss it's the realisation that I'm not a complete git."

Bishop rubbed his end-of-day stubble. "I've been thinking, perhaps the two are related."

Eva wondered if Bishop's change in topic was to distract himself from Roger Moore in a spacesuit.

"What's related?"

"The armed men and your memory loss."

"So someone wiped my memory then turned up to kill me? That doesn't make a whole lot of sense."

"Perhaps you're right." He shrugged in a manner that suggested he didn't believe his own words.

"If someone went to the trouble of wiping my memory, and by all accounts it would have been a fuck-load of trouble, why kill me straight after? It's like spending a fortune to save a guy's life in hospital and then putting him in front of a firing squad. I mean, why bother?" She stretched. "We're trying to solve a puzzle without all the pieces. Or the picture on the box."

"While underwater." Bishop slopped his drink in her direction.

"While being attacked by sharks."

"And naked."

Eva was going to add, "while blindfolded", but stopped herself. "Um, why naked?"

"Why not?"

With Bishop, everything eventually led to being naked.

"Well, we should go to bed." Noticing Bishop's hopeful expression, she added, "Alone. We're going to need the rest."

"Of course. Wait, why?"

"For the flight. To Japan tomorrow, didn't I tell you?"

"No, you didn't."

"Oh, right. Probably because I just thought of it. I think we should head to Japan and retrace my last mission to see if it shakes loose any clues. It's either that or sit here and watch more Bond."

Bishop smirked. "Anything but that."

"And besides, I've never been to Japan."

"Yes Eva, you have."

CHAPTER FIVE

"Absolutely not. Under no circumstances. No."

"So we can put you down as a maybe, got it."

Paul didn't think Eva was particularly funny. She took a seat opposite his desk, beside Bishop. They had eagerly suggested the Japan trip as a way of discovering why her brain had been hacked, but Paul seemed less enthusiastic about the idea.

She and Bishop had hatched the plan over coffee and scrambled eggs that morning. The coffee was barely drinkable, which she'd come to expect from the English, but the eggs were top notch. Who knew Bishop could cook? Perhaps it was the only thing he could prepare—being breakfast, it made sense. Send his conquests off with a hearty breakfast and a pat on the bum. Luckily for Bishop, he hadn't attempted the latter with Eva.

Paul glanced up from his computer. "I fail to see how this would help. Traipsing around the Far East hoping to stumble upon a clue is hardly a precise espionage methodology. Do you intend to wander aimlessly around Japan and ask anyone you come across if they know you? You might as well put a message in a bottle, toss it into the Pacific and hope for the best."

Eva frowned. "Better than weeks of me running around mazes looking for cheese."

"Cheese?"

"Like a rat. In a lab. Was that not clear? I don't want to be a lab rat. Do I need a whiteboard?"

"We'll get her expense reports and banking records," Bishop said. "We know where she stayed, where she ate. We know her mission. This isn't needle-in-a-haystack stuff, Paul. Let us do our job. We can investigate this, we can solve this."

"Banking records?" Eva frowned. "That's hardly super sexy spycraft."

Paul smiled for the first time. "Hate to tell you this, Evie, but spycraft isn't super sexy."

"Speak for yourself." That garnered smirks from them both. "What's the alternative? Sit around and hope for a clue to come knocking? I assume you've got everyone available trying to find the missing douchepoodles who tried to give me bullet acupuncture, so what would you have me do? Your filing? Some photocopying? Let me tell you, I look fabulous in a skirt but there's no way I'm going to be relegated to your secretary just because I can't remember what I had for lunch last Thursday. That smacks of discrimination."

She was baiting him. There wasn't a discriminatory bone in Paul's body (partly because Nancy would never allow it). His executive assistant was male. And gay. And Jewish. And from Slough.

Yet there was a shift in Paul's demeanour. The subtle relaxation in his shoulders, the tilt of his head, the slightly more contemplative disposition. She had him.

Paul ran both palms over his desk. "We have to continue finding out what you do and don't know. We still have a lot of questioning to do."

Bishop sat up. "I can drill her on the flight over."

"Oi."

"I mean pump her for it."

Eva crossed her arms. "Listen…"

"Am I interrupting?"

All three heads turned at the interruption. Loch Davenport rested casually against the doorjamb.

Eva was too tongue-tied to say anything. Luckily Loch spoke first. "You messaged me?" he said to Paul.

"Yes, pack your bags. You're flying to Japan with these two. You leave in an hour."

Loch physically baulked. Bishop actually did a double take. This was a surprise to everyone.

Bloody Paul. When he'd been typing away while arguing with them, he must have messaged Loch. One step ahead, as always. He'd make a good spy.

To Eva and Bishop, Paul said, "We're going to have to call in the CIA on this one. They like to think Japan's their patch. They have more assets on the ground than we do in that neck of the woods, and the last assignment was a joint mission, after all."

"CIA? Really, do we have to?" Bishop's tone carried more than a hint of resentment.

"I'm right here," Loch said jovially.

"Five Eyes dictates we must. We're not savages here, Bishop. Espionage can be conducted with some decorum."

It seemed the decision was made. Eva always thought she had good instincts, and the decision to go to Japan felt right. She hadn't expected it to happen so rapidly, though, or that Loch would be involved. Her head was spinning slightly. How would she survive eleven hours with Loch and Bishop on the same flight?

One thing was certain, she wouldn't be bored.

Eva was bored.

No matter where she travelled, there were unavoidable aspects of flying. Queues were one. Whether it was for checking in, security checks or boarding, people always seemed to feel the need to push in/shove/jostle/generally be complete gits, as if they were scared the plane would leave without them. Then as soon as the plane landed, they had to rush to the baggage claim, eager to get there early to… wait for another five minutes before their luggage arrived, just like everyone else.

Then there was the baggage collection itself. It seemed like nearly every person thought if they just got closer to the conveyor belt, their luggage would come out sooner. It was like they believed that if they missed their luggage the first time around it would go into a giant mincer and be shredded into tiny pieces. Eva had this crazy utopian ideal where all the passengers stood back so everyone could view the luggage, and when their case came out they simply walked forward to pick it up. There was a significant problem with the idea, though: it made sense. It was logical. Therefore it had absolutely no place in modern society.

Eva realised she had some deep-seated anger issues with air travel. The trouble was, she loved flying but hated airports. Really hated airports.

She shifted on the couch in the British Airways Concorde Room for the millionth time. The executive lounge should have been enough to sate her, but no. Eva hated to wait. It was so… passive.

Bishop, on the other hand, appeared to be the epitome of zen. He sat on the couch opposite, eyes closed, as if he were meditating on his place in the universe. He appeared tranquil and at peace. Or he might have just been trying to piss Eva off. Both were equally likely.

Loch was on the phone, trying to explain to his superiors why their senior liaison at MI6 was about to board a plane to Japan with no defined mission. He seemed certain he'd be able to pull it off.

A yell came from the reception area of the Concorde Room. A garishly dressed American was drunkenly shouting at the startled young man behind the counter. All heads in the lounge turned towards the ruckus.

"That's bullshit and you know it, yer bum sniffin' fag! I got ma ticket 'ere!" The American, struggling with three large carry-on bags, waved his mobile phone at the attendant.

In an instant Bishop was out of his seat, presumably off to play peacebroker. Or snap the American's neck. It was sometimes hard to tell with Bishop. It could go either way.

Something about the whole situation didn't quite ring true to Eva. There was something disingenuous about it. Almost staged. Bishop entered the fray, using calming gestures, but only seemed to inflame the situation. The reception area became more crowded with people offering to help and contributing to the raised voices.

Rolling the American's dialogue around in her mind, Eva realised what was troubling her. The accent. It was a hodgepodge of various Southern inflections, as if someone was trying to replicate what they thought was an American accent. And Americans didn't use the word "bum" in that way. One thing was certain— this guy was no American.

Eva put her mug down on the glass-topped coffee table and got up to go and tell Bishop, but something blocked her way. Two somethings. A couple of men, mid-twenties, bland-looking business types in suits, were obstructing her path. She was about to excuse herself and move past when she noticed the syringe.

The shorter of the two held a medical syringe, pointed at Eva. The other man held a rag. The chemical stench hit her. Chloroform.

Amateurs.

They had obviously watched too many movies. Chloroform doesn't work by putting a cloth to someone's mouth and counting one, two, three, boom they're out. It can take up to five minutes to take effect, depending on body mass. It seemed like they were attempting something they'd seen on TV. Then again, Eva had no idea what was in the syringe. She had to act.

They moved one step closer, eyes trained on her, tense. They were nervous—that meant they were aware of her skills. If they *really* knew what they were dealing with, they should have run.

Eva couldn't see Bishop among the throng, and there weren't many people nearby. She was on her own. She cracked her neck and crouched into a fighting stance.

A sneer creased the lips of the taller man. He thought he had her. Becoming more confident by the second, he took another step, completing his mistake.

Eva kicked the coffee table forward, driving it into the tall man's shins. The momentum toppled him forward. As he fell, Eva grasped the back of his head and used his weight to slam him into the edge of the glass-topped table. His forehead connected with a *crack* and his body went limp as it crashed through the glass. He was out cold.

The shorter man reeled backwards and fearfully jabbed the syringe at the air between them. Passengers, drawn by the sound of the crash, rushed to the tall man's side. Eva never took her eyes off her assailant. He took a step backwards. Then another. She shook her head and tutted.

"Your move, you cocksplat shitpouch. I suggest you make it a good one," she growled.

His eyes went wide. They faced off and it was as if the rest of the world had turned the volume down. All Eva could hear was his anxious breaths. The space between them turned to ice. Eva stared. A trickle of sweat carved its way down Mr Syringe's face.

Eva stared.

He swallowed hard.

Eva stared.

He dropped the syringe and ran. Eva leapt over the shattered coffee table and chased him. He was headed for the only means of escape, the front reception area, which was now even more crowded. Bishop was pinned against the reception desk, facing away from her.

Somehow Mr Syringe found a gap near the far wall and slipped through. When Eva arrived seconds later, the gap had already been filled with curious bodies. Wedged between two rotund gents in business suits shouting at each other in German, she watched him race through the sliding doors. After losing precious seconds pushing her way through, Eva sped towards the exit, fearing she'd lost her prey.

But she hadn't. As she entered the Terminal Five concourse she spotted the top of his head descending out of view on an escalator. *Gotcha.* But Eva's revelry was short lived. The sheer mass of people on the long escalator meant there was no way she could run down it. The escalator travelling upward was equally packed.

Minge punching cockwombles.

There was only one thing for it. She'd have to slide down the silver separator between the escalators and head him off at the bottom. It would be just like skateboarding. She tried to block out the fact that she'd broken her arm skateboarding when she was twelve. That wasn't important right now.

As soon as she started to slide she realised her folly. This wasn't the gentle, controllable slide she had anticipated. It was full-on, uncontrollable velocity. She was accelerating way too fast.

Flashbacks of hurtling down a ridiculously steep hill on a tiny red skateboard flooded her mind. Then, like now, she'd underestimated the speed and had no way of stopping. She was definitely going to break something.

Everyone on the escalators became a blur as she careered downward. It was a miracle she even remained upright, but if she tumbled she'd severely injure herself and anyone she fell on. She had to remain vertical. And she had to catch the bastard who wanted to kill her.

Wobbling down the silver slipstream to the shrieks of startled passengers, Eva had to accept that she was going to break at least an arm or a leg on the solid tiles she was steadily hurtling towards. There was no avoiding it. She'd do her best parachute landing technique, but she doubted it would be enough. And she'd lost Mr Syringe in the smudge of light the crowd had become.

Then her luck changed.

Stepping off the escalator, a man dressed in a chequered suit decided it would be a grand idea to stand with his suitcase at the bottom of the escalator while he got his bearings. The case was almost as large as he was. And he was rotund. Eva aimed for the case.

Stay there Tubby, stay there.

The end of the escalator came up abruptly. Her plunge would never have scored points in Olympic diving, but it did the job. Eva landed squarely on the centre of the case. The man went sprawling across the floor, but would be fine; he'd only received a glancing blow.

Her head whipped around to see Mr Syringe's astonished face as he alighted the escalator. He broke into a run.

Eva grinned. She had him.

A meaty hand slammed down on her shoulder. It was attached to a uniformed arm. The security guard spoke into the microphone on his shoulder. "Got her, Steve."

She attempted to shake him off but he wasn't letting her go without a fight. He was an innocent—Eva wasn't about to punch a guy for doing his job.

"I'm MI6, I'm in pursuit of a suspect."

The laugh was hearty and loud. In retrospect, Eva could see where he was coming from. The Aussie accent, for one. Her tank top showed off an abundance of tattoos. Even Eva wouldn't believe herself.

Mr Syringe plunged into the crowd.

There was no time to explain her predicament. Eva had to act now or she'd lose him forever.

"Dude, I'm really sorry."

"Sorry for wha—"

The kick to his thigh was swift and harsh. Nothing that would cause a lasting injury, but it would leave a significant bruise. It had the right effect. He crumpled like a soggy house of cards. Eva was off.

The security guard's angry shouts faded as she charged into the crowd and searched for Mr Syringe. Why did the bastard have to be short? Why didn't she ever get to chase basketballers? A flash of brown hair between a couple of burqas seized Eva's attention. She swerved through the crowd, jaw clenched in concentration.

Mr Syringe shirtfronted a woman exiting a door marked "Staff only" and barged through. The woman, dressed in fluorescent yellow safety gear, went down hard. He glanced over his shoulder as Eva ran towards him. Fear creased his weaselly features and he slammed the door behind him.

Eva reached the door moments later. She leaned down to the woman, who sighed. "Oh, thank you."

But Eva wasn't helping her. She reached for the pass on the woman's belt, pulled the retractable string and touched it to the pad next to the door. The light pinged green and Eva yanked it open.

"Sorry, bad guy." She offered the woman a weak smile then dove through the door.

A cacophony of mechanical sound slammed into her. Dozens of multi-coloured conveyer belts crisscrossed the vast space before her. Tens of thousands of pieces of luggage sped towards their destinations in the second-busiest airport in the world. There were up to five conveyer belts overlapping and intersecting one another in a beautiful confusing dance. Disorientated by the spectacle, Eva had no line on Mr Syringe.

Fucknuggets.

A shout of, "Oi!" came from further down the gangway.

But it wasn't aimed at her. Some wonderful worker had given away her prey's position. The chase was back on.

Another worker spotted Eva and shouted after her. His calls caught the attention of Mr Syringe, who now knew Eva wasn't far behind. He skidded to a halt when two uniformed guards blocked his way 20 metres ahead. Without hesitating, he leapt onto the nearest conveyer belt and was whisked away. But Eva hadn't chased him all this way to let him get away with that. As he shot past she jumped onto the conveyor belt. The speed whipped her feet from beneath her and she tumbled to her knees.

Regaining her balance on all fours, she faced off against her adversary mere metres ahead. The belt rose higher and higher, its speed immense. Every 10 metres one belt met another and whisked away thousands of pieces of luggage. He stood, somehow maintaining his balance despite the switching conveyer belts. Glancing ahead of him, Eva smirked, and fear enveloped his insipid features. He was smart enough to know a smirking Eva was a dangerous thing.

He turned just in time to see the head-height beam. Unfortunately, he ducked. A sharp turn on the conveyer belt jostled him to his knees. This was Eva's chance. She sprinted directly at him and caught him in a diving tackle. But her momentum was too great, she'd hit him too hard, and they careened off the belt, falling, a tangle of limbs.

They landed viciously on the belt below, Eva on her back, him on top of her. All the air was punched out of her lungs. They rushed along at breathtaking speed, which was apt, as Eva couldn't catch her breath. Mr Syringe recovered faster. He pushed himself off her and crawled away, but mistimed a step between belts, lost his balance and toppled over.

Eva wheezed. She'd surely busted a couple of ribs. The world rushed by in a blur. The edges of her vision were just as blurred. Using her fists, she somehow managed to prop herself up. Blood poured from a wound somewhere on her head. She was dizzy, random parts of her body ached, and her ribs were on fire, but she wasn't about to give up.

"Hey, Spunktrumpet. Ready for round two?"

Mr Syringe's expression was one of sheer terror. It seemed like he was reluctant to take Eva up on her polite offer.

Too fucking bad.

Eva spat some blood and got to her knees. Steadying herself, she advanced on him. He backed away. She kept on moving forward. Panicked, he looked around for any means of escape. There wasn't one. Suddenly his expression of utter distress washed away. He seemed amazingly calm. In one fluid motion he stood and, without looking, leapt from the conveyer belt into blackness.

Eva scrambled to the edge in time to see him land awkwardly on a conveyer belt below, travelling at speed in the opposite direction. He gave Eva a little wave as he zoomed out of sight. She was having none of it. She rose, ready to jump after him.

The loud *clang* came at the same instant as the intense pain in her head. She'd hit one of the overhead beams, and now stars filled her vision. Everything proceeded to turn fuzzy and black. The last thing Eva thought before darkness enveloped her was, *Please don't let me end up in Canberra.*

~

Bishop spotted Davenport in the baggage claim area of Terminal Five and waved him over.

"Anything?" he asked.

"Yeah, I found her ten minutes ago, that's why I'm still looking."

Bishop smiled like he thought it was a funny joke. The nails of his clenched fists dug into his palms.

There was a cry of alarm from over near one of the baggage carousels. They turned as a body was spat out of the inner workings beneath the airport and onto the rotating silver carousel. The crowd's reaction was a melange of laughter and horror.

Eva Destruction slid down on her arse and inelegantly smashed into the luggage buffer at the base of the carousel. She glanced up at the crowd, dazed, and continued to revolve around the baggage claim, much to the amusement of the passengers.

Loch raced over but struggled to get past the cluster of passengers standing by the baggage claim. "Get out of the goddamn way!" he shouted, then finally managed to reach her and pull her free. They stumbled off the carousel, landing awkwardly.

A relieved grin crossed his lips. "I have to say, you're the prettiest piece of luggage I've ever picked up."

Eva blew a strand of hair off her face. "I really fucking hate airports."

CHAPTER SIX

Bishop slammed the plane's phone down. "It's official. That was a complete balls-up."

If Eva could have cowered any further into her leather seat, she would have. She'd been reckless, again, and jeopardised the mission. She hadn't considered all the options before chasing after Mr Syringe. With Bishop so caught up in the commotion at reception he had no idea why Eva had raced off. As a consequence, Bishop ran off searching for Eva and brought Loch in on the chase. That left nobody guarding the tall unconscious man lying on a broken coffee table. When they got back to the executive lounge he was long gone. Mr Syringe was never found. Eva's impetuousness had destroyed any chance of finding out why two men had been sent to kill her.

The only saving grace was that they'd been upgraded from commercial airline to private jet. MI6 had deemed commercial travel too risky. Eva had her mate the Foreign Secretary to thank for making it all happen so quickly. Freddie had called to make sure she was alright, and ten minutes later they were told a private plane was being arranged. Eva had flown on plenty of private jets, so this wasn't a particularly big deal, but it did save her from eyeing off every passenger as a potential assassin. And the champagne was better.

They'd been in the air for an hour now. Bishop had spent most of that time down the other end of the cabin, talking on the phone to his superiors. Loch, on the other hand, had hovered close to Eva, asking her every three minutes if she was alright, and if she needed anything. It was both endearing and annoying.

Eva didn't need any man's help, but his heart was in the right place. Loch obviously knew her well enough not to push her. His hand strayed to her knee a couple of times, as if by habit, but he'd quickly withdrawn it, remembering their hands-off deal. It must have been tough for him. To be so intimate with someone and then suddenly find they didn't have the faintest idea who you were. Eva could see him struggling to straddle the line between colleague, friend and person who knew all the excited noises one can make in the middle of the night.

He leaned in close, his warm breath tickling her ear. In a hushed, gravelly voice only she could hear, he said, "It's such a shame about our current arrangements. I never have gotten around to joining the mile-high club. That's one card I never punched."

Several visions flooded Eva's brain, all of them good. Images of tangled limbs, sweaty faces and yoga-master feats of contortion bombarded her very creative mind. She snaked her head away from Loch's. The bastard wasn't making it easy for her.

She thought it best not to mention that not only was she a member of that particular club, but she had probably earned enough frequent flyer points to have a plane named after her by now. Maybe even an airline. Her previous life as the girlfriend of a globetrotting billionaire meant there were a significant number of private jet staff who accidentally witnessed Eva's cure for boredom on long-haul flights. They'd probably even formed a club of their own. Or support group.

Rolling around thoughts of her extensive sexcapades was not helping her recent vow of celibacy. And Loch's self-confident, chiselled face wasn't helping, either. Eva needed a drink. And a cold shower. Or half an hour to herself in a bath with a powerful nozzle.

Eva blew out a frustrated sigh and reluctantly pushed Loch away. Her brain was impressed with her fortitude; her loins, somewhat less so. She had to remind herself that she really didn't know this man. At all. Now was as good a time as ever to find out more about him. Besides, she needed the distraction.

"Sooo, you know far more about me than I do about you. Can I ask some first-date questions?"

"Sure, go for it. As long as you don't escape out the restaurant's bathroom window. Shoot."

"Brothers or sisters?"

"One of each."

"Mother and father?"

"One of each." He cracked a wry grin. Eva liked that grin.

"Any diseases?"

"Does Dutch elm disease count?"

"Ever murdered anyone?"

"No." he paused. "Well..."

"Well?"

"Just some homeless guys. And the Archbishop of Canterbury."

"I didn't hear about that."

"I'm very sneaky."

"Back to family, tell me about your brother and sister."

"Both older, she's a lawyer in Dallas and makes me livid every Christmas by telling me how she defends oil companies from evil environmentalists trying to save the planet from idiots. My brother is an even greater disappointment. He's a mime."

"No he's not."

"No, he's not. He's a plumber, but I like to pretend he's a mime."

"Why?"

"It annoys him."

Eva laughed. "Mum and dad?"

"Dad's retired and provides a service to the fish population by being terrible at fishing. My mom…" He grew sombre. "She passed away last fall. The Big C. Thankfully it was pretty quick, she didn't really suffer, but man, she was the matriarch of our family, one strong lady. I miss her every day."

Eva placed her hand on his. "I'm sorry."

"Why, did you knock her off?"

His joviality was forced, but Eva appreciated the effort. "Was she the German Chancellor?"

He smiled a genuine smile. "No."

"Then no." She gave him a little punch on the arm. "Sorry about your mum, she sounds like someone I would have liked."

"Oh, she would have loved you. We always had the same taste." Loch's eyes went wide as he realised what he'd just said.

"Did you just use the L word in reference to me, Mr Davenport?"

Loch cast his glance skyward and pointed to the cabin's roof. "I do love the neoclassical design. Very Baroque friezes, wouldn't you agree?"

Eva shook her head. "Nice save." She gave him a wink and kissed his forehead before going to talk to Bishop.

From the cockpit emerged an elegantly dressed Asian man who had served them pre-flight drinks. His pilot's uniform was flatteringly cut. His white moustache and expertly quaffed hair meant he could pass as a model for the aged set.

Holding a silver tray, he approached Eva. "Canapé?"

Eva took one. "Thank you, er…"

"Yuji, ma'am."

"Thank you, Yuji." She took a bite. "These are delicious."

He gave a subtle bow and approached the others. Bishop and Loch took their canapés without comment. Yuji excused himself and left them alone again.

Eva walked over to Bishop. "So how much did I screw up?"

"Somewhere between the Australian Prime Minister touching the Queen's back and the assassination of the heir presumptive to the Austro-Hungarian throne. Lucky for you I can spin the situation like a whirling dervish on, ah, some substance that makes you spin a lot, I guess."

"You didn't think that one through before you started, huh?"

"It seems we have that in common."

"Touché."

He flashed her his boy-band grin. "I've spun it so it seems like you thought someone had been sent to guard the unconscious assailant. I told them I must have missed you advising that you were in pursuit of a suspect. That way the blame is spread a little thinner."

"You didn't need to do that. I'm a big girl, I take responsibility for my actions. I really don't want you—"

"It's done," he said matter-of-factly.

"You lied for me." Eva was grateful, but knew Bishop would hate if she made a fuss.

"You'd do the same for me." He paused, concern washing over his face. "One day your recklessness will get you killed, Eva. You have to learn to keep a lid on it."

His sudden shift into seriousness was jarring. Eva could be impulsive sometimes, but it usually garnered results. Was she really that reckless? A quick montage flashed though her brain: her jumping out of buildings, punching various men who meant her harm, and the airport security guard who didn't, car chases, blowing up various tropical facilities... There could be some veracity to what Bishop was saying. Perhaps.

Bishop jerked his head towards Loch. "Your prince awaits your return."

He headed for the drinks cabinet, leaving Eva standing between the two men.

Glancing at the ceiling, Eva muttered, "I should send that guy a fruit basket or something. Maybe some movie tickets for him and his wife, or husband, or whatever."

Bishop stopped mixing his drink long enough to say, "What are you on about, woman?"

"The security guard. At the airport. I smashed him pretty hard. I feel bad."

Loch shook his head good-naturedly. "You slice off a man's hand, but feel poorly for giving some working Joe a bruise?"

"That's it, a working Joe." She sat down. "He was doing a job, he wasn't out to hurt anyone, but to save time I smacked him one and went on my merry way. It doesn't sit well with me."

"You're a unique human being, Chérie," Loch said tenderly. He ran his hand down her arm, then whipped it away when he realised he'd lapsed again.

Eva gave him a playful nudge. "Who tends to get knocked on her arse a lot."

"There is a Japanese proverb, *nanakorobi yaoki*."

All three turned in astonishment to see who had spoken. Yuji stood near the cockpit door. He'd changed outfits. Gone was the pilot's garb, replaced with an immaculate grey suit, vest and beautifully polished shoes.

"It literally translates to, 'fall down seven times, stand up eight'. You could interpret it as simply as 'perseverance is better than defeat', or as prosaically as 'if at first you don't succeed', but it's more profound than that." He walked over and took a bottle of mineral water from the fridge. "Something about only having to get up one time more than you fall down has always spoken to me. You could say it is my personal motto."

He opened the bottle and took a drink.

Eva tilted her head. "You're not a pilot, are you?"

"Technically, yes. I am a qualified pilot like my compatriot in there," he gestured towards the cockpit, "but that is more of a convenience, allowing me to fly in and out of countries without too many questions." He gave a genial chuckle.

"So who are you?"

"Yuji Okumoto." He bowed ever so slightly. "I work for Naicho, or as you may know it, the Japanese Cabinet Intelligence and Research Office."

Eva didn't know much about the organisation, only that it was slightly controversial. Japan had not operated an international intelligence arm in the Western sense since the conclusion of World War II, relying heavily on the CIA instead. But that had changed in the last decade or so. Naicho's public acknowledgement was a relatively recent occurrence, and that was only because of leaked documents via Harry Lancing's data-sharing escapades. The Japanese were new to the espionage game, but if history was anything to go by, they would soon begin to overtake other spy agencies.

"So what was with the whole servant routine?" Loch asked, his arms folded.

"I have found the true test of a person's character is not what they say, or know, but how they treat those below them," Yuji said. "If you have respect for those who can provide you with no advantage, then you have a good soul."

"Did I pass?" Eva asked.

"Madam, you most certainly did."

"Permission for fist bump?"

"Permission granted."

She and Yuji traded fist bumps. He eyed off Bishop and Loch with a less-than-favourable expression, and smoothed his moustache.

"Apologies for the slight deception, but it is always good to know the character of those you are to work with. I did not have an opportunity to be briefed on you before I was assigned this role."

Bishop joined Loch in the arm-folding standoff. "And who exactly assigned you this role?"

"Your superior, Winifred Kensington, requested that I accompany you on your journey to my country and assist in your mission."

Bloody Freddie. Eva beamed. She was looking out for her again.

Yuji opened a drawer and took out a laptop. He sat on a chair in the middle of the plane and fired it up. "It seems you had, as the English call it, a spot of bother at the airport."

"You could say that." Eva rubbed the back of her head. "I know airlines are adding all sorts of new pre-flight services, but I could do without the assassination optional extra."

"Ah," Yuji said. "You are assuming the men at the airport were there to kill you?"

"I'm taking a stab and guessing that wasn't a vitamin B shot." She shivered. "I shouldn't say stab."

Yuji turned to Bishop. "Has your lab tested the contents of the syringe?"

Bishop nodded. "Propoven."

"A common general anaesthesia drug. They meant to knock you out, not kill you."

"Well, they were rubbish at it, either way."

Yuji smoothed his moustache. "I am not surprised, as they were amateurs."

"That's what I said," Eva stated. "Whoever they were working for needs to seriously reassess their training practices."

"No, you misunderstand me, Miss Destruction. I mean to say they were literally amateurs. Please." He swivelled his laptop around. "My people have sent me this link. It was posted on the dark web. There is a bounty on your head. You are wanted alive, but that is the only stipulation. It seems your assailants were after, as Mr Davenport's compatriots might say, a fast buck."

"How much?"

"I am sorry?" Yuji asked.

"The price on my head, how much?"

"One million American dollars, or equivalent in any currency. Including, apparently, Bitcoin."

It took Eva a moment to process the fact that there was a sizable bounty on her head.

"Makes sense, I guess. They mentioned—" Eva stopped herself before the word "Halcyon" slipped out. "Ah, that a thing couldn't happen unless they knew what I did with a shipment of some sort. I'm guessing whoever posted this is on the same side as whoever sent the goons into my apartment yesterday."

Bishop stared at the screen and let out a disgusted grunt. "Outsourcing espionage. What a world."

~

"What I want to know is, how did they get a syringe past security?" Bishop waved a piece of steak about on the end of his fork.

Yuji had insisted on serving them dinner, even though he had dropped the pretence of being their flight attendant/pilot. The meal was probably the best Eva had ever had on a flight.

"I read in Keith Richards' autobiography that he used to have the needle part as a hat pin," Eva offered.

"That's great, but neither of them was wearing a hat," Loch said.

"And I'm pretty sure neither of them were members of the Rolling Stones, either," Bishop added.

"What is your point?" Yuji asked, a little lost.

"No idea. But we've established that I wasn't attacked by Keith Richards." Eva took the last bite of her meal and slouched backwards, sated. "My question is, why aren't there any female assassins?"

"What?"

"Everyone they've sent after me has been a bloke, no chicks," she said.

"You want equality in your hit men?" Bishop asked.

"See? Hit *men*. It's very sexist."

"So you're saying you want a female to kill you?" Loch asked.

"Well, no, I'd kick her arse too. I'd just like to see a bit of diversity, that's all."

"Is this how your conversations are normally conducted?" Yuji asked.

Eva shrugged. "Pretty much, yeah."

"Are you sure you are all spies?" Eva wasn't sure if Yuji was serious or not.

To change the subject, she asked if she could check out the equipment Yuji had with him to see if there was anything of use. She needed the distraction. As she and Yuji conversed, she'd noticed Loch and Bishop sitting next to one another in total silence.

Their rapport had not thawed at all. In fact, they both seemed to be covered in a thick layer of frost. It was odd: in all the time since they had left MI6, the two men hadn't spoken to one another without Eva being part of the conversation. Eva shrugged. That was their issue. She had more pressing matters to deal with.

Bishop shifted uncomfortably in his chair and folded his arms. Loch mirrored his movements. Sneers were exchanged.

The MI6 operative gave the CIA agent a derisive look. "I hear you're an unmemorable lay."

Mouth agape, Eva was about to issue an abusive rebuttal, but snapped her eyes shut and tried to focus on what Yuji was saying. This wasn't her battle. Let the two men act out their adolescent mating ritual or whatever the hell it was.

A smirk appeared at the corner of Loch's mouth. "I hear you're an insufferable cad."

Reacting as though Loch had commented on the pleasant weather, Bishop said, "I hear you're a forgotten man."

"I hear you've gone through more loose women than the clap."

Bishop laughed. "You say that, but where did your little Cherry baby spend the night last night?"

Eva rose from her seat. "Alright you two, shut it down or I swear on Jimi Hendrix's Fender Stratocaster I will open one of these doors and toss you both the fuck out. I don't know why, but you two are carrying on like two dogs fighting over a bone and I'm not having it."

As innocent as the day is long, Bishop said, "No bone here." After a pause he added, "Not when you're dressed like that."

Eva glanced at her sweatpants. "What's wrong with my outfit?"

Loch frowned. "Why do you care what he thinks?"

She clenched her fists. "Right. What *I* think is we should get back to the, you know, spy stuff, seeing as you two can't play nice in the sandpit together. Bishop, can you bring up a photo of the sword from my apartment?"

Raising a laconic eyebrow, Bishop walked over to his laptop and tapped away until he found the picture of the sword. Eva took the laptop and handed it to Yuji. "This Samurai sword was in my apartment. I don't know where it came from, but it appeared after my mission to Japan. Do you have some people who are experts on swords that could—" Eva stopped talking when she saw Yuji's face.

"This is not a Samurai sword. This is not Japanese."

"Okay, so…"

"It is a Chinese sword," Yuji said confidently. "Quite an ancient one, but I am no expert. You see the straighter blade? Japanese swords are normally curved. The wide blade, with three grooves, wide on top, with two narrow underneath? I would believe 17th century, perhaps early Qing dynasty. Highly sought after, I would think. Expensive."

"Sold in Japan?"

"No," he said decisively. "This would not be an item my people would like to possess. It would be like selling Nazi memorabilia in Jerusalem." He paused. "I apologise, that was a crude analogy. But no, this is unlikely to be sold in my country. There are regulations for such things."

"Okay, thanks," Eva said, not meaning it. Lately, none of the questions she asked had a straightforward answer, and most led to more questions.

With that avenue of enquiry exhausted, and keen to keep Bishop and Loch from descending into another pissing contest, she asked them to brief her on her previous mission. With all three agencies providing different perspectives, she might gain an insight into what she had been up to.

Eva's mission was to shadow a party boy, the son of a Chinese party leader who was living it up in Japan. But that wasn't all he was up to. The Russian GRU was worried he was selling something. The CIA had caught wind of these concerns, and were nervous.

The GRU was partly a successor to the old KGB, but had been making increasingly aggressive moves into Asia, particularly since the relationship between China and Russia had become strained, if not openly hostile. In one of the few pieces of news Eva had seen in recent days, the head of the GRU, in an unprecedented move, had appeared on national television and stated in no uncertain terms that China should not be allowed to join the G8. His reasoning was vague, but the underlying message was clear: China is up to something, but we're not telling you what it is.

MI6 and CIA hadn't been able to find out what Hu was selling, but if the Russians were worried, they should be too. So they needed an asset on the ground. They needed a woman who would appeal to Hu's exotic tastes. They needed Eva.

The reason Eva had been chosen for the mission was because the Chinese party boy had a soft spot for tattooed rock chicks. She was seated next to him on a flight from Japan to Macau, where he lived. Her job was to get to know him and find out as much as she could. Yuji confirmed that contact had been made, but after that no intelligence agency knew anything of note.

"Wait," Eva was confused. "That's all you all know?"

All three nodded.

"So why didn't I file a mission report from Macau or Japan?"

"We don't know," Bishop replied. "Apparently you were adamant that the first mission debrief had to occur at MI6."

"And that was meant to be the morning of my memory loss?"

"Correct."

"Why did I need to come all the way back to London?" Eva asked, more to herself than anyone else.

"That's what we wanted to know, but apparently it was vital that no reports were made until you returned to MI6 to debrief. It caused quite a stir with the higher-ups, let me tell you."

Curiouser and curiouser. Eva was beginning to think she was Alice in Wonderland.

"Oh well, we better tell the pilot." Eva slapped her hands together.

"Tell the pilot what?"

"There's been a course correction. We're going to Macau."

For the next few hours Eva devoured all she could about her previous assignment. Hu Xia didn't exactly seem like what you would call a worthwhile human being. Born into privilege, he had greatly benefited from China's new brand of capitalism. His social media platforms (he had many) were filled with photos of him draped in expensive clothes and watches, draped over sports cars, and with scantily clad women draped over him. Basically, there was a lot of draping. If modern China had embraced consumerism, he had taken it to bed and thoroughly ravaged it. He wore his advantage as a badge of honour. It was the worst case of affluenza Eva had ever seen.

A cover story had been created for her. She was a reporter for *Rolling Stone* magazine, doing a story on Nu Metal in Macau and mainland China. Hu was an expert. Her cover name was, she was appalled to discover, Candy Stripe. Which made her sound more like a stripper than a reporter. Not that she could talk with a name like Eva Destruction, but still. Eva would be having severe words with whoever had given her that hideous moniker. She hoped she wouldn't be having that conversation with herself.

A whole fabricated persona had been set up, with fake articles and an online presence. She had apparently spent an entire day and night having photos taken of her, in offices, on the street and in clubs so they could be planted around the web. Search engines were manipulated so terms like "Candy Stripe" and "Rolling Stone" would lead to Eva's image and bogus articles.

A Naicho intelligence officer confirmed that Eva had made contact on the flight and had become friendly with Hu. When they disembarked, Eva and Hu were arm in arm and headed for Hu's gold-plated Ferrari, parked in his personal car space at the Macau airport. That was the last any intelligence agency had heard from Eva in five days. When she finally contacted MI6 she demanded immediate extraction and refused the station chief's demands for debriefing. The exact words he used in the report were, "Miss Destruction advised me it was a national security issue and if I didn't like it I could wrap her answer in barbed wire and shove it up my rectum."

"It does sound like the kind of thing I might say," Eva said sheepishly.

Nobody argued.

"There was no word from me in a better part of a week... what about credit cards, phone usage, that sort of thing?"

"No card usage, and your tracking pin and MI6 mobile phone didn't move from Hu's hotel, The Venetian. However," Bishop pulled up a photo on his laptop, "we do have this from the security camera feed of the Galaxy casino in Macau. Their feeds are easier to hack into, as casinos freely share information about troublesome gamblers." He used his finger to scroll through several images. "Days two, four and five you accompanied Hu and his entourage to the casino's high roller room."

Eva ran her fingers over the image. It seemed bizarre to look at a picture of herself at a place she didn't remember, with people she didn't recall. It was as if she was another person entirely. Did she like Hu? Hate him? What had she done in Macau? What were her secrets?

Bishop went on. "And here, his Instagram feed. You appear, ah, quite chummy."

"That was the assignment, right?"

"Yes, quite."

It seemed like Bishop was sulking. *Diddums.* Eva was a spy, she was spying. Would Bishop be as surly if they were discussing a male agent? She wouldn't accept double standards from Bishop or anyone else. Or was it jealousy again?

"Well, that's probably why you weren't returning my calls." Loch gave her a sympathetic smile.

Eva nudged his knee with her own. It was like they were passing notes in class. He almost made her giggly, but Eva's thoughts were far less innocent than those of a naive schoolgirl.

"Do we even know where he is at this moment?" Yuji asked. "We assume he's at home in Macau, but..."

"I'll get my people on it." Bishop began typing.

"He's still in Macau," Loch said quietly. "At the Hotel Lisboa, to be exact."

"Did you get this from the CIA?"

"No, Instagram. This was posted two hours ago."

He held up a picture of Hu holding two magnums of Krug Clos

du Mesnil, an expensive cigar hanging from his lips. He was standing in front of a sign that read "Hotel Lisboa, Macau".

"Okay, so we're pretty sure then."

Bishop was all business. He hadn't made a sexist quip in hours. "How are you going to play this, Eva? You don't know what happened or where your relationship with Hu ended."

"I'll do what I always do. Wing it." Eva thought of throwing out some jazz hands, but decided against it.

"That's hardly what we would call playing by the rule book." Yuji was far from impressed.

"I don't play by the book," Eva said. "I burn it."

"She means literally, Yuji." Bishop sighed. "She literally burned the MI6 rule book. In a wastebasket. The alarms went off, the fire brigade came. It was a palaver."

Eva did her best to appear adorable.

An apprehensive expression crossed Yuji's face. "I am unsure if this is the correct manner in which to conduct an operation."

Eva grinned. "I wouldn't have it any other way."

CHAPTER SEVEN

The Venetian Hotel wasn't exactly subtle. Then again, neither was Hu Xia. Gaudy to the extreme, it was like a Vegas casino turned up to eleven. Gondoliers propelled tourist-filled boats through unnaturally blue water, past high-end shops, flashy casino signs and McDonald's restaurants. Not *exactly* like the real Venice, then.

Bishop, Loch, Yuji and Eva silently looked out on the artificial canal. The plan, which was what Eva had called it, though the others were reluctant to use such a definitive term, was simple enough. Eva was to rock up on Hu's doorstep and accuse him of lying—exactly what about was unimportant—and wing the rest of it. They had no intelligence as to the success of Eva's previous mission, or the current state of her relationship with Hu. She'd have to use her brain to gauge his opinion of her and adjust her story accordingly.

Granted, it was as thin as a gossamer G-string, but it was all they had. Yuji had argued for more surveillance, but Eva countered that further scrutiny of Hu's movements wouldn't uncover what he and Eva had talked about. The only way to do that was for her to speak to him.

Standing next to the hotel's entrance, they all seemed reluctant to enter. Eva was nervous because their strategy was ridiculously flawed; the others were probably justifiably concerned about her safety. It all came down to how well Eva had gotten on with Hu. Eva suspected that she wouldn't have liked him much. It said plenty that the man lived in the garish surrounds of the largest casino in the world. Whether Hu believed Eva wanted to spend time with him would all depend on her training and acting ability.

But they wouldn't find out by standing around. Eva clapped her hands together. "We're not here to fuck spiders, let's do this."

Eva strode off, but the three men stood motionless by the railing.

"What did you just say?" Bishop placed his hands on his hips. "We're not here to what?"

"What? It's a common saying—we're not here to fuck spiders. It's a saying."

Bishop folded his arms. "Not from where I'm from."

Loch shook his head.

Yuji furrowed his brow. "I am afraid I am unfamiliar with this particular proverb, also."

"It's like he's got a few roos loose in the top paddock."

More blank looks.

"Fine. Whatever, let's go."

They split up and headed to their assigned locations. Bishop was to go to Hu's room on the thirty-second floor, and would pretend to be lost if Eva needed immediate backup. Loch would do the same one floor up, near the stairwell. Yuji was to stay down at the bar nearest the elevators. Much to Bishop's chagrin, none of them were armed, but they all had micro earpieces courtesy of Naicho's tech arm. It was sloppy spycraft, but it was all they had.

While the other two went off, Eva hung back with Yuji. He ordered two mineral waters and they sipped them in tense silence.

"I have a question, if I may," Yuji said after several minutes. "Do Western espionage organisations normally allow cross-agency fraternisation?"

Was it that obvious?

"Well, I'm not sure 'allow' is quite the right word. I'm confident if everything is kept separate, no intelligence is shared, I, ah, it's complicated." Eva thought more about it. "Very complicated."

Yuji straightened his moustache sagely. "I'm sure it is. But my organisation would never allow such a thing. Due to the risk of intelligence being compromised, of course, rather than the homosexual aspect."

Eva nodded, lost in her own thoughts, then froze. "Wait, what?" She shook her head, unsure she had heard Yuji correctly. "Bishop and Loch?"

His face was dead serious, not a crease to be seen. Eva did her best not to laugh out loud. She had to wonder where he'd gotten such an absurd idea. Yuji must have the world's worst gaydar. It wasn't even worth considering. Then she tilted her head, envisaging the possibility in detail.

She coughed and covered it with a sip of her mineral water. "I should," she motioned her glass toward the elevators.

"Of course. Good hunting, Miss Destruction."

Eva waited for the elevator, on edge. She should have had a bourbon while she waited. Sure, it was too early for that sort of thing, but she needed something to take the edge off. She took the tiny earpiece Yuji had supplied out of her pocket. She needed a way to relieve the building anxiety.

"Testing, testing," she said, stepping into the elevator. "Target transport acquired and proceeding in a forwardy motion soon to be followed by some upwardy momentum. Tango, banana, foxtrot, jellybean, dildo, over."

Loch's voice came through as clearly as if he was standing beside her. She wished he was. "Intel received by Team Alpha. Team Bravo, you are to proceed with assignment. Sierra, marzipan, Zulu, fisting, chlamydia, over."

Eva laughed out loud and covered her mouth. She was glad she was alone in the elevator.

"Why are you Team Alpha? I want to be Team Alpha."

"Too late, I bought a hat."

"Does it have a propeller?"

"No, but the ear flaps are to die for."

A smile spread across Eva's entire face and she shook her head. Loch got her sense of humour. A rare thing.

"Everyone, a little decorum, please." Bishop was not amused.

"Is this a code I am unaware of?" Yuji inquired.

"Sorry guys, just releasing a little tension."

Eva was sure she heard Loch sigh.

She clenched and unclenched her fists. "I'm ready."

The elevator reached the thirty-second floor and before she knew it, Eva was standing before the great double doors of Hu's apartment. She wasn't prepared. The mission was ramshackle at best. *This is insane.* Without consulting her brain, her hand pressed the doorbell. Eva's breath hitched as she waited an eternity for some hint of movement behind the door. There wasn't any. She tried again and waited. Nothing.

Then there was a muffled scraping sound, followed by a faint croaky voice. Eva spoke just enough Mandarin to know it was a guttural usage of the dialect. She also caught an implication about her mother and what she thought was the word for goat.

Eva sighed. It was now or never. "Hu, it's me." She gritted her teeth. "Candy."

The door flew open to reveal a dishevelled and bleary-eyed Hu. He was dressed in an elegant purple velvet dressing gown and matching slippers. He had bags under his eyes, but when he saw Eva his face lit up like a Christmas tree doused in petrol.

"Darling!"

He threw his arms around Eva and embraced her in a bear hug, lifting her clean off the ground.

Darling? What the hell had Eva done with this guy?

"What the *tā mā de* are you doing in Macau?" He waved his hands dismissively. "Doesn't matter. Come in, come in."

His accent was heavily influenced by his expensive education at the Diocesan Boys' School in Hong Kong. Even with the trappings of privilege, Hu had enough brains to graduate in the top five per cent of his class. Not bad for an elite, high-performance school. Pity he squandered it all living the life of a teenager's wet dream.

"Sorry, I was asleep."

There was a slight slur to his words, and as he sauntered through the immense apartment Eva detected a wobble in his stride. He was either hungover or still drunk.

He slid behind a great mahogany bar and mixed a drink. When he caught Eva's glance, he sheepishly said, "Hair of the dog. Last night I, well, I'm not sure what I got up to."

"I am." Eva tilted her head at the well-endowed tattooed Asian beauty laying naked on the couch. Parts of her anatomy defied gravity in a way that suggested there was some medical enhancement at work. Hu glanced over and appeared as surprised as Eva. He quickly rushed over and woke her up, then scribbled a note on a piece of paper and shoved it in her hand. Eva assumed it was his phone number. He spoke to her in a harsh whisper as he threw her clothes at her, thrust some money in her fist and pushed her towards the door. After a terse exchange of words, she raised an angry middle finger and slammed the door behind her.

Hu headed back to the bar and resumed making his drink. "Sorry, my cousin."

"Sure." Eva wasn't concerned about Hu's recent conquests, she wanted to know about his previous activities.

"What's going on?" Bishop asked, far too loudly, in her ear.

"Later," she whispered harshly.

"Later what?" Hu asked.

Eva grinned like an idiot, hoping he wouldn't ask again. She needed to focus on why she was here. "So, Hu, I think we have some unfinished business."

A sleazy sneer crossed his lips. "Finally, you've come to your senses and want a Hu special."

So maybe they hadn't slept together. His swagger was nauseating. Eva really didn't want to know what a Hu special was.

Eva shook her head. "I said business."

Hu gave a slight shake of his head. "Business? What, you want to buy another nuke? That shit doesn't grow on trees, babe."

Nuke?

Another?

Babe?

What?

Loch's voice came through loud and clear. The alarm in it was just as distinct. "Did he just say nuke?"

Ginger minger ninjas.

"Well..." She started the sentence not knowing where it would end. "About that nuke..."

"Don't tell me you lost it?" Hu asked in good humour. "You paid good money for it, don't tell me you've misplaced it already..." His face turned grave. "Wait. I told you there were no returns. Don't think you can bring it back. This isn't Kmart. A deal is a deal." There was a slight note of panic in his voice. "I've already spent the three and a half mil. Had some debts, so, you know, ah, no returnsies."

Cutthroat businessperson he wasn't.

Eva tried to process this new information. She'd bought a nuke off Hu for three and a half million—dollars, she assumed. That was what the Russians had caught wind of? If so, why had Eva gone through with the purchase? Why hadn't she alerted the local authorities? Or MI6 for that matter? And where had she got three and a half million dollars? Sure, she was frugal with her shopping, but she didn't have that kind of cash lying around. It had to come from somewhere. She was pretty sure this was the kind of minor detail MI6 would have covered in the expense reports. So, if MI6 didn't pay, who did?

"Please advise the gentleman that you doubt the validity of his claim as to the origin of the device." It was Yuji.

Eva nodded despite there being no one to nod to. "The nuke—" she almost choked on the word. "I'm not sure it comes from where you claimed it did."

Hu stopped stirring his Bloody Mary. "What's that? Of course it does. You think I have a stockpile of nukes just lying about that I can pick and choose from? Babe," he shook his head, "I don't know where you're coming from with this, but if I say Da Qaidam, I mean Da Qaidam. Ain't no other place it could come from, lady."

Yuji whispered, "Da Qaidam is on mainland China. It contains

ICBM missile silos. My country is understandably not fond of this place."

Loch piped in. "If this is true, the thing would be big. We're not talking a briefcase bomb here. Those suckers have some heft."

Hu checked his watch. Something about the move made Eva jittery. He gave her a fake smile.

He was up to something.

"What's going on, Hu?"

"Don't know what you mean, babe."

His casual manner was clearly forced. Eva's hackles were up. She glanced at his hands—they were shaking. It wasn't the hangover.

There was a knock at the door, which made them both jump.

"I'll get it!" Hu ran to the door.

Eva got there first. She blocked his way.

"Hey, babe. It's just breakfast."

"You said you were asleep. Been sleep ordering, have you?"

He lunged for the door. Eva grabbed his wrist and twisted, then shoved her thumb under his armpit and pinched. As Hu winced in pain, she rammed his face into the wall beside the door and glared through the peephole. In the hallway six heavily armed Asian men clad in black—*why is it always black?*—appeared ready for a fight. Each of them had earpieces, submachine guns and nasty dispositions.

Eva retreated from the door. "I'm not hungry." She shoved Hu back into his apartment. "Boys, I've got company of the heavily shooty bang bang variety on the other side of the door. I have thirty seconds at best. Making my way to the far end of the apartment for potential extraction."

Holding Hu's arm behind his back, she pushed him along. As they hurtled down the hallway Eva scanned the apartment for weapons of any description. An occasional vase or small statue were the best there was—nothing that would be effective against a couple of well-aimed bullets. She pushed on.

When did Hu have a chance to raise the alarm? She cursed

herself. The hooker. He'd passed on a message. The scribbled note was to contact them. *Stupid.* She should have realised.

"My only question is why, Hu? Why did you rat me out?"

Despite the pain Eva was inflicting on his extremities, his sleazy sneer returned. "I have a million reasons why."

A million?

The bounty.

Jesus on a pogo stick.

Hu shrugged. "Like I said, I have debts."

He must have uncovered her real identity. Moreover, he knew there was someone willing to pay a million dollars to have her captured. Eva twisted his arm harder. Hu squealed like a rat in a microwave.

They reached the end of the hall. The beautiful vista afforded by the thirty-second floor location was breathtaking. Far below, tiny specks navigated the artificial winding paved streets and canals that all led, eventually, to the gaming rooms. Jumping wasn't an option unless death was the objective. Eva looked up and down, but there were no nearby balconies or alcoves. They were trapped.

The sound of splintering wood and aggressive shouts told Eva her thirty seconds were up. Perhaps she could use a statue to break a window, fashion a rope out of bed sheets, tie it to the statue, use that as a pendulum to break another window a floor down and then shimmy down to relative safety. It was a ludicrous and dangerous idea even, if she had an hour. She had seconds at best.

"Guys, I'm out of options here."

She placed her finger to her earpiece only to find it wasn't there. It must have fallen out when she'd run. Not that it mattered. Three unarmed men without backup could offer no assistance. But that didn't stop her hoping otherwise.

For some reason the doorbell rang. Elevated shouts came from the front entrance, more instructional sounding than the ones before. Warnings.

Bishop's voice was loud and clear. "Housekeeping!"

Automatic weapon fire was the only reply. Eva gasped. Her grip on Hu faltered.

There was no further sound from anywhere. It seemed like the entire world had stopped. Eva waited for any sound at all, but none came.

After an eternity, there was a cough. "Would you believe me if I said dry-cleaning?"

More weapons fire.

"Room service?"

The gunfire was longer.

"Massage?"

Now it was deafening.

"Fine, if you're going to be like that, I'm coming in!"

There was silence. No shots were fired.

"Here I come. One, two, three. For Devonshire tea! Arrrgghhh!"

The burst of gunshots was furious. There was a loud *bang* followed by a sizzle. White smoke emanated from the entrance-way. Its chemical smell had a distinct tang.

The gunfire didn't let up. There were confused shouts, interspersed with more confused shouts.

Eva smiled. The crazy bastard.

A small piece of plastic on the ground caught her attention. She pushed Hu out of the way to retrieve the earpiece and put it in, and immediately heard heavy respiration, as if someone was running.

"Nice improv with the fire extinguisher. Where'd you pick that one up?"

Breathlessly, Bishop replied, "Old friend taught me. 'Throw the fucking thing, Bishop,' she told me. She was sweet like that. I wonder what ever happened to her."

"Right now, I think she's wishing she had wings."

Eva was startled by a knock on the other side of the glass.

She and Hu turned. Loch's smiling face was on the other side of the glass. He tipped an imaginary cowboy hat. The window-washing rig he stood on was uneven, as if he hadn't quite worked out the controls. Not that it mattered. All they had to do was get on it.

"How are you going to break the glass?" she asked.

Loch's face fell. "Ah."

He looked about the rig for something that could do the job. When he glanced up he shouted, "Duck!" and did exactly that himself.

Eva grabbed Hu by the back of the neck and shoved him down. Bullets pockmarked the hallway and shattered the window. A screaming breeze burst through the fragmented void. There was a pause while their assailants regrouped.

Loch poked his head up. "Like that, I guess." He inhaled and shouted, "Return fire!" using Bishop's tactic of assumed resistance.

Eva didn't even wait. She tossed Hu through the window, where he landed gracelessly on the window-washing rig. The attackers were most likely hiding behind something solid, awaiting a volley of bullets that would never come.

Eva leapt on. "Hit it," she said to Loch.

The rig jolted as it lurched skyward. Being for a modern building, the rig moved relatively rapidly, but to the passengers it seemed positively glacial. Thankfully they were only a few floors from the roof, but that didn't mean they were going to make it.

Bullets hit the bottom of the window-washing rig. It was designed to be light, not to withstand submachine-gun fire. Bullets ripped through the floor, somehow missing them.

With a *bump* they reached the top of the thirty-seventh floor. There was no need for discussion; all three leapt onto the roof as a torrent of bullets shredded the remainder of the rig. Some must have hit the cables, because one side dropped forcefully, then the other side snapped, and the whole rig plummeted down the side of the building.

Loch and Eva were already on their feet. Eva she grasped the back of Hu's dressing gown, propelling him towards the fire escape door. The flat roof was huge, and sparse, except for some construction material at the far end.

All three skidded to a halt as the door swung open. They were completely exposed—no cover, no weapons and no escape.

Eva clenched her fists anyway. If she was going out, it wouldn't be quietly.

Bishop burst out of the fire escape with a gun in hand and his shirt covered in blood. He beamed. "Is this the Bill Murray Country Club?"

Eva could have hugged him.

"Anyone for a quick exit?" he asked, holding the door open.

All four halted as the sound of charging feet came thundering up the stairs.

"So, down isn't an option then." Eva scanned the roof. "The construction stuff, grab it, we'll barricade the door."

As they ran, Eva pointed to the bloody pistol in Bishop's hand. "Pick that up in a yard sale?"

"I ran into a fellow who didn't take kindly to my handsome face."

"Inconceivable."

"I know, right? Unconscionable."

Bishop tucked the gun into his belt and they all grabbed what they could. As they raced back to the door Hu lagged behind and had to be forcibly encouraged to speed up. The heaviest items they could find were wedged against the door. Between the handle and outer door frame, Loch threaded brackets. The aluminium was flimsy, just like their plan.

"This won't hold for long." Bishop had a point.

"The rig is out of commission, so, uh…" Eva scratched the back of her head. "Anyone Ever tried base jumping without a parachute?"

"Surrender."

They all glared at Hu.

Loch shook his head. "I don't think that's an option we're considering."

Hu sneered. "I didn't ask you to consider it. It was an order."

It was then that Eva noticed the blood-smeared gun in his hand. Bishop grabbed at his belt. There was nothing there.

Bellend heaving bloodclaat.

Eva shook her head. "Dude, have you not noticed those guys are shooting at you as much as they're shooting at us? They won't care if you called it in. I'm pretty sure you're not going to get your bounty. At least, not in this life."

"I've got a million reasons to help them, remember?"

Bishop lunged to get his gun back but Hu recoiled just in time. He waved the weapon nervously in their direction. His glance darted between the door, the roof's ledge and back again. It seemed he didn't have a plan beyond obtaining the gun.

"Do you have any other weapons?" he asked.

"Pretty sure we would have used them by now, guy," Loch said soothingly. "How about we work together to get out of here and—"

"There is no out of here, man! That's the point!" Hu ran the gun against his temple. His cheeks blew out and he blurted, "Everyone take your clothes off."

There was total silence except for the distant sound of footsteps.

Eva gaped at him. "Excuse the fuck me?"

"Clothes," Hu brandished the gun, "off. Now!"

"Why?" Loch asked.

"I don't want any surprises," Hu said, his voice becoming increasingly high-pitched.

Bishop folded his arms. "Believe me, if I take off my pants there will be a surprise."

Hu shrieked and fired a round at their feet. "Now!"

The rumbling of footsteps from the stairwell momentarily stopped. Loch and Eva froze. Without hesitation, Bishop began to disrobe. It wasn't like he was unused to it. The other two followed suit, and soon all three stood before a leering Hu, naked as the day they were born, although Eva had slightly more tattoos these days. Eva and Loch attempted to cover themselves while Bishop stood legs akimbo, his significant manhood gently swinging in the breeze.

"Alright, everyone step back." Hu flicked the gun, motioning for them to move towards the fire-escape door.

The deafening sound of rifle butts hammering against the door assaulted their ears. It would be seconds now. Eva desperately looked about for anything that could help, but there was nothing. She would be captured, and her companions were most likely going to be killed naked. That was no way to die. Well, except the naked part. Eva was OK with passing away naked, but many years from now, ideally, and in bed. With several equally naked friends.

The thumping against their makeshift barricade was drowned out by a sudden rush of wind. All four turned as a bright red helicopter roared over the roof ledge and hovered there for a moment.

It was just the distraction they needed. Loch rushed Hu and punched him square in the jaw, sending him reeling. Before he fell, Loch snatched the gun and aimed it at the startled man. For a brief moment Eva thought he would fire, but instead he turned towards her and gave her a wink. She took a fraction of a second to glance down Loch's torso and back again. It wasn't leering if she'd already seen it, was it? The fact that she couldn't remember the member was neither here nor there.

The helicopter landed smoothly on the roof and all three raced towards it. Even though they had no idea who was flying the thing, it was still a better option than an armed black-clad assault team.

They needn't have worried. When Bishop slid the door open, Eva saw that a headset-wearing Yuji had the stick in his hand. "Please get in!"

Eva pushed Bishop and Loch into the tiny cabin.

"Wait!" Hu staggered towards them, blood pouring from a cut lip. "Take me with you!"

"You were about to give us up, you fucking cocksplat," Eva shouted over the noise of the helicopter blades.

"I've got no bargaining chip without you. You have to let me on!"

Eva tilted her head. "I've got a million reasons not to."

She climbed on board and slid the door shut. Hu stood on the roof, stunned.

Yuji didn't wait. The helicopter lifted off and sped—recklessly, Eva thought—away from the Venetian, just as their makeshift barricade finally collapsed and four men burst through. The assailants raised their weapons, but dropped them just as quickly. The short-barrelled submachine guns didn't have the range. They turned their attention to a snivelling Hu. The last thing Eva saw before Yuji banked away was Hu taking a rifle butt to his stomach.

Eva tapped his shoulder. "How did you pull this off, Yuji?"

"I did mention I was a qualified pilot, yes?"

They raced across the Macau skyline. No aerial craft seemed to be in pursuit.

"Where did you get the helicopter?"

"A tourist operator. He was very accommodating."

"By accommodating, do you mean he's unconscious somewhere?"

"Please. Perish the thought. No, he has been generously compensated and now the glorious State of Japan owns one heli-copter formerly owned by the Spin Out Helicopter Tour Company."

Eva waited a moment. "You're not going to ask why we're naked?"

"I assume it is your own business."

She glanced back into the cabin. Loch had attempted to cover up, but Bishop was leaning back, his ankle resting on his knee as if he were at a pleasant garden party.

Finding a "Spin Out!" t-shirt, Eva slipped it on. It was only a small, but it did the job. Kind of. "Well, at least I know one thing now."

"What's that?" Loch asked.

"That shipment they're searching for? Now we know the cargo. We're looking for a nuclear weapon."

CHAPTER EIGHT

Eva's arse was probably on YouTube by now.

It was inevitable. Yuji had landed the helicopter on the fourth fairway of Caesars golf course. Grey-haired golfers shared much amusement as three naked or semi-naked bodies piled out. It was only a short run to the limousine driven by one of Yuji's agents, but long enough for golfers to pull out their mobile phones. Their naked flesh probably contrasted beautifully against the deep green of the fairways.

Yuji deemed it too dangerous for the four of them to fly directly to the airport, not knowing what awaited them. The golf course was their best shot at avoiding hostile forces. Yuji's man advised that they didn't appear to have a tail. Eva wondered if he was having a crack at her nude derrière.

With any luck her bare arse would be attributed to Candy Stripe, and she'd still be able to attend her family Christmas without being the butt of too many jokes. But that potential drama would have to wait. They had more pressing matters to attend to right now.

As the car's engine fired up, Eva relaxed. Well, as much as she could with a bounty on her head. Loch's reassuring hand on her knee also helped. It was still odd how quickly the goons had shown up at Hu's. Had they been waiting for her? If so, whoever was after Eva had far better intelligence than they did.

The blades of the helicopter sped up, in readiness for take-off. Their main aim now was to leave Macau as soon as humanly possible. Yuji had a helicopter to take care of, and he couldn't just stash it in a storage locker, so with any luck he'd rendezvous with them at the nearest field office. Eva hoped it wasn't the last she'd see of Yuji. He was a gentle and brave man.

A black smudge in the corner of the sky caught her eye. As the smudge grew larger, so did the smoke tail behind it. Its trail wove through the sky, the missile's destination plain to see. Words stuck in her throat, Eva pounded the limo's glass with her fists.

She managed to squeak out a helpless, "No" before the missile slammed into the helicopter. It exploded in a sphere of intense orange, knocking golfers off their feet, engulfing some in flames. Chunks of fuselage hurtled in all directions and debris was strewn across the course. People both ran away from and to the wreckage, either trying to save themselves or others.

With a screech of tyres the limo jolted forward and out of the car park.

"We have to go back!" Eva implored the driver, tears streaming down her face.

Bishop placed his hand on her shoulder. "There's nothing to go back for, Eva. He's gone."

As the car skidded around the corner, Eva took one last glimpse at the burning wreckage. It was her fault, again. Every place she went, death followed. It was too much. Everything was too much. She just wanted to be somewhere safe, somewhere she didn't have the spectre of death tickling her neck with his ghastly breath every minute. She needed a safe place. Her place.

A splinter of a concept began to form. She parked it for another time.

Loch slipped his arm around her and she nestled in, warm, wanting to feel the illusion of safety. Bishop glanced in their direction and his back stiffened.

The limo zoomed down the Estrada de Seac Pai Van with all eyes on the sky, scanning for airborne destruction. None could be seen. After five minutes without any further hostile engagements, the tension in the limousine eased slightly. But only slightly.

"We'll need to inform MI6." Bishop reclined on the soft leather seat.

"Like fuck," Eva replied.

Loch's head snapped around. He pursed his lips, but was silent. This was an MI6 discussion.

Bishop frowned. "Is that your professional appraisal, Ms Destruction?"

"Yep, that's my professional as fuck appraisal. We don't know how those guys knew we'd be at Hu's. That could have been anyone who just tried to shove a large missile up my arse without due consent. Yuji's dead." She was shocked at how callous those words sounded. But right now it was all about survival. Mourning Yuji would come later. "Look, Bishop, a very wise person thought I should keep the nuke information secret until I was safely within the walls of the MI6. That wise person was me, by the way."

"I got that."

"Well, she's someone I trust. I can't say the same for anyone else."

"Oh, thank you very much." Bishop frowned indignantly.

"You know what I mean," Eva said with a tilt of her head.

"I don't know that I do, Eva." Bishop's comment was not light-hearted. "You're basing your decision on sentiment. You are trying to make an intelligence decision while overcome with emotion—"

"Because I'm a woman? Fuck you, Bishop." Okay, *that* was based on emotion.

"Eva—"

"No, seriously, fuck you." She was pissed now. Her fingernails dug into the leather trim. "Do you know how condescending that is? Basing my decision on emotion, because that's what silly women do, right?"

"That's not what I—"

"Well it's bullshit, Bishop. I'm a trained MI6 agent, and I think

I've earned my stripes, so why don't you drop the patronising attitude and actually listen to the frivolous little skirt, who might just have something to contribute?"

"Now listen here, that's not fair. I've always—"

"Been a condescending twat, yes, I know. But listen to a female opinion for once. They knew we were coming, Bishop. They *knew*. They were there to kill. They had rocket launchers, for Christ's sake! I think there's two bastards out there, one who wants to find out about the shipment, and another who wants me permanently silenced. I'm not fond of either. Obviously I had reasons for breaking protocol, and demanded a briefing at MI6 because I didn't trust the chain of command. I've seen nothing in the last twenty minutes to sway me otherwise. So this skirt votes we get on the fastest jet and don't stop until we hit the MI6 boardroom."

The car slowed at a set of traffic lights, the driver remaining vigilant, scanning for any threat.

Bishop exhaled loudly and ran his hand over his face. "Apologies, Eva. Espionage is not a democracy. As senior agent, it's my decision. I'm calling this in as soon as we hit the field office. Missing nuclear weapons can't wait a minute, let alone another day. I'm ordering an immediate extraction."

"Well let me out here, then." Eva pointed at the sidewalk.

Humour danced in Bishop's eyes. "You may have forgotten, but you don't have any pants."

Eva glanced down. "You're right, but I think there are more than enough cunts in this car already."

She opened the door against Bishop's howls of protest and stepped out onto the Estrada Flor de Lotus wearing nothing but a too-small t-shirt and a pissed-off expression. Loch jumped out too, wearing even less.

The shopping precinct erupted with gasps, laughter and a hell of a lot of pointing. Her head held high, Eva strode confidently to the nearest high-end shop. Loch attempted to replicate Eva's self-assuredness, but with less success. He didn't seem to know which parts he should be covering, and failed in his attempts.

As they entered Gucci they were greeted by a shriek from the shop assistant. Eva offered a genial smile and proceeded to regale her with a sob story about the two of them being mugged on the short walk from the Venetian. After calling the hotel for verification, the assistant supplied Eva and Loch with new designer outfits, all charged to a Mr Hu Xia, room 3209 at the Venetian Hotel.

Eva was still livid at Bishop. Pulling rank was the final straw. Couldn't he see MI6 was leaking like a hobo's shopping bag? The only person she could trust right now was herself. She observed her companion, standing uncomfortably in a two thousand dollar leisure suit, and amended that assessment. Possibly Loch, too. But he had to earn that trust. Siding with her and parading naked around Studio City was a good start.

Thankful for the 21st century, Eva borrowed the assistant's mobile phone and used it to access her untraceable PayPal account. She transferred some money to the assistant, who gave her cash in return. That would do for a few days at least.

The next step was passports. Entering the airport was out of the question. They hailed a taxi and offered the driver an additional five hundred dollars to go inside the airport and retrieve a sealed envelope from a locker. When they'd first landed in Macau, the group of spies had stashed their passports in a locker that they all knew the code for, in case of a situation exactly like this one.

They paid the taxi driver and had him drop them off at the nearest internet café. Only when he was out of sight did Eva open the envelope. She took out a bundle of passports each for herself and Loch, leaving Bishop's and Yuji's. The sight of the Japanese passport stirred up so many painful emotions, but she swallowed them hard. *Later.* Survival first. Bishop would need to make his own arrangements.

She flicked through her options. Eva Destruction was out, as was Candy Stripe. Luckily she had two others to choose from, and thankfully, neither sounded like a stripper. She chose Deana O'Neill and binned the rest. They ditched their phones, too. Any benefit they offered was outweighed by the possibility of some pimply kid with half a brain being able to track their every move.

Using a computer at the internet café, they organised an Uber to take them to the Taipa Ferry Terminal. Uber on fake accounts was less traceable than a taxi, and less likely to have cameras.

Loch had wanted to at least notify the CIA he was alive. His conflicted feelings played out across his features. But if they were going dark, they had to do it completely, or not at all. No contact until they reached MI6. It was probably less dark, more rogue. Eva would lose her job over it, that was certain. But she still had her coffee shop—if she wasn't deported. She gave Loch the choice; there was no use them both losing their careers. He kissed her cheek.

"Maybe you could teach me how to make coffee?"

"Oh darlin'", she rubbed his leg. "You're American, you don't know coffee. You think you do, but it's either been filtered until all the life has gone out of it or it's a Starbucks abomination. No, you can be a waiter and we'll see how you go."

"Is there room for promotion if I suck up to the boss, Chérie?"

"Oh, there will be plenty of sucking, I assure you."

In the back of the Uber, winding through the streets of a city where any turn could be their last, Eva and Loch shared their first real kiss. Or at least, the first where they actually knew each other, at least more than a few minutes. Despite, or maybe because of, the dramas of the day, the rest of the world melted away. Eva nestled into his strong arms and wished she could stay there forever. Eva could be tough and emotionless when the mission required, but that didn't mean she couldn't take comfort with those she cared for. He held her tight for a long time, neither of them talking. It was exactly what she needed.

After a while the relentless rhythm of the tyres lulled Eva into a post-adrenaline haze. Nestled into Loch's embrace, she felt safe. It was several minutes before he spoke.

"You hit Bishop pretty hard back there. I know you felt strongly about Yuji, we all did, but I don't know that he deserved to bear full responsibility for the patriarchy."

She was still pissed at Bishop. "Like my mum used to say, if you can't handle me at my radical feminist, you don't deserve me at my radical whore."

"Your mother said that?"

"I'm paraphrasing."

"I'd like to see how." Loch didn't even try to mask his smirk. It was a lovely smirk.

She traced his beard with her hand. "I know I was hard on him, and yes, I'm sure losing Yuji was a big contributing factor, but that doesn't negate the fact that I'm right. We don't know who our friends are. You said it yourself, don't trust anyone."

"I did, and I'm very clever."

"Exactly. We need to lay low until we have this thing sorted." She glanced at her bright pink Gucci leisure suit, then at Loch's matching vivid purple one. "And these ensembles are the perfect start."

"When we get to the terminal we should probably buy leather outfits." Loch gave her a slanted grin.

"Why?" Eva asked cautiously.

"Because if we don't want to be seen, what's better than an outfit made of hide?"

All that was missing was a drummer in the corner. *Boom-tish.*

She crossed her arms and shook her head. "That was terrible."

"Oh, come on, it was gold."

In spite of herself, Eva laughed. She understood how she'd fallen for him, even if she didn't remember doing so. He was a very handsome man, capable and caring, but it was his humour that would have swayed her. She was certain that's what would have tipped her over the edge and into his bed.

She sighed and patted his chest. "I really don't know if this is the right course of action, Loch. It feels right, and that should be a sign that it's probably not." She looked up at him. "I tend to never do things right in my life. I've done a lot of things wrong. Well, a lot of wrong guys." She didn't know why she was telling Loch this —he must already know—but she felt the need to start fresh. "I have, ah, quite the sexual history. Not that I'm bothered by it—my body, my choice and all that—but, you know, I, um, thought you should know. If you didn't. But you probably do. Hey, look who's babbling."

He kissed the top of her head. "Personally, I'm more concerned about what comes out of a woman's mouth than what's been in it."

"Pretty sure I just ovulated."

The driver advised that they were coming up to the ferry terminal, so they straightened themselves out as best they could. Leisure suits weren't the easiest things in the world to make presentable.

The terminal was bustling. The daytime crowd appeared to be mostly made up of tourists travelling to or from Hong Kong. The trip on the hydrofoil would take less than an hour, but for Eva, it may as well have been weeks. They were in danger every second they stayed in Macau, and they no longer had the protection of the CIA or MI6. They were on their own in a hostile land. The sooner they disappeared the better.

The short journey on the jetfoil craft was uneventful. They weren't blown up, stabbed or kidnapped, which was always a bonus. Even though she'd been to Hong Kong countless times, Eva had never ridden the hydrofoil. It was actually fun—or it would have been if she wasn't searching for assassins. The speed of the craft pushed her back in the seat, just like on a plane, which made it far more exhilarating than a normal ferry. When she entered Victoria Harbour she felt safer, even nostalgic. In the last ten years she'd probably spent more time in "Honkers", as she called it, than in her native Australia. Her ex did a lot of business in Asia, and used Hong Kong as a hub. Eva liked the chaotic nature of the city, the frenzied traffic, the claustrophobic crowds, the general frenetic buzz. And she liked the way all that could be countered at any moment by finding a peaceful park, or by an act of kindness by one of the locals. This was Eva's turf, somewhere she could get her bearings, which she had been sorely missing of late.

They cleared customs without incident, sideways glances at their garish outfits notwithstanding, and made their way to the line of red taxis. The midday heat had settled in, pushing down on the crowded city and covering everything in a slick coating of sweat.

Eva knew her destination. The Mandarin Oriental Hotel had served her well for years. It was probably her favourite hotel in the world. They always managed to find her a room. Even a few years back, when the Rugby sevens were in town and the entire city was booked out, they found her a suite.

She craved comfort. Needed it.

The doorman opened the large glass door and bowed slightly. "Welcome back, Ms Destruction. Good to see you again so soon."

So soon? That was a good sign.

"Hi Tay. Now, you know I've asked you to call me Eva, right?"

He giggled and gave her a gap-toothed smile.

She'd always had a soft spot for Tay. "How is that little grandson of yours?"

"Oh good, good, thank you. Not so little now. Starts school in a month. He will achieve great things."

"With a grandad like you, I'm sure he will." She gave him a playful nudge and headed straight for reception.

Loch hung back and took a seat on one of the luxurious couches in the lobby. He knew this was Eva's patch and let her take the lead. Eva wondered if this was a change for the CIA agent, or if he was used to it from her by now? It didn't seem to faze him. He'd eagerly gone along with her mad plan to go rogue. She must have done good things in the past to garner such devotion. She made a mental note to ask him what they were, so she could do them again.

The prim receptionist stood behind the large oak desk, his hair slicked back and his leer even slicker.

"Ah, Miss Destruction, always a pleasure."

"Bernard," she replied evenly. Bernard was the one person at the Mandarin who Eva could not abide. He was always trying to prise business contacts or corporate favours from her, and his weaselly ways never sat right with her. On the other hand, he had a superhuman ability to provide anything she requested, at all hours of the day or night. She hoped it was a talent he could replicate once again.

"I don't have a booking."

Without glancing at his computer terminal, Bernard replied, "I am aware, Miss Destruction".

"So I was wondering if you could do me a solid and find me a room?" Eva plastered on her best fake smile.

Bernard replied, replicating Eva's insincere gesture. "I have already taken the liberty of securing you the penthouse, Miss Destruction." He handed over her room card.

"Bernard, I'm taking a break from things for a while. Life has been rather, ah, hectic. So if we could just keep this off the books, and if anyone contacts the hotel…"

"We have not seen you in some time, Miss Destruction."

"Outstanding. Thanks."

Bernard glanced behind her. "There is no luggage?"

"Travel light, travel fast." Eva turned away.

"And Miss Destruction?"

"Yes, Bernard?"

"Love the outfit."

Smarmy prat. Eva prised a polite grin from her lips.

"Oh!" Bernard exclaimed, appearing to remember something. "Your package." He motioned to a door behind him. "You left it on your last stay. Would you like me to retrieve it from our vault?"

She hesitated, not knowing what he was talking about. "That would be most helpful, thank you."

Interesting. She didn't remember leaving a package behind, but apparently Past Eva had deemed it necessary. Present Eva approved.

Bernard returned a minute later with a large envelope-shaped package. It was bound in layers of packing tape, with a small piece of paper taped to the front that simply read, "Eva Destruction". It was her handwriting.

She thanked Bernard, tucked the package under her arm and motioned for Loch to meet her at the elevators.

Halfway up, he elbowed the package. "What's that?"

"Frequent stay rewards," she said, and wrinkled her nose playfully.

She felt a pang of guilt for not telling him that it might be pertinent to their mission, but she was just following his advice. He had told her not to trust anyone. She felt like she could trust him, but in the spy business, feelings could get you killed. She trusted her gut more than she should, but even that had limits. She would open the package in private, and then decide whether to tell Loch.

By way of silent apology, she looped her arm through his and pulled him close. He leaned down to kiss her. That was three cities now she'd had his lips on hers. They were practically dating.

The elevator pinged and they made their way to their room. With a click of the pass, the door opened to reveal a massive suite. Beyond the cool glass of the hotel room lay sweeping vistas of Victoria Harbour, the bustling metropolis busy with people hurrying about their business.

The suite had several rooms branching off from an enormous central space with an open fire, sunken lounge and impressive chandelier. The main bedroom was the most prominent, with a ridiculously large king-sized bed as its key feature.

"Am I going to be sleeping on the couch?" Loch asked with a tilt of his head.

Eva grabbed him by the lapel of his flashy purple leisure suit. "No, I think we'll be okay," she whispered throatily.

Her tongue intertwined with his, their bodies pressed firmly against one another. Loch ran his hand down the side of her face and drew her chin up. His kiss was far less innocent than the last. He was hungry, ravenous. He devoured her and she loved it.

When they managed to come up for air, he said, "I'm sure we will."

He leaned down and picked her up. There was only one destination. Eva unzipped her leisure suit as they headed for the bedroom.

~

Several hours later Eva untangled herself from Loch's muscular form. He was a surprising lover. Eva had wondered if his recent passivity would translate into the bedroom as well. It turned out the exact opposite was true. Loch was no shrinking violet behind closed doors. He was a take-charge lover, but that never meant forgetting her pleasure, which was extensive.

His gentle snores were the result of a job well done, on both sides. Their chemistry had been magnificent, like old lovers, except for Eva they were anything but. Before slipping into a contented sleep he had told Eva she had exhausted him like no one ever had. That was one of the best compliments a girl could receive.

Strolling through the penthouse naked, Eva retrieved the package, which she had tossed on the kitchen bench, and sliced it open with a knife.

There were a handful of pages, all of them relating to the same thing. A shipping manifest listing industrial parts for a generator. The transport company's name was familiar. It was a business Harry, her ex, had used. The manifests and instructions were all in the name Hillary Trump, which Eva was reasonably sure was a fake. She was certain the writing on the document was in her handwriting—even the signature had similar loops.

Eva scratched the back of her head. Why on earth would she need to ship generator parts, let alone keep the evidence stashed away in a hotel vault?

Then it twigged.

The nuclear weapon. The shipment. This was it. This was what people were trying to kill her for. It *had* to be.

Eva turned the page. The destination halted her breath.

What the hell?

Why would she send it there of all places? Was she *insane*?

She heard rustling from the bedroom and quickly stashed the paperwork under the microwave. By the time Loch came limping out of the bedroom, Eva was behind the counter, pouring herself a glass of water.

"Hey," he said with the smug smirk of someone who had provided multiple orgasms in the very recent past.

"Hey, yourself," Eva replied.

She poured Loch a glass without asking and handed it to him.

"So," she began, as innocently as she could manage. "What would you say to a holiday?"

"Hi holiday, it's a pleasure to meet you. Why do you ask?"

"Just a random thought. Thought it might be nice to spend a few days relaxing before we head back to MI6."

"What happened to the huge sense of urgency?"

"Oh, you know." She refilled her glass as casually as she could manage. "Getting shot at, kidnapped, saving the world and stuff, sometimes it's nice to kick back and take some me time, right?"

"Uh, I guess. Anywhere in particular?"

"Ever been to France?"

CHAPTER NINE

The crisp early summer air filtered through the olive and lavender trees that bathed everything in vibrant colours. Usually the beautiful tree-lined streets of Rasteau sent Eva into a relaxed state. Not today.

What the hell had she been thinking? There are plenty of bad places to stash nuclear weapons, of course.

Childcare centre—bad.

Mecca—bad.

Dave Grohl's bidet—bad.

Giant novelty penis museum—kind of funny, but not helpful right now.

Vatican City—bad.

But then there's downright idiotic. And her own castle in the middle of the Rhone Valley, France, was right at the top of that list. Especially considering she'd opened it up to several refugee families, who were now living with a device that could give them the world's worst sunburn.

She wasn't one hundred per cent sure the manifest was for the bomb, but all the evidence was there. The shipping docket didn't come right out and say, "CONTENTS: ONE VERY EXPLODEY NUCLEAR WEAPON. HANDLE WITH CARE. DO NOT DROP OR YOU WILL START WORLD WAR THREE. PLEASE LEAVE UNDER MAT."

Sure, Eva could be impetuous. She could be hot-headed and careless with her own life at times. But that was the thing: she was only reckless with her *own* life. Both Bishop and Paul had recently chastised her for being reckless on missions, but it was always for a good reason. Eva couldn't think of a solitary motive for stashing a thermonuclear device in the middle of a peaceful countryside. And in wine country, too. Past Eva appeared to be a reckless dick.

Loch missed another gear shift. It was endearing that he couldn't properly drive a manual. What sort of secret agent doesn't know how to use a stick shift? "Quick, get in the car and chase that evildoer!", "Oh, it's not an automatic? I guess we'll have to let him go and plunge the world into international chaos, then. Oh well."

He missed shifting from third to fourth and went back to second instead. The engine protested like a four-year-old at bedtime. Loch's driving was becoming less endearing.

"You want me to drive?"

Loch stuck his tongue out and found third again. He frowned at the suggestion. "I'm perfectly fine, thank you."

"Poor little baby, scared the big bad girl will take away his pwecious masculinity?"

He leaned over and said throatily, "I would hope over the last day I've proven my masculinity."

Eva's body tingled. "Well, yeah, there's that."

"Thank you. Now, if you don't mind..." He growled as he crunched the gearbox. The car shuddered up the slight incline before Loch found the right gear, but overrevved the engine, dropped the clutch and the car juddered to a halt.

"Way to ruin the moment, dude."

Loch restarted the engine and took off with more convulsive gear changes. "Shhh, driving."

"Is that what you're calling it?"

Loch poked his tongue out at her, then leaned into the steering wheel, his face creased in intense concentration.

Eva shook her head. "Dude's in the CIA and can't drive stick."

Despite the reason they were going there, Eva was looking forward to seeing her castle again. It was her little oasis. She also wanted Loch to see it, to share it with him. She wanted to share everything with him. She'd made a very good start in the last twenty-four hours.

Except one thing.

Eva was yet to tell Loch about the manifest. It was clear he thought her story about taking a brief holiday was as believable as a politician's sex scandal apology. But he hadn't questioned her on it, just supported her. That said something, right?

They shuddered around a corner, and through the trees caught a glimpse of a stone wall in the distance. Eva's head tilted forward as she peered between the foliage, eager to see more. The castle was far from the main road and isolated; just the way Eva liked it. With each passing tree her home away from home loomed larger and larger until it engulfed the entire windscreen. Loch's jaw flapped open.

"That's not..." He swerved the car to keep it on the road. "That's not it, is it? It's massive."

"Castles usually are."

"I thought when you talked about a castle it was an exaggeration, like 'I go to the gym five times a week' or 'I'm kind of a big deal'."

"Or 'it gets bigger, really'. I've heard that one a few times."

Loch cocked an eyebrow.

"Present company excepted." Eva gave him a punch on the leg.

"Thank you."

He shook his head as the road curved towards the front of the château, where the castle's full magnificence became clear. He slammed on the brakes and the car went into a skid.

"You have a drawbridge? A real, goddamn draw— is that a moat?"

Eva's grin widened. "You like?"

"Why on Earth would you be working at MI6 if you have this?" His outstretched hands gestured towards the castle.

Eva shrugged. "Because I didn't earn it. My hard work didn't pay for this place. I love it and I've put it to good use, but I'm not ready to retire, you know? Besides, who would I make coffee for out here?"

"Knights. Damsels in distress. Serfs. The Rolling Stones."

"Fucken' A." Eva turned to him, impressed. "See, right there, knowing that the Stones recorded in a French castle. I understand why we hooked up."

Loch jutted out his chin. "It's only the greatest rock album of all time."

Eva's nose nuzzled his cheek. "Just for that you get three extra positions tonight."

"Only three?"

"Seven."

"Better." Loch nodded to a young girl walking towards them. "But we might have to hold off for a bit."

The little girl crossed the drawbridge and approached the car. The door creaked as Eva stepped out. Upon seeing her, the girl broke into a run. She was probably about five years old. From a metre away she launched herself at Eva and wrapped her tiny brown arms around her.

"Oh, okay." Eva was surprised, but returned the hug.

In French, the little girl said, "I'm very glad to see you again, Miss Eva!"

Eva replied in French, "I'm glad to see you again, ah, yes, good to see. How have you been?"

"The best! I can count to eighty-seven!" With that she cackled playfully and ran back to the castle.

Loch smirked. "Seems you have fans."

"Seems so."

As the girl ran through the gate, a woman emerged and tutted at her with a mixture of amusement and disdain, as only a mother could. She wore a beautiful purple kaftan and carried herself with the deportment of a runway model. Around her long, elegant neck, she wore several colourful necklaces.

She approached them with a warm smile.

"Hello," Eva said genially.

"Miss Eva, an unexpected pleasure," she replied in measured English. She extended a graceful hand. "It is most pleasing to see you again."

Using her favourite trick, Eva introduced her companion, hoping to learn the woman's name.

"This is Loch, he's in the CIA and can't drive stick."

Loch extended his hand. The woman took it, with less enthusiasm, Eva noted. "Akachi. Welcome, Mr Loch."

"Just Loch is fine. Lovely to meet you, Akachi."

She didn't respond, but turned her entire body towards Eva, effectively blanking him.

"Akachi, this may sound odd, but, ah, do you know of any, ah, messages for me of late?"

Akachi eyed Loch, waited a second longer than Eva thought necessary. "No, no messages, Miss Eva. Come, we are about to have lunch, we would be honoured if you would join us." She paused and frowned slightly at Loch. "Both of you."

They followed Akachi inside, where she introduced them to all seven of the families who were staying in Eva's castle, as well as the four staff from the refugee relocation organisation. Most of the families were friendly and grateful, some guarded but respectful. All the families were from Somalia. While none went into detail, Eva read in their eyes that they had seen far too much for one lifetime. The staff, led by a tall Frenchman called Malik, seemed polite and competent. Loch seemed to have already garnered a fan club among the staff members, so Eva deemed them to have good taste too.

The meal in the grand hall was sumptuous and bountiful, a mixture of couscous and locally harvested vegetables. No meat, Eva noted. The soundtrack was a nonstop onslaught of 80s music, which everyone seemed to know far better than Eva did. There was a lot of laughter, and the children found any excuse they could to be around Eva. She had never really considered herself a kid person, but she must have made an impression on her previous visits because even a raised eyebrow sent them into fits of giggles.

Near the end of the meal, Akachi gently touched her hand and asked Eva to assist her in the kitchen. She followed the elegant woman into the vast kitchen space, but Akachi made no move towards the benches.

"What is it, Akachi?"

"My apologies, but your instructions were absolutely clear."

"My instructions?"

"About the... delivery."

Eva did her best not to appear shocked. Akachi remained resolute.

"Yes. I guess they were," Eva said, wishing she knew what she was talking about.

Akachi tilted her head quizzically. "You said I was not to speak to anyone other than yourself. You were exceptionally clear on this, Miss Eva. No one. I followed your instructions."

"Yes, thank you. Look, it's been a weird... life... so what did you want to tell me?"

"The shipment, it arrived two days ago."

Suddenly the idea of a nuclear weapon being so close became real. Too real. Were all the families safe? Why had she endangered them? She could be reckless sometimes, but not with other people —especially not innocent people who had been through so much already.

"I took the delivery as you ordered. I ran a fire drill so no one was this side of the castle to observe it. I did everything you asked, Miss Eva. It is locked in the old scullery quarters." Seeing Eva's concern, she added, "It is secured. I put a lock on the door."

The idea of a padlock being the only security between her and a weapon of mass destruction did not fill Eva with the sense of safety Akachi was trying to convey.

Eva had to get a grip. "Thank you, Akachi, you did wonderfully well. Amazingly so. I'm sure there is a way for me to properly thank you. I—"

Akachi held up her hand. "Miss Eva, you put a beautiful roof over my family's head, over all our heads, when you did not have to. My people… my people have been through so much and we have seen much hatred, much fear, but you and the staff here have reminded me that there is much kindness in the world also. You will please not mention your thanks again, for if we stood here until the end of our days I could not convey my thanks properly to you. It was a very small thing I did, let us not speak of it again."

She bowed her head slightly. A lump formed in Eva's throat, an unfamiliar desire to cry was trying to force its way loose. She fought it down. Now was not the time.

She took Akachi's hand. "One more." She smiled. "Thank you."

Akachi turned her head to hide the proud grin on her face. Her face quickly returned to her usual stoic composure.

Eva asked, "Why didn't you say something before?"

"I had to wait until I could speak to you alone. You told me to advise no one. I am a woman of my word. Keeping one's word is important to my people. You trusted me to be faithful, and this I have done."

Eva wanted to give her a friendly punch in the arm but thought it might be culturally insensitive, so went with a slight bow instead. Anxious to check on the shipment, Eva turned to stride off to the scullery quarters. There was only one problem.

"Uh, Akashi, where are the old scullery quarters?"

It turned out "the old scullery quarters" was what Eva had thought of as the old maid's quarters, an area of the castle that hadn't been renovated. It was isolated from the rest of the building, and not easily stumbled upon. Eva still couldn't believe she'd organised for an intercontinental ballistic missile to essentially be stored in her spare room.

It wasn't as big as Eva had been led to believe, but this wasn't the first time that had been the case. From the way Hu had described it, she had expected a full-sized missile, but the crate was only about two metres square. The wooden box looked just like any other piece of industrial packaging, which Eva supposed was exactly the point. Now all she had to do was open the bastard and see what was inside.

She looked around for something to prise it open. Behind her, Akachi gave a polite cough. Eva turned to see her holding a crowbar.

Eva took it graciously and asked, "What did you do in your homeland before you left?"

"Avoided bullets and faced down bad men."

"Did you just sass me, Akachi?"

She issued her first genuine smile. It disappeared as quickly.

"I was a hospital administrator." The response didn't seem to bring back pleasant memories.

"A very good one, I imagine."

She bowed. "I will leave you, Miss Eva. I will ensure you are not disturbed."

With that, she left Eva alone with her bomb.

The crate had been sealed exceedingly well, and took some work to prise open. When the side finally came away, it crashed to the floor with such a racket Eva was sure half the castle would come to see what the din was about. Nobody came.

Eva peeled the internal packaging away to reveal the content, then gulped. Inside the crate lay a smooth white metallic ICBM. Or a chunk of one, anyway. The lower section had been crudely cut away, like the work of an apathetic high school student in metal-work class. It had either been done in a hurry or by someone incompetent. Or both.

It was the upper section of the missile, the warhead. The top of the triangular cone had been removed. It was probably for the guidance system, which wouldn't be required when it was converted to a bomb. Chinese markings were emblazoned across a small hatch. Eva couldn't understand what it said, but assumed it was important, given the blood red lettering and the smattering of skull and crossbones. She assumed it was something along the lines of, "Dude, seriously, this is a nuclear weapon. Back the fuck up."

Before her lay the internal workings of an intercontinental ballistic missile capable of wiping out all life in any city in the world. The missile contained plutonium and uranium and enough explosive force to ensure that anyone within twenty kilometres would have a very bad day.

She noticed a hand-scrawled notation in English on the side of the casing. Eva burst out laughing.

The laughter soon turned to tears.

She needed to sit down. The tension had obviously gotten to her.

She looked at the note again. What was inside the box had originally been the warhead from a DF-4. Eva already knew it was a Chinese ICBM, but she didn't know what the DF in DF-4 meant. The note told her. It was short for Dong Feng 4.

The nuclear weapon was one big dong.

Eva sat cross-legged in front of her bomb. She didn't know what to think. She'd been staring at the nuclear warhead for five minutes and still hadn't managed to come to a firm course of action. It may have been the complexity of the situation. It could have been the sheer terror of being so close to a weapon of such staggering destructive power. It might just as easily have been the radiation.

She resealed the crate as best she could and tried to work out what to do next. Had she had a plan beyond storing the bomb in the castle? A set of written instructions would have been helpful. Possibly a diagram or two. And a margarita.

At least now she understood why so many people were after her. Harbouring a nuclear weapon was far more understandable than cutting someone off in traffic or seeking revenge for Eva's karaoke rendering of "I Want It That Way".

Whatever she did next, she had to be careful. Who could she trust? Who knew more than they let on? Would one phone call to the wrong person bring everything crashing down? One thing was certain—Eva needed a drink.

Heading slowly back to the main hall, Eva ran her hand over the familiar stone walls of the castle. This was more than a home away from home for her. She felt a deep connection with the place, and with the locals. Loch had asked why she hadn't retired here. She had certainly thought about it, and perhaps one day she would, but she had plenty of living to do first. Before then, there were the slight issues of being a rogue MI6 agent, identifying who had stolen her memory, who was behind the people trying to kill or kidnap her and working out why and how she'd purchased a nuclear weapon and stashed it in the middle of French wine country. Minor issues, sure, but Eva was a stickler for sorting out trivial details.

As Eva approached the main hall, she could hear the 80s music blaring. She halted her steps when she sensed another presence. She hadn't detected any shadows or footsteps, but she suspected that someone was nearby. On high alert and in defensive mode, Eva clenched her fists and crouched into a fighting stance. She was ready to Krav Maga the fuck out of whoever was sneaking around her castle.

Eva breathed, and waited. Waited and breathed.

She fought to filter out the dulcet tones of A-Ha—and then she heard it. Almost imperceptible, but there it was. Someone else was inhaling and exhaling, just like her. They were nearby, and doing their best not to be detected.

Eva tilted her head, trying to determine where they were. Her opponent must have been doing the same. Every muscle tensed. *There.* A slight movement. They must have shifted their weight, or scratched an itch. It was enough.

"Whoever you are, come out before I kick your ugly face in."

Loch stepped out of the shadows with a sheepish expression. He was behind her. How did he get behind her? Then she remembered: spy.

There was something not right about finding him here. Eva pushed the feeling down. Loch wasn't like her ex. He'd shown that he had her back. But still, her spider senses tingled. She did her best to silence the doubt.

"Bollocks out Jesus on a pogo stick, dude! I was ready to kick your arse."

"I have no doubt." He kissed her gently. "You've been missing for a while. I thought you'd shacked up with a local truffle farmer."

Eva rolled her eyes and kissed him back, less gently. "I was just thinking about you."

"Inappropriate, I hope."

"Is there anything else?"

"I certainly hope not." He groped her arse and ran his hand down her thigh. "Listen, we need to talk."

"What have I told you about using that phrase? Unless it's in reference to a dirt bike, I don't want to hear it."

"Dirt bike?" Loch asked, confused.

"Miss Eva?"

Akachi stood awkwardly in the doorway to the main hall.

"I am sorry to interrupt, but you must come." She motioned for Eva to follow her. "Come, please."

Eva and Loch followed a surprisingly fast Akachi up the stone spiral staircase to the upper parapet of the castle. On the way up, Eva could hear George Michael telling anyone who would listen that he wanted their sex. When they emerged into daylight, they met a young man wearing an ankle-length thobe. He handed a pair of binoculars to Akachi and bowed at the others before rushing down the stairs. Akachi handed the binoculars to Eva.

"There, past the line of trees," Akachi pointed. "At the mouth of the valley."

Eva took the binoculars. "What is it, Akachi?"

"Please." She motioned again to the trees.

Eva peered through the field glasses and rotated the adjustment ring until the image came into sharp focus. She immediately wished it hadn't. She staggered backwards, and would have fallen down the stairs if it hadn't been for Loch grasping her waist at the last moment.

Before Loch could form a question, one of the staff members

came bounding up and saw the commotion. "Is everything alright, Miss Eva?"

It took Eva a moment to gather her thoughts. Had she really seen it? Was she going mad? Was it a paranoid delusion?

She did her best to calm herself. "Hmmm? Fine, fine. What did you want, er…?"

"Kristi," she supplied pleasantly. "Apologies for interrupting, but Mohamed mentioned you were up here. Sorry to be a bother but would you happen to know who looks after our phone service? The phone lines have stopped working."

Downstairs, Big Country, who were in the midst of singing about a big country, suddenly fell silent. Someone below asked who turned out the lights.

It was starting.

Loch's face turned grave. He sensed it too, despite not having seen what Eva had beyond the treeline. He pulled a mobile phone out of his pocket.

"No signal on my cell. Eva, what's happening?"

She didn't answer, but turned to Akachi. "Get everyone into the castle. Keep everyone away from the windows. Go now."

Akachi grabbed the confused worker's arm and led her hurriedly downstairs.

Loch stepped forward. "What's going on, Eva?"

Eva took the binoculars and wasted frustrating seconds finding them again. She hadn't been hallucinating. There they were. Five large black SUVs. A phalanx of burly men, clad in black, all in full body armour.

At the centre were two men deep in conversation and gesturing towards the castle. One turned so she could clearly see his face. Eva inhaled unsteadily. The man next to him with the grey streaked flat-top haircut issued an order, and the two men beside him snapped to attention. The fit man in his late fifties holding the binoculars aimed them directly at Eva. It was as if he knew exactly where she was. They stared at one another across the valley. The man next to him had a face like a kicked in door. The bastard tilted his head and smiled. He raised his arm and waved the stump at Eva.

Eva lowered the binoculars. "Better pull up the drawbridge. Before the day is out we're going to be repelling boarders."

"Boarders? What are you talking about?"

"Captain Flat-top and his boys are back, and they're not here to fuck spiders."

CHAPTER TEN

"So that's it then?" Eva looked at their stash with a growing sense of dread. "Three cleavers, seven kitchen knives, a broken lacrosse stick and a tennis ball. We're screwed."

Her head landed heavily on the old rustic kitchen table. Eva, Loch, Akachi, Kristi and Malik were seated around the table, staring at the measly set of "weapons" they had accumulated.

The men who were about to attack were specialist killers. The fact that they had failed to do exactly that in Eva's apartment would only make them more dangerous. Revenge is a fervent motivator.

Loch placed his hand on her shoulder. "What if we wet the tennis ball? I mean, that can really sting."

He was trying to lift her spirits, but right now they were heavier than a lead colostomy bag. And about as useful. Raising her head, she gazed at what she'd optimistically referred to as her "war cabinet". Before them lay a crudely drawn map of the castle and surrounds.

The rest of the staff were out entertaining the children, doing their best to convince them that being confined to the castle was fun. They were running siege preparation exercises disguised as games. At that moment the kids were seeing how many rocks they could take to the parapets every five minutes. They'd be exhausted by the end of the day.

"How long can the main gate hold out?"

"Each gate is a good foot thick," Loch answered, "and we have three of them. They're basically a concrete wall. It will hold."

"It better," Eva replied. She rubbed her face. "So tell me about the fuel situation."

Malik shifted in his chair and spoke in his native French. "We have enough fuel in the generators to last two, maybe three days if we conserve enough. We are prepared for just such an occasion."

A grin creased Eva's lips. "You prepared for a paramilitary assault on the castle?"

"I... er... no, I mean to say... if the power failed or some-thing... not..."

Eva gave his hand a gentle pat. "It's okay, I was joking. Good work. The generators are inside the walls?"

"Yes."

Eva nodded. "Okay, that's something. What about the castle itself? Is there a secret tunnel out of here that no one told me about?"

"We have no tunnels out of the castle," Kristi said. "The only entrance and exit is via the main gate." Her shaky voice and forced calmness told Eva she was barely holding it together. "Has anyone thought of opening the gates and making a run for it? Like, some of us could just gun it and go for help? Could we do that?"

Loch shook his head slowly. "It's not a good idea, I'm afraid. They've stationed sniper nests along the road. You wouldn't get a hundred feet before you were shot to shit."

"Especially if you can't drive stick," Eva offered. She turned to Loch. "And sweetie, we're outside the US, you can use metres like the rest of the civilised world."

Eva felt that the bird he flipped her was an appropriate response.

She gave him a wink. "The castle is both an advantage and our greatest threat. They're not going to have trebuchets or siege towers, so we're safe there. I doubt they'll have ladders or grap-pling equipment, but we'll need to be vigilant just in case. The piles of rocks should help us. We'll go medieval on their arses if they try. But my guess is they'll go for full cock-out brute-force penetration of the main gate. We have to hold them off for as long as we can."

"We will need rations." Akachi was matter-of-fact. "I will organise fast meals to be prepared for the families, and," she paused, "the fighters."

Eva did her best not to dwell on that last word. "Good sugges-tion, thank you." She pointed to the area near the main gate. "The gardens outside, how are they watered? Where's the source?"

Loch tilted his head. "And the award for the best non-sequitur of the day goes to…"

Malik leaned forward. "It is plumbed into the main water supply. It can be re-plumbed into the moat if need be. We did that last month when they shut off the water for two days. Mrs Martinez did not wish to see the flowers wilt after she had put so much work into them."

"So the plumbing for the sprinkler system is inside the castle," Eva asked.

"Yes, ma'am."

"Why are you focusing on sprinklers, Chérie? They have auto-matic weapons and God knows what else. They probably won't care if they get a bit wet."

Eva moved on. "We need to run a few drills for the families. When shit goes down they need to be in the east annex residential quarters, far away from the firefight. They'll be safe there, they're not the prize."

"What is?" Kristi asked.

Eva straightened her back. "Something we can't give them."

"Can't, or won't?"

"Yes," she replied. The hardness in her voice silenced any further questions.

Loch clapped his hands together. "Okay, good work everyone. Malik and Kristi, please run those drills, and make sure everyone knows their place when the call goes out. Akachi, do you need any assistance with the food preparations?"

She sneered in response. "I require no help from you."

It took a moment for Loch to process the harsh response. Before he could respond, Eva said, "Thanks all. I'll come to see everyone in the next ten minutes." After a pause, she added, "Akachi, a moment?"

She waited for everyone to leave the room. "You don't like Loch very much, do you?"

"He is a man like any other."

Eva tilted her head. "That's not quite what I'm asking. You don't like him specifically. Is there a reason?"

Akachi sighed deeply. "When you introduced Mr Loch you advised he was from the CIA. My people have no love for the CIA, Miss Eva. In Somalia we had what the CIA referred to as rendition sites. These were not pleasant places, but there was not much my people could do. The CIA knew this. They are not my favourite people, so if it is alright with you I would prefer to not spend much time in his company."

"Oh, apologies, Akachi. I was only fooling around when I introduced him that way. I meant no harm."

"Miss Eva, please, I am much stronger than that. He may very well be a good man. You trust him, it is enough, no?"

If that question was any more loaded she could have used it to take out the bastards lining up outside her castle.

"Let's just say he's done much to earn my trust. He's put his life in danger for me on more than one occasion, and I feel deep down that he would do anything to protect me. I've come to know him as a caring and sensitive soul who wants only what's best for me."

"Do you read Shakespeare, Miss Eva?"

"Religiously."

"Then you are familiar with the line, 'The lady doth protest too much, methinks'."

"Act three, scene two, *Hamlet*. The Murder of Gonzago scene." Eva couldn't help her tiny grin. She was usually the one quoting

Shakespeare at someone, not the other way around. "You think deep down I don't fully trust Loch, is that it?"

"How long have you known him?"

"That's an unbelievably complicated question."

"Nevertheless, I see it in your eyes. You care for him deeply, but there is a little doubt there, yes? I am quite adept at reading people."

"Oh, I'm getting that."

How right was she? Eva couldn't even answer the question for herself, let alone verbalise it. Every instinct she had told her Loch was the person she would have fallen for. He ticked all the boxes, and had even invented new ones she hadn't known existed. And yet... Was it the memory loss that made it impossible for Eva to accept what she felt so deeply in her gut, and other rather more interesting places? Was it not remembering pivotal moments that made it impossible to accept what seemed so blatantly obvious? She didn't know, and wasn't sure she ever would.

A change of subject was in order. "Akachi, why did you have people on sentry duty?"

"Your secretive messages, the package. I took precautions."

"I'm glad you did."

She bowed. "Will we survive the night, Miss Eva?" For the first time, Eva detected fear in Akachi's eyes. Given what she'd seen in her life, that was saying something.

Eva ran her hand down her arm and summoned her best reassuring expression. "Yes, we will."

Akachi accepted this, albeit reluctantly. "Forgive me if I am too forward, but I think it may be related to your package, hmm? These men will not stop until they possess it?"

"I hope that's not the case. I've met these men before—well, some of them. Last time they pointed loaded weapons at me in my bedroom. They are not my favourite people."

"How did you survive this encounter?"

"I kicked their arses."

"How many men?"

"Only four. They're lucky they didn't send any more. I hadn't had my coffee yet and was a bit cranky."

"Cranky?"

"Bad-tempered, irritable. But that's what we're going to do again, kick their arses."

"We are women who do not cower from men who wish to do us harm. That is good." Her face was determined. "I will leave you now. I will aid in arse-kicking preparations. Good luck to you, Miss Eva."

"Good luck to us all."

She found Loch in the kitchen teaching several men how to manu-facture Molotov cocktails. They'd siphoned off some petrol from the generators, and were in the midst of tearing bedsheets for the fuse. She loved seeing him all business, manly and focused. She could have done him right there, but it might have been a bit inap-propriate, and besides, they were on a bit of a tight timeline.

"Hate to interrupt, fellas," Eva interrupted, "but you might want to ask your wives for better fuses."

Confused expressions were her only reply.

She grinned. "Tampons make a far better fuse. Rags have a habit of going out before they reach their target, but if you douse a tampon in some lighter fuel and tape it to the side of the bottle, you'll have a far more effective trigger mechanism." There was still silence. "Plus, I'd suggest you add some sugar into the mix. Do you have any motor oil handy?"

Loch tilted his head. "Okay, I'll play along. Why the sugar and motor oil?"

"The motor oil extends the burn time, and when combined with the sugar it sticks to the surface and creates a nice thick smoke." She knew she appeared smug, but didn't mind in the slightest. "Any other questions, class?"

"No ma'am," Loch replied. He shook his head in a good-natured way and pointed to one of the men. "You heard the lady, please grab some tampons. Mohamed, can you see if we have any motor oil? I think we're okay for sugar." He turned to Eva. "Anything else we can improve on?"

"I think that's it. I'm satisfied in all other areas."

"I'm most pleased to hear it." He shook his head with a smirk. "Do you have a moment, oh great teacher?"

"For my favourite student, but of course."

Loch led Eva away from the kitchen to a side corridor and gave her a light kiss. "I'm sorry, but I don't have time for an oral exam."

She nudged him with her hip. "Tease."

His charmed face turned grave. "Chérie, are you sure we're doing the right thing here? We don't know what the other guys want. We assume it's bad, but they haven't made any demands..."

"It's not common in civil diplomacy to cut the power and all communications. You usually start by bringing donuts."

"Maybe, but they're ex-Special Forces. These families aren't soldiers, they're not trained for this. We can't expect them to—"

"So what's the alternative? Open up the gates and find a good spot to lie down? Not my style."

"That I know, but surely there's a middle ground. Surely we can find out what they want first."

"I know what they want, and they can't have it."

"I assume you mean yourself?"

"No." *Oh boy, here we go.* "The nuke... it's here, in the castle."

"It's here!" He backed away, startled. "I knew you were hiding something, but... Jesus fuck, Chérie! Why didn't you tell me? Don't you trust me?"

Eva eyed the door, hoping for a convenient distraction. None came. She exhaled. There was really no way to respond. He was completely right. She should have told him. She should have confided in him. Trusted him. She hadn't, and now she was paying the price.

"Look, Loch, I regret not telling you, but you told me yourself, don't trust anyone."

He crossed his arms. His face could have been added to Mount Rushmore.

"Okay, so that was a lame response. I get that, I do. But I was going to tell you." Eva wondered if that was true. She wasn't entirely convinced. "I've been running to catch up to where you're at. I'm nearly there, I am, but come on, dude, you have to admit this isn't exactly a run-of-the-mill relationship."

"That's not the point, Chérie."

"What is, then? Everything has happened so fast. The memory loss, the goons, kidnapping, assassins, Macau, the fuckers outside right now, everything. It's all too fast. I haven't had time to properly tell you."

"You had between Hong Kong and here to tell me, Chérie, but you didn't."

It was as if they were having this conversation in a freezer. The air between them was positively arctic.

"True." She added a sly grin. "But in my defence, during much of that time we were engaged extracurricular activities."

"You're using sex as an excuse?"

"Let's face it, it wouldn't be the first time that's ever happened." Eva shook her head. "Now isn't the time. I'm sorry for not telling you and I'll totally make it up to you, but first we have to survive the next twenty-four hours, and that's going to be next to impossible unless the two of us are focused, okay?" His features thawed somewhat. Eva added emphatically, *"Okay?"*

A nod. "Okay."

"Good man." She kissed his cheek, then in a quieter voice, added, "And I really am sorry—and this comes from a girl who doesn't apologise, so you know it's a big thing."

Footsteps rushed towards them. It was Mohamed. "Come, please. It is happening."

They rushed through the castle and up the stone steps. Akachi greeted them with a small nod and handed Eva the binoculars. She didn't need them. In the fading dusk light, it was plain enough. Six large SUVs were crawling down the main road, surrounded by burly men in full body armour, comms equipment strapped to their heads and bulky assault rifles in their hands.

Not a box of donuts between them.

"I better get back to those Molotovs, then," Loch said.

He disappeared downstairs. Every muscle in Eva's body clenched. Her rear end threatened to do the opposite. Fear gripped her so thoroughly she couldn't think straight. They couldn't defend themselves against that. Her bravado had put these innocent families at risk. Her hubris would get them all killed.

Akachi's gentle hand settled on her shoulder. "Do not doubt we will prevail, Miss Eva."

"I'm definitely doubting. I should never have put you in harm's way."

"My name, Akachi, means hand of God." She smiled a toothy grin. "To use the phrase you English use, I got this."

"I wish I shared your confidence."

"You do not need confidence. You need this."

She handed Eva an AK-47.

"Where in the holy hell did you get that?"

"The French gun laws, they are strict, but there is much on the black market from Eastern Europe. My cousin fell in with some silly people, so I decided it best for them to not have this."

"I see. Is that the only one?"

"Yes, just the one, and some ammunition, but that is all."

"My, my, woman you are full of surprises."

"Let us hope surprises are enough, yes?"

"Let's hope."

They fell into silence as they watched the slow procession of militants marching on the castle. The SUVs stopped, but the men kept advancing. Eva supposed if all else failed, they had one hell of a destructive fallback weapon.

Despite the encroaching danger, her thoughts turned to her last conversation with Loch. Had she seriously damaged their fledgling romance by not trusting him? Was she so jaded it was impossible for her to trust men? She had to consider the possibility. And if it was the case, what did she do with that knowledge?

As she stood on the parapet, a nagging thought festered. She knew it was important, but it wasn't fully formed. Whatever it was, it wouldn't let go. It was something Loch had mentioned last time they were standing there. *Think, dammit!*

"Here they come," Akachi said in a low murmur.

The forces fanned out, taking key defensive positions facing the main gate. Behind a mound of dirt here, behind a tree there. Several took position behind a large stone bench in the rose garden. Mrs Martinez would not be happy.

Eva tried to replay the moment in her head. The phones were cut, then the power. Loch did something, what was it?

Loch had pulled out his phone to call for help.

His phone.

His fucking phone.

The same phone she'd thrown in the bin in Macau. The one they'd agreed could be traced. The one that under no circumstances could travel with them.

"Akachi."

"Yes, Miss Eva?"

"I'm going to need to borrow your gun."

CHAPTER ELEVEN

Loch Davenport's battered face looked helplessly up at Eva, who towered over him with a blood-spattered rolling pin and a furious disposition. A trickle of blood ran from his nose. His hands were tied behind his back and he was chained to a chopping block, which Eva may have found ironic at another time. She wasn't sure where Akachi had found the chains, but it was a castle, after all.

They'd found him diligently attending to the Molotovs as promised. He was startled by the sight of an incensed Eva. Startled quickly tumbled into fearful when he saw the AK-47.

When she'd confronted him about the mobile phone he'd feigned innocence. Of course he had. But it wasn't like it had been an accident. One does not accidentally double back at an airport to retrieve a discarded mobile phone from a rubbish bin. That takes intent.

She'd told Loch he had to come with her and answer a few questions.

He hadn't come willingly.

Which was a change.

With pure anger coursing through her veins, she hadn't had a chance to process the fact that she'd been betrayed by a man she was truly falling for. She'd trusted her gut and it had screwed her over yet again.

How had she been so stupid? Had she not learned to ignore her instincts? He'd even told her directly not to trust him. She had the world's worst taste in men. It was reasonable to assume that wasn't hyperbole—it was literally the world's worst. If they weren't plotting to overthrow world governments, they were stealing from her purse and hocking her record collection. If she lived through the night she'd head straight for the nearest convent.

"I can explain, Chérie, I can. You just need to untie me. We don't have much time. If those men manage to break into the castle the consequences will be catastrophic."

"Maybe you should have thought about that before you called them."

"Is that what you... no, I can explain. I didn't call them."

"Oh, so they managed to find me by pure fluke, nothing to do with the mobile phone you had in your pocket?"

"No—well, yes. Ah, it's complicated."

"I have no idea what complicated looks like. Please, enlighten me."

"It wasn't the cell phone that brought them here—well, not directly. You need to untie me before it's too late. Chérie, you've really messed up now. Shit, I can still protect you. If Grey's faction gets their hands on the nuke, we're in for a world of hurt. Literally a world of hurt."

"Grey's faction? Who the hell even are you?"

"Miss Eva!" Malik called as he raced into the kitchen. He stumbled to a halt when he saw Loch's bloodied form. "Ah, there's someone who wants to speak to you. At the moat. One of the, um, men."

"I'll be right there."

Malik's glance lingered on Loch, but he chose not to comment. He raced out as quickly as he'd entered.

Eva sniffed indifferently. "Now, if you'll excuse me, I have another stupid man to put in his place."

"Eva, please! You have to hear me out! You don't understand

what's going on. There's way more to all this than you realise. Please! Let me explain!"

She walked away with Akachi in tow, who smiled pleasingly at Loch's shackled form.

Eva shook her head and said over her shoulder, "Oh, it's Eva now is it? No more Chérie? I'm sure it was never real. Another lie, am I right?"

Loch's head slumped. To Eva, it seemed that his whole body deflated, just like his deception.

How could she have been so wrong? She'd trusted her heart and this was where it had led her. Her emotions had told her Loch was the real deal, that she had feelings for him. How could she have been so far off? It had gone beyond attraction, her heart had told her she *knew* this man. That she trusted and loved him. How could she have been so far off the mark? The answer was obvious. Her heart knew nothing.

Her pounding footsteps on the ancient steps couldn't drown out the deafening thoughts shouting for attention in her mind. They had to be silenced. She needed to focus. Without Loch as her second-in-command the defence of the castle had become a whole lot more difficult, if not impossible.

Night had taken hold and the new moon offered little light. A handful of tiki lights illuminated the battlement, and showed enough of the faces present for Eva to see the terror in their eyes.

On the ground in front of the castle a solitary figure was bathed in spotlights. The soldier cast a foreboding shadow. They'd obviously spent time setting up the lights to create just the right amount of menace.

Captain Flat-top stood with his hands behind his back. Arrogant. Confident. Condescending.

Fuckmuppet.

Gripping the stone parapet, Eva leaned forward so she could be seen. With false self-assuredness, she said, "Mr Grey."

Grey by name, and grey by nature. His close-cropped grey hair stood out among his troops. Eva had been observing him closely through the binoculars. It was obvious he was military through and through. His men saluted so sharply Eva was surprised no one got cut. Discipline was paramount here.

Grey frowned approvingly. "It seems you're a little better informed than when we last met, Ms Destruction."

"That's not entirely hard, if I'm honest with you."

He tilted his head in agreeance. "Quite. While we're being honest with one another, I should inform you that the rules of engagement have changed. When we first met I had been ordered to use kid gloves. Those rules no longer apply. Let's just say that due to your interference, we are less interested in rules and more focused on the end game. Right now, you stand between us and our goal. So does every one of your precious refugees. Either you step aside and let us retrieve what is rightfully ours, or you and everyone in this castle dies trying to stop us. The end result will be the same either way. I am giving you an out, Ms Destruction. Considering our history, I think that's rather magnanimous of me."

"I'm sure Lefty is really pleased about that."

"Lefty?"

Eva pointed to the man standing in a pool of seething hatred, casting daggers in her direction. "Lefty."

Lefty stepped forward and went to raise his weapon, but Grey placed a hand on his shoulder to dissuade him. It seemed to take every ounce of effort for Lefty to step back into line.

"Ah, most amusing. Yes, even Lefty." Grey clasped his hands in front. "Now, I hate to cut our pleasant little discourse short, but—"

"I have your man inside," Eva interrupted. "I'm afraid you might not get a full refund; he's slightly shop soiled."

"My man? I don't have anyone inside… yet. Give me an hour."

"Sweetie, by the look of you, you wouldn't last two minutes."

"I… I don't know what that means."

"I'm sure you don't."

He shook his head, betraying his frustration. "Listen, I've been reasonable. Far more than you deserve. Open the gates to avoid bloodshed or the death of every human in this castle will be on your head. You will answer me now."

Eva held up her hand. "You want an answer? Here's my flaming answer." She snapped her fingers.

The Molotov cocktail flew in a beautiful arc, the flaming tampon casting tumbling loops of flame. Grey scampered out of the way just before the bottle hit in a dazzling explosion of fire. The fire spread quickly and remained alight, illuminating Grey and his troops in orange light.

Through the flames, Grey screamed, "You'll die tonight, you little bitch."

Eva blew him a kiss. "You first."

They both retreated to their respective camps, preparing for the battle to come. She didn't believe for a moment that his offer was genuine. She knew too much now, and anyone in the castle could have seen their faces. Right now, with no communications, they were isolated from the rest of the world. They were contained. Grey had the advantage and he wouldn't give that up for mercy. Their only choice was to fight.

Everyone of fighting age gathered around Eva. They were plainly petrified, but gained confidence from Eva's conviction that they would fight when the time came. It wouldn't be long.

On the plus side, the castle had been constructed to withstand sieges. In fact, it had survived many, usually for weeks or months at a time. On the down side, none of those sieges had been against modern weaponry. Nor were they defended by petrified refugees who knew nothing of tactics, or even why they were fighting. The best they could hope for was to hold them off until the authorities found out there was a firefight going on. Their isolation meant that was a long shot. They would almost certainly be dead before anyone raised the alarm.

Contrary to logic, Eva occasionally glanced at the horizon, hoping for Bishop to miraculously appear with the better part of the 1st Division. It was a ridiculous delusion. She'd gone rogue; he didn't know where she was … and yet… it wasn't without precedent for him to turn up right when she needed him the most. But the treeline remained steadfastly free of tanks and sanctimonious chauvinists. Eva steeled herself to focus on the battle at hand.

"We don't have to defeat them. We don't even have to draw. We just need to hold out until someone outside realises what's going on."

"But how long will that be?" Kristi asked, fear throttling her words.

"I can't say, but remember, this is a motherfucking castle. Sieges are what it was built for. We are the ones with the advantage here. All we have to do is make it hard for them, and hold out until someone comes to deliver the milk."

"We purchase the milk from town," Malik replied.

"That was an example."

"Oh, I see."

"But you get my point. They can't stay indefinitely. They know they're on the clock. We just have to hold out until it becomes too hot for them to stay."

"Doesn't that make them desperate?" Kristi asked.

"Maybe, but not reckless."

Eva had to cut it short before they descended into discussions about worst-case scenarios. Every single person gathered around her was scared. Some put on a brave face, but their eyes betrayed them. These people were frightened and confused. Eva needed them attentive, for their sakes as well as hers. She needed to rally them and keep it punchy, keep it positive.

"Guys, we can do this. We have the higher ground, we have five metre-thick walls. And we have Akachi," she smiled at her new friend. "She's worth twenty of them."

Akachi beamed in return.

Eva lowered her voice, ensuring every syllable was unwavering. "For most of you, this will be your first battle. If you're scared, hold onto that. Anyone who says they're not scared is a lying bastard. Be scared. Wear it like a suit of armour. It means you're human, you're smart. Make no mistake, the men out there want to kill everyone here, but that's not going to happen. Why? Because we're right? No. We are, but history has shown that being right is no guarantee of victory. We're going to win because we have the advantage, we have a motherfucking castle and they have to cross open ground to even get close to us. This castle has held strong for centuries, a few more hours isn't much to ask. Keep your head down, follow the plan and we'll be here this time next year reminiscing about our triumph. I'll even buy the drinks. Know that everyone is depending on you, but at the same time, everyone here has your back. Don't ever let up and don't think your job is unimportant. We all have vital parts to play. Don't be reckless and we'll get through the night. You with me?"

Every single person present whispered positive affirmations. They were as ready as they were ever going to be. Eva almost believed her own words. But not entirely. A couple of missiles to the main gate and a swift breaching vehicle and this thing would be over before it began.

Everyone took up their positions with extra confidence. They even pepped one another up, repeating versions of her stirring words. It was enough for Eva to start believing them herself. A hand landed lightly on her shoulder.

"These people would follow you into the gates of hell, you know?" Akachi said.

"Let's hope it doesn't come to that, yeah?" Eva nodded at the AK-47 in Akachi's hand. "You going to be alright on sniper duty?"

"Please, Miss Eva. I am Somalian. I know guns. I know how to defend my family. Let me do this thing."

Eva was overcome with admiration for her friend. "You're a brave woman."

"I do not think so. I am a woman. That is enough, no?"

"More than enough."

"Then let us do this thing." With that, Akachi moved silently towards the tower turret to take up her position, leaving Eva alone.

For the next twenty minutes, nothing happened, but everyone remained vigilant. On edge. The trees all merged into one. Every falling branch sounded like a tank, every flutter of a bird's wings like an invading army. But mostly, there was silence. Deafening silence.

Then the rumbling started.

Faint at first, it quickly grew. In the distance, to the left, far from the main road, the rumbling quickly turned into a roar. A war cry.

Several engines overrevved, creating a cacophony of sound. A group of men chanted guttural grunts and clanged some sort of metal objects together, sounding like symbols.

"Eyes right, people!" Eva cried.

"But they are coming from over there," said a young Sudanese man.

"No, they're not."

Near the road, a solitary SUV gunned the engine and sped towards the castle. Without lights, and given the distraction of the noise, the vehicle was difficult to detect. But Eva saw it.

"Hold your fire!"

The SUV raced down the road directly towards the main gate and the raised drawbridge. He must have been doing at least eighty kilometres an hour.

"Hold it!"

"But, Miss Eva," Akachi pleaded, aiming the AK-47.

"I said hold!"

The car bounced down the road, gaining speed as it did. It was unwavering in its aim. The driver sped up again. He was going to jump the moat. They were going to fling the SUV at the heavy wooden gate and breach the castle.

The car ran out of road, and the huge black SUV launched into the air over the moat.

But the driver misjudged the gap.

The SUV crashed into the stone wall just below the raised drawbridge. The thunderous collision reverberated through the entire castle, and the shockwave caused people to stumble on the battlement.

The front section of the car disintegrated, then the SUV bounced backwards into the moat. No amount of velocity could overcome the pull of gravity over that distance.

Eva leaned over the fortified wall and shouted, "Physics, bitches!"

The crumpled car sank below the waterline in a burbling mess of steam and grinding metal.

One SUV down. One less mobile vehicle. One less movable barricade.

Eva eyed the water. "Let the man swim free when he comes up."

But nobody swam out of the moat. The driver hadn't survived the crash.

Silence descended once more.

Over the next hour, brief skirmishes broke out. Occasionally a shot was fired, reminding everyone to keep their heads down. The only injury sustained was a graze to the upper arm of a refugee. When hit, he acted like any other sixteen-year-old boy in front of sixteen-year-old girls; being shot was no big thing. In public, he shook it off like Rambo, but when Eva brought him down to their temporary infirmary he burst into tears. The wound was superficial, barely breaking the skin. When Eva reminded the boy, whose name was Lekan, that chicks dig scars, he perked up and was rearing to return to the frontline.

The lack of another attack made Eva wonder if Grey and his men were planning something big or if they were out of ideas. She found the latter unlikely. It wasn't long before she had her answer.

Akachi spotted them first. The tiki lights had been doused to improve their night vision. It worked. Even with the lack of moonlight they saw them coming. Their opponents moved swiftly from tree to tree, machine guns covering their compatriots as they moved silently. They must have assumed they would be fired on, even though no one in the castle had fired a single shot.

Word passed along the castle perimeter—get ready, and give them hell.

The first wave began on the stroke of two. Barrages of bullets strafed Eva's beautiful castle. There was no need to issue an order to duck; everyone kept low. Akachi fired sporadic shots from the protection of an arrowslit, but wisely kept them infrequent, knowing more would make her a prime target.

Through Eva's improvised trench periscope she saw at least a dozen men clear the treeline and head for the main gate. Their teammates peppered the parapets with a constant strafe of bullets. Two men broke away from the main group. One held a heavy field bag.

Eva called out, "Team AC/DC, light up!"

Below, a square-jawed man grasped the zip of bag, eyes constantly darting left and right, scanning for threats. He was looking in the wrong direction.

"Team AC/DC, fire!"

Over the castle wall came a barrage of Molotov cocktails, all aimed at the main gate. They exploded in dazzling fireballs, engulfing a good half of the assailants in flame. Right on target. Eva was proud.

It retrospect Eva supposed she could have named her squads after members of the A-Team—it would certainly be more apt— but she'd already named them after Australian rock bands, and it would just be confusing to change it now.

"Team Cold Chisel, light up and fire at will!"

The volley of Molotovs landed ten metres behind the last, right where most of the surviving assailants were retreating to. Some soldiers who were already on fire became engulfed in more flames. Several collapsed in pitiful screams.

"Team Divinyls, go!"

More Molotovs launched over the castle wall. The idea was for them to land ten metres beyond the last, but with greater distance came reduced accuracy. They landed far apart, inflicting no further casualties, but they did speed up the retreat of those left standing.

"Team Powderfinger," Eva called out as she watched the last attacker limp beyond the trees, "stand down. That's it for now. Great work everybody."

Cheers erupted down the line. Their first victory. Lekan, the boy with the superficial shoulder wound, stood up, arms raised above his head, and moved in what Eva could only assume was a victory dance. Those around clapped encouragement, whooping and hollering.

A cheerful feeling spread within Eva's chest. She wanted to keep them safe while maintaining discipline, but at the same time, it was their first major achievement. They needed to celebrate.

It took less than a second. One moment Lekan was dancing, the next his head disappeared in a puff of red. She didn't even hear the shot. Fragments of brain matter and skull burst in all directions. His body remained upright for what seemed like an eternity, as if it hadn't been informed that it was no longer in possession of a head.

Lekan's body teetered for an instant before falling backwards over the small inner wall. It tumbled end over end before landing with a booming thud in an internal courtyard below.

The cheers were replaced by screams.

Eva scowled at the attackers below. There was a solitary figure at the front of the pack with a large smoking rifle resting on his arm, which was missing its hand. He chuckled. It was like a game, as if killing a sixteen-year-old Somali was sport. The smug expression on his face was like he had won a prize, not killed a boy. A boy who had never held a gun before Grey's men arrived. A boy whose only care was not embarrassing himself in front of teenage girls. Lekan was innocent. He should have had his whole life in front of him. Instead he had been murdered by a one-handed sadist.

Eva's eyes met Lefty's, and his grin widened. He held up his stump and shook his head. "Still not even."

Eva looked away and did her best to calm the distressed men and women. These weren't trained soldiers. They were refugees, university students, charity workers, cooks. They were not equipped to witness death and shake it off to be dealt with later. Death was something you saw in movies, glorified and noble. It wasn't meant to be senseless, like Lekan's.

"Miss Eva!"

She turned to Akachi.

"They come again."

They approached from the left, in great numbers. These were

the ones who had been revving engines and clanging metal. This time, it was guns making the noise.

Everyone ducked low.

"Team Midnight Oil, light 'em up, go!"

The residents of the castle did what they were asked. They flung the Molotovs at the incoming horde. Only one landed near the men, and even then it merely singed a soldier.

They kept coming.

The trouble was, they were out of Molotov cocktails. There were no bottles left to hurl. All they had was a beaten-up AK-47, which had limited range. The two clips of ammunition would soon be spent, leaving them virtually defenceless. Virtually. Eva still had her broken lacrosse stick and the tennis ball.

They kept coming.

"Akachi, if you please."

"My pleasure."

Akachi opened fire through the arrowslit. Her shots were measured and unhurried. Three men fell before they managed to return one shot. But when they did, it was a fearsome volley. Akachi sat cross-legged behind the stone wall, appearing relaxed and at peace. Even Eva couldn't fake that level of serenity. After a minute, the barrage settled down and Akachi took another position further along the wall, again using an arrowslit for cover.

Only one adversary fell. They had taken up more defensive positioning now that they knew their prey had teeth.

For ten minutes Akachi valiantly and expertly wielded her substandard weapon, but too soon it was spent. She crawled to Eva.

"You're out?"

Akachi bowed her head. "Mostly, yes."

"Mostly?" Eva asked, confused.

"I have three bullets left, but they are mine."

"I don't understand."

"Three bullets. If these bad men break in, it will be very bad. Very bad. I have one bullet for each of my two children, and one for me. If we are to die this day, I will be the one to choose the method of our death, not those men. You understand?"

"Jesus, I do, but Akachi, I don't want you to—"

"Three bullets, Miss Eva. That is all I ask from you. I have done everything you have asked, yes? You do a good thing here for us, you defend us well. But please give me this one thing."

"Alright, but promise me it will only be as a last resort, when everything else has failed."

"These are my children. I will not do this thing if there is still hope."

She was right, it was a stupid thing for Eva to have said. "I'm sorry, of course."

"Ms Destruction, a moment?"

The shout came from the other side of the wall. Through the arrowslit, Eva saw Grey standing on the path before the raised drawbridge, hands on hips, smiling like only a smug bastard could.

"What do you want, Grey?"

"I'm not here for a cup of sugar, you daft bitch. Open the gate. You're spent. You have no more party tricks. Let us in and we'll do our business and leave you in peace."

It was as if he expected the gate to open at any moment. He was unarmed, but the five bulky warriors flanking him were equipped like a twelve-year-old's GI Joe wet dream.

Under her breath, Eva muttered, "Worst pick-up line ever."

They had brought with them two long strips of metal, like a car trailer ramp. It had to be to try and span the moat. Eva wasn't fond of the idea, and would do what she could to prevent it. The problem was, she didn't have many options left. Grey's numbers were depleted, but they had all the firepower.

Louder, she shouted, "You said the rules had changed, the gloves were off and other assorted clichés, and that if we didn't let you in you'd murder us all. Am I summarising our little chat accurately?"

"Open the fucking gate, you bitch!"

Eva shook her head. "So much frustration. You should really go and rub one out, dude."

"I'm going to kill you slow, Destruction."

"Whatever. By the way…" To her compatriots on the wall, she shouted, "Team Mental as Anything, go!"

Down below, every man braced for a barrage of bullets. But there was no ammunition left. For several seconds nothing happened. No gunfire. No Molotov cocktails. Nothing. But then a slow rumble started. They aimed their weapons in every direction, as that was where the sound was coming from. Even from that distance, Eva could see every muscle tense in readiness.

The staccato rhythm of the sprinklers broke the silence. The spray spurted forth, casually spraying the garden, the grass and the militia with equal informality.

The first reaction was laughter. The soldiers had been so tense. They'd been expecting explosions; instead they'd received a light shower. Grey joined in, laughing riotously for a moment. It didn't last. Realisation soon crossed his face—he must have smelt it. It wasn't water coming from the sprinklers. It was fuel.

Eva stood, the broken lacrosse stick in her hand, bound by ancient masking tape. In its scoop, the tennis ball, alight with dancing flame.

"You wanted a party trick?" She hurled the flaming ball at the centre of the spreading fuel. "Abracadabra, motherfucker."

The petrol ignited with a deafening *woof*. The flame spread like a wave, leaving merciless fire in its wake. Every militiaman dove as if it were a grenade. It wasn't. It was worse. Most of them were soaked to the skin, and that's where the flames penetrated to. The screams were pitiful. Grey, at the front of them, furthest from the garden, had the most time to react. Seeing the approaching inferno, he grabbed the bag the previous soldier had been carrying and dove into the moat.

The bag.

That Grey had bothered to retrieve the bag meant that it was valuable. Eva watched him escape the wall of flame. It must contain some kind of tactical advantage. Perhaps their only one. If it was so important that Grey would risk burning alive, it was important to her, too.

What was in the bag?

Grey's head broke the surface, and he treaded water while struggling to open the bag. There probably weren't rose petals in there. As he unzipped the top, Eva could see dials contained within. He twisted them, then performed an uncoordinated doggie paddle, heading towards the main gate.

Without taking her eyes off Grey, Eva called out, "Akachi, I need one bullet! One." She pointed at Grey struggling in the dark waters of the moat, lit by the orange flames. "I need you to take him out before he uses whatever's in that bag."

"Then it will be my bullet, Miss Eva."

Akachi fired once, but it was wide. She shot another two times; all missed.

"Nuggets," Akachi spat. "I am sorry I failed you."

Struggling to keep his head above water in all his combat gear and webbing, Grey glanced up and smiled. He fiddled with the dials, then hurled the bag at the huge wooden gate. It landed on a small ledge at its base. He swam away like crazy.

"Everyone take—"

The explosion rocked the castle. The walls shook. Stone crumbled. Debris flew. The whole structure vibrated with violent intensity. She held together, but only just.

Smoke obscured everything; it was impossible to see the damage caused. Eva knew it wouldn't be good.

Beyond the treeline two SUVs hurtled down the road. They drove past the rolling, screaming bodies and skidded to a halt at the moat, weapons out. Grey shouted and was hauled out of the muck. After a muffled order, the soldiers picked up the car trailer ramps and laid them across the moat.

Eva and her people were out of weapons. They were out of options.

It was over.

Grey's men had breached the gate.

The enemy was in the castle.

CHAPTER TWELVE

Fuck.

CHAPTER THIRTEEN

It all happened so quickly.

Smoke swirled, making it impossible to see more than a metre ahead. The ringing in their ears made it impossible to hear. Their chances of survival? Worse than impossible.

They couldn't fight—there was nothing left to fight with. The best Eva could hope for was to gather her people, keep them out of the way and hope to hell Grey's men didn't extract vengeance. It was the slimmest of possibilities but it was all they had.

Knowing they had precious little time, Eva gathered her noble fighters and told them to run for their lives. Their fallback was the residential quarters. The children were already there. It had two heavy wooden doors, which they'd barricade with furniture as best they could. Then all they could do was wait. They would defend themselves with knives and sticks until there wasn't an adult left standing.

Rushing down the stone steps, they passed Lekan's prone, headless body. Some bowed their heads in respect, some looked away. Nobody stopped.

Nearing the quarters, Akachi touched Eva's arm. "What about Mr Loch?"

She didn't hesitate. "Fuck him."

"I do not wish to, but you have. That means you care, yes? Should you not at least release him? He said these were not his men. They are not good men. What is the saying about not wishing a fate on your worst enemy?"

Eva knew she was right. Again.

Snatchtrumpets.

With a huff she stopped walking. "Barricade this door. Do not open it for anything other than a shave and a haircut, you got it?"

"Shave and a… I am sorry, I do not understand."

Eva knocked out the rhythm. "Shave and a haircut, two bits."

"Ah yes, the children, they use this sign. Very good. And Miss Eva?"

"Yes, Akachi?"

"Your head, please keep it down."

"If you insist." She gave her a grim smile. "But first I'll seal you up."

It was a crude deception, hardly likely to work, but they had set it up anyway. A tapestry had been nailed above the door to hide the entry to the residence. To Eva it seemed obvious, but then, it would—it was her castle. When everyone was through she pushed a chest of drawers in front of the tapestry to distract prying eyes from the entrance. Eva ran towards the kitchen.

She knew risking her life for a man who had betrayed her was more idiotic than a Jar Jar Binks dildo. But she also knew why she was doing it. Human emotions aren't operated by switches. They can't be turned off at will, and they don't adhere to logic. They're far more complex than that. And stubborn. Only a few hours ago, Eva was falling in love with him. It takes more than the revelation of truth for the brain to say, "Oh, we don't like this guy anymore? Okay, cool." The heart simply isn't that cooperative. So there Eva was, skulking around her castle, liable to be shot at any instant, looking to save the man who may have condemned every man, woman and child to death. *Stupid brain.*

She should have taken the AK-47. It was spent, but at least it may have given one of Grey's men a fraction of a second's hesitation. Without it, she had zero defensive capability, besides her rapier wit. So, less than zero, then.

Given her lack of weapons, she resorted to skulking. Finding her way wasn't the problem. Big blokes with guns were. Luckily an unarmed lithe woman could move with more stealth than a fully laden soldier.

Each turn could be her last. Every corridor or dark corner could mean death. And all the while, a little voice in the back of her brain kept repeating, *he's not worth it, he's not worth it.* She wasn't disagreeing with the little voice. But the fact that it sounded like Elmer Fudd made it very annoying.

The only way to the kitchen was via the main hall, with all its varied entrances. Eva stared at the vast space, looking for any sign of life. The hall was deserted. Some tables had been pushed aside to make room for breaking large rocks into more usable sizes. Not that they'd needed them. They were to be used if anyone had tried to scale the outer walls of the castle. The charge of C4 at the front gate had negated the need for such shenanigans.

The huge expanse of a room was eerily quiet. Eva could have crossed it five times in the time she'd been watching for Grey's men. Still no sign of life, no sound.

This is bollocks.

She ran fast and low, expecting to receive a bullet in her back for her trouble. Diving through the kitchen door, she took cover behind the island. She needn't have gone to the trouble. There was nobody in the kitchen.

Loch was gone. The chains were gone, too. The chopping block had been crudely cut away, and she assumed the chains had been threaded through. Wood was easier to saw through than iron.

In the distance, a truck backed up. That would be the nuke, then. They'd found it. If they had a truck it wouldn't be long before it was loaded up and taken away. She doubted they planned to hand it over to the Weapons of Mass Destruction Commission.

The question was, who had freed Loch? The most obvious answer was Grey's men. If Grey were his enemy, as Loch had claimed, they would simply have put a bullet in his brain. But what if it wasn't them? One of her people? She highly doubted it. Had he freed himself? It was possible, but improbable; they'd left him with nothing within reach. The most logical explanation was that Grey's men had released one of their own.

Knob-slapping chowder monkeys.

What now? She had no one to rescue. Returning to the residential quarters would risk exposing their position. Perhaps she could wage a guerrilla campaign against Grey's men. Or give herself up.

They were all viable options, she supposed.

In the end, Eva didn't get to choose.

She heard the breathing first, like an expectant lover standing behind her.

"Hello." It was like a first meeting on a blind date. He sounded both relieved and thrilled.

Eva was neither of those things.

Don't think, Eva told herself. Use your muscle memory. Use your instincts. Rely on your training.

She turned to see the dark eyes of her opponent. He had the good sense not to come too close. She didn't know this one, they hadn't tussled before, but he was dressed the same as Grey's men. Full combat webbing, comms gear with an earpiece.

"You're better-looking up close." His voice was young, it sounded like it had only just broken.

What sort of intimidating talk is that? He tilted his head as if assessing her. Eva didn't enjoy being appraised like a slab of meat. She also didn't enjoy being shot.

"The closer you get, the more intriguing I become." Eva stepped forward.

He raised his weapon. "Stay back."

So he wasn't naive. Good for him. She raised her palms as if to say *all good here,* and stepped back. Her arse hit the kitchen bench and plates rattled.

The young mercenary pressed the button on his lapel mike. "I've got her, she's in the kitchen."

He nodded his head in acknowledgement of a reply Eva didn't hear. Time was not her ally; she had to act.

She threw a plate in a beautiful arc that sailed over the soldier's head. He didn't take his eyes off her. The plan, as simple as it was, was to have him follow the plate. She would then run at him, overpower him in some way and then keep running until she reached this nice little bar she knew in Camden Town. The kid didn't take the bait.

Eva addressed the space over his shoulder. "You trained them better than I gave you credit for, man. This one's smarter than he appears."

The young soldier gave a slight shake of his head. "I'm not falling for that one either."

Eva shrugged. "Shame."

The chain looped over the soldier's head and jerked back hard. He instantly dropped his weapon and clawed desperately at his neck, but the restraint was harsh and unwavering. The soldier wheezed for air that didn't come. His eyes bulged, pleading with Eva as he struggled, but his frantic movements had no impact.

The man who was strangling him came silently out of the shadows.

Finally, the militiaman stopped struggling and blacked out. His attacker reached down and pulled the knife from his gear and held it to the soldier's throat.

"Loch, he's a kid," Eva said calmly.

With a reluctant sigh, Loch rummaged around in the soldier's pockets until he found flexi-cuffs and hogtied the unconscious man. Loch's hands were still manacled, but there was enough slack in the chains for him to move freely enough.

Loch went to pick up the soldier's Heckler & Koch UMP assault rifle but stopped when he saw Eva's suspicious face. With pursed lips, he handed it to her and picked up the pistol instead. Eva grabbed the knife and slipped it through the belt of her jeans.

"How'd you get out?" Eva asked in hushed tones.

"Lucky for little old me, the chopping block wasn't as immovable as it appeared. A few good kicks drove it close enough for me to reach a cleaver. Then it was just a matter of not letting up until I was through the bastard."

Eva knew how focused Loch could be, never ceasing until the end goal had been achieved. It was a tenacity she'd benefited from many times. She shook her head to keep her thoughts from meandering down that particular memory lane.

"Time to exit stage left." Loch's joviality was forced.

Following him out the door, Eva whispered, "This doesn't change anything, you know."

A slight nod conveyed both his acceptance and an urge for her to follow silently.

Loch took the lead, pistol raised, scanning ahead for threats. Not all threats were in front of him. If Eva was to take him out, now was the time. It could be done silently with the knife, and would be fast and relatively painless. She could do it.

But she didn't.

Was it because she still needed answers? Because she cared? Needed an ally? She was sure Akachi would have something wise to say about the enemy of her enemy. Eva might be able to unravel it in that Soho bar over a few pints with Nancy. If she ever spoke to her again. But before any of that, she had to get past Grey's heavily armed and well-trained militiamen first. Easy.

With two fingers, Loch gestured for her to keep her eyes right; he'd take left. She pushed the Heckler & Koch into her shoulder. Back to back, they moved as one into the expanse of the great hall, weapons sweeping every door, window and solid object. No threats.

Their moves across the floor complemented one another, each covering the other, each surefooted, knowing the other had their back. They were synchronised as only lovers could be. *Ex-lovers*, she had to remind herself.

A shrill whistle halted their advance. Suddenly the vacant doorways and windows filled with hulking armed men, their weapons trained on Loch and Eva. The two of them shifted their guns from one target to the next. There were far too many to take out. At most, they'd hit one or two each before dying in a hail of bullets. Not as romantic as it sounded.

Eva muttered, "Cockmonkeys."

She and Loch dropped their weapons.

A tut echoed across the hall. From the courtyard entrance, a man strolled towards them. "Now, now, is that any way to speak to your executioner?"

"I don't know, Grey, is it?

Each step was accompanied by a squelch. His clothing was singed and soggy. In spite of the forced casualness, his features conveyed an intense loathing. It was the eyes. They burned with hatred. No amount of fake smiles could hide the murderous intent in his expression.

"You've made this much harder than it needed to be, Ms Destruction."

"Why do you insist on phrasing things like that, dude? Seriously. There's no way it's coincidental. Do you have a list in your pocket, or what?"

"Enough." Grey squished towards them. "Stay quiet and come, Ms Destruction."

"See, this is what I'm talking about. You know you're flirting with me right now, right?"

"Why are you provoking him?" Loch asked.

Eva fluttered her eyelashes. "It's a special talent I have. Besides, you think I can make this any worse?"

Grey's face lapsed into rage. "Do I have to shove something in your mouth to keep you quiet?"

"Oh, come on, that one was totally intentional."

"Stop it!"

"I'm not the one who's using every sleazy pick-up line in the book."

With pursed lips, Grey took a moment to steady himself. It was an effort.

"Where are the refugees, Ms Destruction?"

"All over. Some are in camps, some in boats, a lot have been resettled in other countries, but I think a lot more should be done in supporting their integration, and quite frankly, I don't know what made multiculturalism a dirty word, but I think—"

"Shut up!" Grey's fists shook as he tried to still them beside him.

Loch regarded her with disbelief. "Do you want to get us shot?"

"Not particularly, but if the old Greyster wanted us dead he would have done it by now." She turned to the seething Grey. "Isn't that right, Captain Flat-top?"

Grey's face lived up to his name. All colour had drained away. Every feature screamed that he'd love nothing more than to strangle her right there, but something was holding him back. He had orders. Orders he didn't particularly like.

Diddums.

So they hadn't found the residential quarters. She'd take that as a win. It seemed her quick ruse was more effective than she'd thought it would be. She hoped it would stay that way.

Dull sunlight slowly crept into the hall. It wouldn't be long before day broke. As long as she kept Grey antagonised, he wouldn't be issuing orders for his men to search further. Once daylight hit it would be too dangerous for them to stay. Explosions and gunfire throughout the night and now scorched earth, a blasted front gate and suspicious SUVs all meant their operation was exposed. They would be on a tight timeframe, and time was running out.

Grey stepped within centimetres of Eva, his face a picture of barely controlled rage. "Where are the refugees? This is your last chance."

"Did you ever see 'Land of the Giants'?" In a whisper, she added, "Shrink ray."

The slap was as hard as it was expected. As forceful as a punch, she would have reeled backwards if not for one of Grey's faithful men grasping her shoulders. For a moment everything went black as pain radiated from her aching face. Loch twisted futilely against his captor. He appeared ready to tear Grey's head from his shoulders.

Blood trickled from her mouth. "I'm taking a wild stab here and guessing that's not the first time you've hit a girl. Am I right?"

Grey stomped away from Eva, as if he didn't trust himself to be any closer. One of his minions approached from the direction of the scullery quarters. A terse exchange quickly followed, then Grey saluted and sent the young soldier back where he'd come from. After a quick series of hand gestures, half of Grey's men followed.

Colour had returned to Grey's face. It was either the release of the slap or whatever the soldier had told him. Possibly both.

"Well, Ms Destruction, regardless of your pathetic efforts, we now have your nuclear weapon. We'll be on our way."

"Goodo, I hope you enjoyed your stay. Be sure to sign the guest book on your way out. Miss you already."

"Oh, that's where you're mistaken. You're coming with me."

Eva scanned the other soldiers. "I'm not the only one seeing this, right? The dude's a walking double entendre."

A soldier near the rear puckered his lips slightly, as if trying to stop a smile. He quickly shook it loose.

Before Eva could offer another smart-arsed response, a hood was shoved roughly over her head. Pushed forward, Eva stumbled.

"Where are you taking her?" Loch demanded. "Listen, this is way outside the—"

The brutal sound of a punch put paid to Loch's pleading. But they weren't finished making their point—the repeated muffled punches and Loch's pained grunts wrenched at Eva. She didn't know how much of an enemy he was, but she had no desire for the man to be hurt. At least, not by anyone else. The blows continued to echo in the hall as she was shoved away. The way the footsteps echoed back at her told her she was in the hallway. A minute later she was yanked to a halt. Scraping footsteps and grunts were drowned out by the sound of a truck's engine starting.

"Where's this one going, boss?" a gruff voice asked.

"Cabin's too good for her. Strap her to the wall of the truck. No less than two guns on her at any time. If she talks, punch the bitch until she shuts up. Make no mistake, this one's as dangerous as a rabies-riddled gorilla. She will kill all of you if your attention lapses for a second. And then I'll resuscitate you and kill you myself. Got it?"

"Yes, boss."

A new voiced screamed across the courtyard. An angry voice. "Is that the whore? Is that her?"

Eva knew the voice. She could even picture the face like a kicked-in door.

"Is that you, Lefty?" she said in mock friendliness. "It is, isn't it? Let's bury the hatchet, guy. What do you say? Game of Twister?"

The punch to the gut shot all the air out of her lungs. Gasping for breaths that didn't come, Eva wondered if she'd ever breathe again. Painful wheezing followed.

Worth it.

The scuffle that followed sounded like a group of soldiers hauling Lefty away before he killed her. He was lucky. She was ready to kill him. He'd taken the innocent life of Lekan. If they ever met again he wouldn't get off so lightly.

There was a sigh. "You have a way with people, Ms Destruction. It's an astonishing talent." Grey's voice was cold.

"Yeah, well, if you like that you should see me juggle."

"That won't be necessary." In a louder voice, he said, "Find something to fasten the bag, soldier. I don't want the cow to chew through her restraints."

Hurried footsteps moved away. Eva sensed she was alone with Grey.

"It's okay, Grey, I won't tell them your little secret."

He scoffed. "You know nothing about me."

"Don't I? Let's see, you come from Scottish heritage. It's the r's, academics call it the syllable coda, the rhotic accent. You try to hide it among the English upper-crust rounded vowels, but it's there, like a big burly red-headed kilted Scotsman in Westminster Abbey, not hard to spot if you're searching for it. Not from your father's side, no, he left early, it's your mother who is the Scot, I think. You're still close, some say a little too close." The lack of response told her she had hit her mark. "Now, the bitch and cow talk, it doesn't sit right with you. I know, because you pause a fraction of a second before you say it, like it's what you think the tough boys do. But you know what other men, gentler men, do, don't you Grey?"

"Shut. Up." The growl sounded like it was delivered between clenched teeth.

"It's okay, sweetie, your secret's safe with me. But despite what you think, I do know you, Grey. Maybe a little better than you know yourself."

She was seeping into Grey's pores. Her observations were intended to rattle him and keep him off-kilter. She wasn't dead yet, which meant she was valuable, at least for now. Keeping Grey challenged meant he could make mistakes. Mistakes that Eva could use to her advantage—as long as she stayed alive.

It was a valid question, though: why was she still alive? Their first encounter was to extract information about the shipment and the location of the nuke. They had that info now, so what value did she represent? Was there more to the story? What other secrets had she known before they'd been torn from her memory? Whoever was running this must think she knew something of worth, something that justified keeping her alive, if only for a short time. If so, she represented a risk—a risk she intended to exploit.

But what of Loch? Was he dead? Even with all the things he'd done, she desperately hoped he wasn't. As far as she knew, he hadn't been shipped out with her. Was he lying dead in the great hall, to be found by Akachi and the others when they finally emerged? Had he survived? Did he manage to somehow make it out? Too many unknowns. Too many variables Eva would never resolve if she didn't get out herself. She'd focus on that. Staying alive.

Grey's frustrated voice cut through her meditations. "Soldier, seal her up before I kill her, would you? There's a good lad."

A zip tie was fastened around her neck, at the base of her head covering. The effect was to cut all light completely. The result was claustrophobic, and nauseatingly disorientating, but she wasn't about to give Grey the satisfaction of knowing the effect it had on her. He was responsible for all her recent suffering, probably for Loch's death, and for whatever vile plans he had in his little reptilian brain.

"Guys, this is a quality bag," Eva said. "I have to tell you. No light at all. It's like an isolation tank, very relaxing. Great stuff."

"Does she ever shut up?"

"No light in here at all. I can see better if I shut my eyes."

"Throw her in the truck. Maybe she'll get travel sick and shut the hell up."

"Though, I have to say, the tie's a bit tight. Pretty sure this is how Michael Hutchence went."

"Glad you can make jokes, Ms Destruction. What I find amusing is that you actually think you're coming out of this alive." Grey's voice was as warm as a mortician's slab. "I can only assume you believe you haven't been killed yet because you're somehow protected. It's staggering how wrong you are. Or are you under the delusion that MI6 are going to swing in on ropes and rescue the princess? Hate to inform you, but you've been disavowed, love. SIS issued a burn notice yesterday. There will be no miraculous rescues, no knights in shining armour, just unrelenting pain and torment."

Was it true? Had MI6 disowned her? Sure, she'd overstepped the mark by abandoning Bishop in Macau, but for them to issue a burn notice, essentially telling all agencies she was persona non grata, was a huge leap. Then she realised she didn't have the entire story. Her reason for leaving Bishop was that MI6 had likely been infiltrated. Was the burn notice evidence of that? She doubted Lady Kensington, her Freddie, would have abandoned her so easily, but perhaps it wasn't her call. Who knew what wheels were spinning within wheels.

She tucked her hand in the waist of her jeans and clenched her trusty keepsake in her hand. Not for the first time in her life, Eva was completely alone in the world.

Grey continued. "Believe me, by the time we're done with you

you'll wish we had put a bullet in your brain. You'll be begging for it."

"Sounds like your mum."

This time she was ready for the slap.

Worth it.

CHAPTER FOURTEEN

For a while Eva tried to guess her position from the changes in direction, sounds or smells, like an old episode of 'Get Smart' she'd seen, but it quickly became impossible. There were too many stops and turns. After what seemed like several hours Eva couldn't be sure she was even in France anymore. The sound of highways gave way to increasingly congested road sounds. Even later, the faint smell of the sea wafted her way, disorientating her completely.

Standing pinned to the wall of the truck with her arms outstretched, Eva felt like a Catholic dash ornament. A blasphemous one at that. Her movements completely curtailed by handcuffs, all she could do was listen, and wait for an opportunity. Any opportunity.

The truck came to a halt and the motor was turned off. Outside, Eva struggled to hear a muffled conversation in French. She could only make out the occasional word: "Marcel?", "here", "arrangements", "confirmed", "on your way", "cleared", followed by a loud double thump on the cabin door.

The truck started again and dipped downward, as if it was on a long ramp, airbrakes slowing its descent. The road evened out and they took a few small turns. The truck's motor echoed back at her, as if it were a confined space. It kept moving forward without stopping, but the pace was slow, careful even. When the engine was cut, the soldiers in the back shifted, as if tensions had changed.

Minutes of silence followed. A distant horn sounded and there was a sudden shunt. They were moving again, but the movement wasn't powered by the truck. Eva knew where they were. The train began its journey through the Eurotunnel.

So Eva was heading home. She doubted she'd be deposited on her doorstep with a pat on the head and a letter of apology. The UK was a big place, they could be headed anywhere. Why would Grey's men need to bring a nuclear weapon into the country? Whatever their reason, Eva would find a way to stop them.

Reluctantly, she conceded that being strapped to the inside of a truck travelling at a hundred and sixty kilometres an hour with trained soldiers aiming guns at her wasn't the best place to start. Eva liked challenges, but this was ridiculous.

With no immediate opportunity presenting itself, she thought it best to adhere to the soldier's creed: sleep when you can, for any moment could be the next battle. Mere moments after she made the decision, Eva's body was enveloped by the crushing weight of exhaustion. She soon fell into fitful vertical slumber.

The shrill screech of a car horn woke her, and the steady thrum of the road confused her at first. Had she slept all the way through the Eurotunnel and customs checks? She tried to recall the last good night's sleep she'd had. The previous night had been defending the castle, the nights before that Loch had kept her up all night, and prior to that she and Bishop had stayed up watching old Bond films. For all she knew, she may not have had a decent sleep in six months. No wonder Eva had slept longer than she anticipated.

The truck wasn't travelling at speed. The lack of outside noise indicated they were in a relatively rural area. The occasional increase in background noise told her they were passing through the sporadic town.

Her shoulders ached. Her legs felt like fossilised logs. As for her back, it was spasming like a like an epileptic at a rave party. Everything was numb, hurt or throbbing.

It was near impossible to know where she was. Her best educated guess was somewhere out of Folkestone, where the Euro-tunnel disembarked. Their destination was a complete unknown. Time to find out.

"Hey," she croaked. Her mouth was parched. "Any chance a girl could get a glass of sparkling mineral water? Evian or Perrier? Something with mountains on the label. Oh, and plenty of ice. Maybe an umbrella."

A couple of the soldiers sniggered.

"In case you missed it, you've got a bag on your head."

"Oh, is that what it is? I thought I had my head up my arse this whole time."

More sniggers.

"Come on, guys. A girl's gotta breathe. Can you take it off for a minute?"

"The Major would have our head on a plate if we did. No dice."

"Guys, you have me strung up here like Christ on an Easter long weekend, where am I going? You've got all the firepower, all I've got is a nose itchier than your sister's crabs."

"Two minutes?"

"Dude, no!"

"What can she do in handcuffs?"

Under the bag, Eva smiled. "Whoever said that has not lived a fulfilling life."

Some of Eva's fondest memories involved handcuffs.

The light was like a slap in the face. With eyes scrunched tight, she gradually allowed more light in until her vision finally returned.

The first thing she saw were three soldiers who all had subma-chine guns trained on her. They were practically prepubescent. The men who had invaded her apartment had all been ex-military; hard men who probably found the private market more lucrative. These guys were so young Eva wondered if they even shaved.

The second thing she saw was the looming packing crate containing the nuclear warhead. She wondered if the customs offi-cials who'd been bribed to let them through really knew what they had done. She doubted it. They probably assumed the truck contained illegal immigrants, guns or drugs. The canvas flap gently fluttered enticingly at the rear of the truck.

A pasty white soldier presented his canteen to Eva, tilting it to supply much needed fluid to her dehydrated body.

"Just two minutes, yeah? Then the bag goes back."

Eva gulped. "You're sweet. Two things. Firstly, thanks, I was dryer than my grandfather's toolbox. Second, and this is a valu-able life lesson, boys. Never, and I mean never, trust a kinky girl with handcuffs."

Eva held up a handcuff-free hand.

The three men recoiled in horror, lifting their weapons to the firing position.

Using her free hand, Eva manoeuvred her bobby pin to work on the other set of handcuffs. She'd extracted it from her jeans back in France, then it was just a matter of biding her time.

Deliberately casual, she addressed the soldiers. "It comes from a lifetime of poor dating choices. Always, and I mean always, have a bobby pin on you. Don't get me wrong—" she paused while she held out her tongue and moved the bobby pin, "cuffs are fun and all, but when you're handcuffed to a bed and Chad is stealing all your worldly possessions, you realise there are skills you need to," she paused as the cuff popped open, "master." Her grin was wide. She rubbed her wrists. "I mean, he wouldn't even leave me the signed Nick Cave CD. Took the lot. Bastard."

"Stay where you are!" one of them shouted.

"Yeah, look, I understand you boys probably have orders to

shoot me or whatnot, but there's something you need to know." She halted and put her hands on her hips. "My, I am full of wisdom today. I should do seminars or something." She shook her head. "Anyway, did you see Mr Lefty before you loaded me onto the truck?" She shook her fist for emphasis. "He lost his hand when he and three of his mates invaded my bedroom. They were experienced and battle-hardened soldiers; I had a wicked hang-over and wasn't wearing any pants. I kicked each and every one of their arses."

The three young soldiers exchanged fearful glances. To Eva, they looked like work experience kids who had just discovered what the job actually entailed.

"So, we have several options here. One, you just shoot me. I mean, it's an option, so let's explore it. Bang, headshot, I'm gone. Probably not the best option, at least from my perspective, but probably not your best career choice either. You'll need to explain to Grey why you killed his prime asset." It wasn't true, but these lowly soldiers weren't to know.

Eva paced the truck's cabin, regaining circulation in her legs, limbering up. "Option two, you try—emphasis on try—to restrain me and hope to hell Grey doesn't find out you fucked up big time. Unlikely, but hey, you could give it a crack. The third option," Eva said, casually leaning her hand against the wooden crate, "is to…"

In a lightning-fast move she slid her fingers between the sides of the packing case and pried the box open. Before the soldiers could react, she tore off the white control panel and slammed her palm into a bright red button. The nuclear bomb emanated an unpleasantly urgent beeping.

"…blow us all up in a nuclear Armageddon. Surprise!"

Two of the three soldiers leapt to their feet, guns up and lunging for the crate. Eva curled her arm around the nearest weapon and twisted. The soldier cried in pain, but was quickly silenced by the side of Eva's hand to his throat. Her knee cracked into his ribs and a succession of swift head punches sent his limp body to the floor. Too close for their long-barrelled weapons, the second soldier fumbled for his combat knife. Too slow. A punch to the solar plexus knocked the wind out of him and he doubled over. The knee to the side of his skull sent him reeling as Eva finished him with a heel to the head.

That left one more. The poor kid was shaking so much she doubted he could have aimed straight if he'd tried. He didn't. His head swivelled between Eva and the nuke, as if trying to decide which was the most dangerous.

Casually, Eva asked, "Could you?" and jerked her head towards the beeping nuclear device. "The big red button."

A hurried nod was his reply. She gave a thumbs-up and he leaned over to depress the button, silencing the alarm. Too late he noticed that Eva had snuck up beside him. She rammed down his machine gun and thrust an elbow into his chin. Pulling back her arm, she delivered a punch to his jaw that sent him twirling to the truck floor. All three unconscious bodies looked as though they were having a nap. She hoped they didn't get in too much trouble.

"Right." Eva slung the submachine gun over her shoulder. "Sleep well, boys, mummy's going out for a bit."

Peeking through the tarpaulin she expected to see a conga line of black SUVs, but there was nothing but a deserted quaint English country road. No tail vehicle? That seemed odd. Something about her escape didn't sit right with her, but she knew better than to look a gift horse in the arse, as her grandmother used to say. But that was probably the dementia.

No time to query her good fortune, Eva pinned back the canvas and waited for her moment. She'd have to time the jump just right, wait for a curve in the road, when the sunshine was directly behind the truck and in the eyes of the driver.

It took a few minutes, but her chance finally came. On the outskirts of a small town, the truck took a right at a roundabout. Using the momentum, Eva propelled herself clear of the lorry and into the grassy trench by the road. It wasn't the first time she'd been in the gutter, and she hoped it wouldn't be the last.

She refused to breathe, instead concentrating on the sound of the truck, waiting for the brakes to be applied or for it to slow down. It did neither of those things.

This is too easy, Eva thought to herself warily.

After several minutes, she had the confidence to stand and brush off the grass. No broken bones, so that was something. One ankle was tender, but serviceable, so she hobbled back along the road, hoping to reach a town. When she finally reached the nearest one and read the sign, a small grin crept across her face. Knockholt. She knew where she was. Better yet, she knew exactly what her next move would be.

The lazy slide into night had begun. The roads were quiet. A faint drizzle fell, dropping the temperature and giving every surface an almost-but-not-quite level of dampness.

Eva contemplated hailing a stranger for a lift, but decided it was too risky. She kept to side roads and did her best to remain as inconspicuous as possible. Easier said than done in a tank top and with arms full of tats in a quaint rural area. The submachine gun slung across her back may also have piqued some interest. She had one destination, and hoped it worked. She'd only have one shot.

She made a list in her head of the things she'd need, and began searching for them in the gardens and sheds of Knockholt. There was no way she'd find everything on her list, but whatever she could manage would come in handy on the mission to come. A hessian sack in the second shed made the endeavour a lot less cumbersome. She felt a spasm of guilt at effectively stealing from innocent people, but justified it by telling herself it was for the greater good.

Missing fertiliser, garden tools and aerosol cans were a small price to pay for world peace, surely? Perhaps one day she'd pop around for a cup of tea and tell the residents they helped save the world from nuclear Armageddon. If she survived, that is.

As she pilfered items in the sleepy country town, Eva went over what intelligence she had gathered so far. She understood now what Grey and his goons had been after when they broke into her apartment. Likewise, she knew what Hu had been selling that had spooked the Russians so much.

What she didn't know was why her memory had been wiped, and by whom. Had she done it herself to protect the shipment? She dismissed the idea. Why would she send it to the castle if that was the case? How had she paid for the nuke in the first place? Why had she mistrusted MI6 so much she'd taken it upon herself to ship a nuclear weapon across the world, risking the safety of everyone in the castle in the process? Who was Grey working for, and how was it all linked to her memory loss?

Then there was Loch. What was his deal? She had been so sure of her feelings she'd jettisoned all reason, and it had ended up biting her skinny white arse once again. She was certain he *knew* her. What did he mean back at the castle about factions? Factions of what? All she knew for sure was that she had a better chance of finding a suitable lifelong partner by jumping on Chatroulette. Her instincts with men were so appalling Eva was convinced she should never date another human ever again.

Back to the minor issue of a rogue nuclear weapon being driven about the English countryside. What could their target possibly be, and why did Grey's men need the weapon so urgently they would attack a castle?

Then she realised. There was a little gathering coming up where a nuclear detonation would really mess up their day.

Holy arsebadger jizzmongers.

Eva broke into a run, her bag of tricks thudding uncomfortably on her back. This just became a whole lot bigger. She might not know who Grey was working for, but she knew what he was about to do. And she was going to stop it, or die trying.

The mansion was more impressive than she'd expected. When the English call a building a "house" or a "manor", it could be anything from a small outhouse to a structure that makes Buckingham Palace look like Aunty Ethel's Blackpool caravan. This leaned towards the latter.

Chevening House was located on private acreage nestled among lush green rolling hills. It was picture-postcard stuff, or it would be if people still did postcards.

Traditionally, Chevening is the primary residence of His Majesty's Principal Secretary of State for Foreign and Commonwealth Affairs—the position currently held by Lady Kensington. Or, as Eva knew her, Freddie. She hoped she was home.

Given her disavowed status, it was impossible for Eva to simply stroll up to the front door and knock. Well, not impossible, but it would result in her being flung in the nearest police cell for treason.

That wouldn't do. Eva looked hideous in stripes, and besides, she had to do something about that pesky nuclear weapon currently taking a leisurely drive around the countryside.

No, Eva had an alternative plan, which was riskier, slapdash and overly complicated—just the way she liked it. All she had to do was break into a high-security mansion with no gadgets, no blueprints or intel of any kind, no backup team and no communications. The only tools she possessed were her cunning and her devastating sense of style.

The poor bastards didn't stand a chance.

She recalled the story of Michael Fagan, who had scaled the wall of Buckingham Palace in the 80s and had a lovely chat to the Queen while sitting on the end of her bed. Eva was sure a few heads had rolled after the biggest royal security blunder of the 20th century. Given Freddie's critical position within the UK government, Eva doubted the security at Chevening House would be limited to a geriatric guardsman who suffered bouts of narcolepsy.

Night had fallen hard, plunging most of the countryside into complete darkness. The only light came from the mansion itself. A high brick wall surrounded the estate, with a camera on every third pillar. It wouldn't do for a hostile power to effortlessly kidnap the woman responsible for overseeing MI6, so it was logical that safety measures would be airtight and formidable. Alice in Wonderland was told to believe six impossible things before breakfast. Eva would have to do ten before supper.

First step: find a blind spot. It wouldn't be by the front gate— that would be heavily monitored from all angles. The cameras were mostly aimed at the wall itself, instead of outside the compound. That was something she could use. Eva had to find a less frequented section and exploit a fault in their defence. It wouldn't be a piece of cake, which was a shame. Eva hadn't eaten in at least twenty-four hours. She was starving.

It took fifteen minutes, but Eva found it. By the south wall, a security camera faced outward like all the others, but a mulberry bush had grown so large it obscured the camera. Would it be enough to hide Eva as she scrambled over the red brick wall? There was one way to find out.

Pacing back towards the front gate, Eva prepared her first surprise. Across the opposite side of the road from the main entrance, away from the cameras, she set to work. The ingredients were volatile, but not explosive. The bottle of stump killer had been the find of the night—pure potassium nitrate. When combined with salt for driveways, it made a fairly suitable smoke bomb. The fuse had been harder to come by but she had improvised well enough, pulling apart a citronella candle to procure one.

The improvised ingredients meant that the smoke bomb was unpredictable. Eva's main concern wasn't blowing her face off, it was the bomb going off before she'd had a chance to get into position. She was running on fumes, and realised her abilities were diminished.

Her mind drifted to the next phase of her plan. What would Lady Kensington do when she saw her? Eva's hope was that she'd hear her out. Was their friendship strong enough that Freddie would give Eva a couple of minutes? It was possible. Equally as likely, she would be so shocked she'd call in the guards immediately, without giving her time to explain. Even more likely, Eva wouldn't even get that far.

There was only one way to find out. She lit the fuse and broke into a run.

When she reached the south end of the compound Eva was wheezing. She wasn't in the right condition for this, but there was no alternative. She couldn't slip into a nice B&B for a couple of days to recuperate, not with a weapon of mass destruction on the loose. She sucked in lungfuls of air and waited.

When clouds of smoke began to billow from the entrance, Eva made her move. She tossed the modified end of a garden hoe attached to the strap from the Heckler & Koch over the top of the wall. It took a few attempts, but finally the improvised grappling hook took hold. She gave it two tugs—it seemed secure enough to hoist herself up.

She tossed the submachine gun over the wall, but would leave it there. There was no use bringing a loaded weapon with her—she wasn't about to shoot a security guard for doing their job: protecting the Foreign Secretary. She knew being unarmed was the better approach, even though she felt naked without a weapon. Then again, Eva did some of her best work naked.

Sprinting across the grass, Eva didn't take her eyes off the mansion. The red brick English Renaissance building was certainly imposing. The gardens had been painstakingly maintained. There was a lake to her left and a series of well-manicured hedges to her right, both of which she'd avoid. At any second security personnel could burst from the building. But they didn't. As she approached, she scanned for the best entry point. The front door was out. The building had no balconies, so the next best option was the back door. She headed that way.

A silhouette crossed her path: the outline of a bulky man, pistol drawn. Eva dashed towards the hedges. Finding a gap, she inched her way along the straight hedgerow. She couldn't tell which way the silhouette had been facing, but she assumed the person had heard her running.

"Ah, excuse me," said a loud voice with a South London twang. "Love, you're in a maze."

There was no use being silent, she'd been made. "Did you say I'm amazing?"

"No. Maze. You're in a maze."

Eva observed the sharp trimmed hedges surrounding her on all sides. "I realise that... now."

"Are you going to come out?"

Eva didn't reply.

"Where are you going to go?" he asked.

"I thought I'd try left, then go right a bit."

"No, I mean, we know where you are, it's not like you're going to escape."

"What if I stay here until the next open day?"

"That'll be October."

"I don't suppose you could throw in a few chocolate bars to tide me over?"

The man sighed. "Miss, could you come out, please? I was just reading an Agatha Christie novel and it's up to the big reveal, so if you could make your way to the nearest exit we can wrap this up."

"Which one?"

"To your left."

"No, which Agatha Christie are you reading?"

"Er, *Crooked House*."

"Josephine did it. Her grandfather wouldn't pay for her dance lessons."

She heard a pistol hammer click. "I'm going to shoot you now."

"Terrence, that will be all." The voice was new. Older, more authoritarian. Female. Eva recognised it immediately.

"Judging by the accent, I've either got Eva Destruction in my maze or one of ten thousand barmaids from the greater London area."

Eva stuck her head above the hedge. "Hey, Freddie."

"Eva, what the jolly hell are you doing here?"

She scratched her head. "Funny story—with an explosive ending."

"Another chocolate mousse, my love?" Freddie asked.

The main study of Chevening House was resplendent in floor-to-ceiling bookshelves that Eva could have spent the rest of her life serenely inspecting. The Foreign Secretary was seated behind a huge oak desk while Eva sat hunched on the other side, eating furiously. Plaques adorned the wall, a sextant decorated the table in the corner and an old nautical telescope stood by the large window. It was clear that the woman on the other side of the desk came from the Royal Navy. A degree from Cambridge took pride of place on the wall. The whole room had an old sea captain's feel. All it needed was a giant ship's wheel and an eye patch.

"Thanks, but three is my limit."

Freddie grinned. "Especially after two steak sandwiches and three bowls of chips."

Eva eyed her sideways. "Are you having a go, Freddie? Because I have no problem with taking down the Foreign Secretary, let me tell you."

"I have no doubt." Freddie smiled.

The first thing Eva had asked was about the refugees back at the castle. It took a while, but word finally came back that everyone was fine. The local gendarmerie had initially put the incident down as an anti-immigration attack. Grey's men had removed their dead, but the blood remained. That and the fact that someone had blown a hole in the castle meant the local authorities knew something was up, but the residents of the castle were remaining silent. Eva suspected Akachi was still protecting her. There was no word on Loch.

Freddie took a drag on her cigar. "Quite the week, you've had, hmm? So what do you think is their next move?"

Eva put down the remnants of her chocolate mousse, wiped her mouth with a napkin and leaned backwards.

"Is she doing the dramatic pause thing? She loves the dramatic pause thing." Paul's voice came through crisply over the secure phone line to SIS Headquarters. The Foreign Secretary had called him in to the office so he could hear the story from Eva as well. She'd brought them up to date, now she had to drop the bomb. She hoped not literally.

"What major event is occurring tomorrow?" she asked.

"Eurovision," Paul said from London.

"Yes. Wait, what? No. Why would anyone want to bomb Eurovision?"

"Obviously you've never watched Eurovision."

"Focus, please," Freddie interrupted.

"We know G8 is occurring tomorrow, Evie. The former Foreign Secretary and I have been going over the security at length for months," Paul told her.

"Yes, but… did you say former?" Eva eyeballed Freddie.

"I resigned yesterday."

"You what?"

"It's been brewing for some time. The Prime Minister and I have been at loggerheads over this business of bringing China into the G8. It came to a head, I tendered my resignation, she accepted and there you are." She clasped her hands together on the desk.

Eva paused. "So bringing Paul into the conversation…"

"Means an active member of His Majesty's government is able to take some action," Freddie finished for her. "Plus, I thought you would prefer a friend on the line instead of a bureaucrat. We know how you love authority."

Eva frowned, conceding the point.

"As for the action, that starts now." Paul's tone was all business. "As soon as I'm off this call I'll notify MI5 to implement the Switchback protocol."

"I shouldn't be hearing this," the former Foreign Secretary said. "I no longer have top-secret clearance, Mr Cavendish. Please refrain from divulging classified information."

"Apologies, ma'am. I spoke in error. I meant to advise that precautions will be implemented."

"Very good."

Eva swirled her spoon in the dish. "I'm in a lot of trouble, aren't I, Paul?"

"You could say that, Evie, yes."

"Am I going to lose my job?"

"That's for the board to decide." Paul added a dramatic pause of his own. "But I'll put in a good word for you."

"As will I." Freddie winked.

There were bigger issues than her career in espionage. Worst-case scenario, she'd go back to her coffee shop full time, which wouldn't be a bad thing. "So what do we do now?"

"I need to coordinate things from my end," Paul said. "Evie, I suggest you stay with Lady Kensington. It is the safest place to be... despite the recent security breach."

Eva smiled, chocolate clinging to her teeth.

"There's a lot at stake here," Paul continued. "You've done your duty admirably, now let the rest of us do ours."

"Not really my style to sit on my hands, Paul."

"Oh, I know." Eva could detect Paul's amusement down the phone line. "I hear Lady Kensington has an impressive billiards room. You could show her how you cheat at pool by calling it pub rules."

"Pub rules is totally a thing, Paul!"

"Okay, Evie," Paul chuckled. "I have to go, the Director General is on the line. I'll see you soon, Evie, yeah?"

Before Eva could answer, he hung up. Freddie rose and opened her drinks cabinet.

"You'll join me in a drink, of course?" she asked.

"Is the Pope a Protestant?"

Freddie handed Eva a glass of amber liquid and perched on the edge of her desk. "Salut," she said, raising her glass.

Eva didn't have to be told twice. She downed the drink in one, and wiggled her glass for more. If she was out of the game she may as well enjoy herself. She was exhausted, physically and emotionally. She planned on sleeping for a week. The drink would help her on her way.

Her glass topped up, she took another swig of the smooth nectar. She couldn't place it. Was it a Scotch? Her hands were very heavy.

"I plan on thleeping until nexth thentury... thent?" Why did her tongue refuse to say century?

Freddie smirked at Eva and placed her untouched drink beside her. "You've been through so much, my love." She tilted her head in a grandmotherly manner.

Eva fought to keep her eyes open. Her vision stained black, the room fell in and out of focus.

"You've done your duty." She folded her hands together. Freddie leaned down, a sneer painted across her face, and took the glass from her hand. "Nighty night, you stupid little bint."

Everything went black.

CHAPTER FIFTEEN

A dirty long weekend in Sussex was a far better idea than she had originally thought it would be. They had spent the last two days holed up in Castle Cottage and now lounged on the hillside with a picnic, watching a beautiful sunset. She poured the last of the wine and handed it to him.

He gripped her hand and pulled her in for a tender kiss. It was sweet. Then he leaned in and whispered what he intended to do with her when they returned to the cottage. That was less sweet, but equally welcome. Eva nestled into his arms and kissed his lips. The sky turned pink, and a gentle breeze blew in from the south, bringing with it a slight chill. She shivered and held her tighter. It had been the perfect day—maybe even her favourite day. There was no one she'd rather spend it with than Loch.

Eva sat up with a start and her head screamed in protest. She wasn't on a hillside or in Sussex. To the best of her knowledge, she'd never even been to Sussex. Was it a dream? It had seemed so real. Was it a flashback to a part of her memory that had returned? It couldn't be—Loch had been lying the whole time since her memory loss. Hadn't he?

With great effort Eva concentrated on the here and now. Her

limbs were made of lead. Her fingers were like balloons. Her tongue had swollen up and filled her mouth like a fat man driving a Mini. It took a while for her eyes to adjust to the gloom. When they did, she wished they hadn't.

There was a small slit of a window high up on the wall, indicating she was in a basement. The shabby bare brick walls on three sides meant it wasn't luxury accommodation. The floor-to-ceiling bars across the rest of the room didn't necessarily put paid to the possibility of this being an aristocratic version of a kinky sex dungeon, but they did make it unlikely. As she was on the side of the bars without a door out of the room, she assumed she was a prisoner. A solid wall split the cell in two and she couldn't see the other side. Eva assumed hers might not be the only cell in the basement.

Why had Freddie drugged her? To what end? What threat did Eva pose? MI6 and MI5 knew about the nuclear weapon, which was basically everything she knew. There was nothing else to share. She didn't know who was behind it all or what they wanted. And how did all this relate to Freddie resigning as Foreign Secretary? One thing was certain, she wasn't going to find any answers by asking herself these questions.

"Hey! Hey, fucksticks! Where's my breakfast in bed? Also, there's no dunny in here. Where's a girl meant to put her…"

The door opened before she could finish the colourful thought. A tired-looking Lady Kensington slouched in.

"What in God's name is a dunny?"

Eva folded her arms. "How can you know so much about Aussie music and not know what a dunny is?"

Freddie shrugged. "It never came up."

"You know what also never came up? How you're actually the bad guy in all this."

"That was a terrible segue."

Eva planted her fists on her hips. "Too fucking bad, you twat-faced shitpouch wankstained fucknugget."

"I'm getting the impression you're somewhat upset."

Eva's whole body shook with anger. So furious she couldn't

articulate a sentence, Eva resorted to a series of increasingly obscene hand gestures.

"I can explain." Freddie's voice was calm. "Not that it will matter. Despite your current incarceration, I've only ever had your best interests at heart, my dear. Don't you realise this was all for you? Since my daughter passed, you were my charge, you were the one I protected. I looked after you, Eva, and all you can do is abuse me and make... I don't even know what that one is supposed to be."

Eva changed the gesture to the finger.

Freddie went on. "I saved your life several times over, not that you knew."

"That's bullshit. You weren't in my apartment, you weren't in Macau and you sure as shit weren't there in the middle of the night manning the parapets in France. So how, pray tell, did you save my life?"

"I just did, let's leave it there. Not that it matters."

"You used those words before, 'not that it matters'. What do you mean?"

"It doesn't matter what we discuss right now. Tomorrow, you won't remember."

"Like flaming hell I won't." Suddenly all the pieces fell into place, as if she'd thrown a thousand-piece jigsaw on the floor and it had fallen to form a complete picture. "It was *you*! You stole my memories. You tore six months of my life from me! *You're* the other faction, the one Grey's working against."

"The relationship with Grey is, ah, quite strained currently. Please understand I took your memories in order to keep you safe. You knew too much, about, well, everything. It was either make you forget or kill you. Eva, you're like a daughter to me, there was no way I could sanction taking your life. Can't you see? I saved you. You would have been blissfully ignorant if you hadn't switched the bloody shipments."

"What do you... The nuke. I was meant to ship it somewhere else, wasn't I?"

Freddie nodded. "We supplied you with an untraceable

account to pay for it and you were meant to ship it to Scotland. Unfortunately for us, the supposed nuke arrived at port after your memory had been erased. And of course, it wasn't the nuke, but a quarter ton of bright pink dildos. You had become suspicious of your instructions and then disobeyed my direct order."

"I tend to do that." Eva gripped the bars. "What's Halcyon?"

"I do wish you didn't know that word. It was meant to be buried long ago, in the bowels of MI6." She shook her head.

"So my entire mission to Macau, all of it, was just for you?"

"Essentially, yes. Assigning Yuji was a stroke of brilliance, if I do say so myself. With your memory loss we needed you to retrace your steps, particularly around where the shipment went. In essence, you were working for me, trying to find out exactly what I wanted to know."

"And it killed Yuji." The words were bitter in Eva's mouth.

"That wasn't my doing." Freddie shook her head. "He was a trusted ally and a man performing his rightful duty. What happened to Yuji Okumoto was unfortunate."

"Unfortunate!" Eva screamed. "He was a good man and you shot him down with a missile when he no longer posed a threat. That's not unfortunate, you douchepoodle, it's cold-blooded murder."

"As I said," Freddie clenched her teeth, "not my doing. Grey's faction are, let's say, far more trigger happy than I deem necessary."

"Speaking of trigger happy, you aren't really going to blow up the G8 meeting, are you? It makes no sense."

The smallest of smirks creased the outline of Freddie's mouth.

Eva hated the smug expression. "But now you're stuffed because they'll move the meeting. Your little plan has fallen apart."

Freddie smiled. It was broad and all-encompassing.

Eva gasped. "Oh shit. You wanted it to happen. That's why you let me talk to Paul. You want them to move the meeting—that was your plan all along. The nuke's already there, isn't it?"

Freddie's features were unconcerned. "We're prepared. Given the bedlam that comes with relocating a major event like this, no one is going to check every nook and cranny, not when it's already been done. Our strategy is proceeding according to plan. My apologies for using you one last time, but you served a purpose, my dear. Even Grey recognised that. He *really* wanted to shoot you back at the castle. You do have a unique ability to aggravate people, my dear. But I managed to convince him you were more valuable to us alive. Didn't you think your escape from the truck was far too easy? Or that it was beyond coincidental that you ended up mere miles from here? Surely you're not that naive?"

Eva had questioned it but had stamped the thought down, focusing on her mission. Which was apparently to do exactly what the bad guys wanted. She was a pawn, and had placed herself on the board willingly. Reckless again.

Eva paced, feeling the urgent need to throttle something. "But why did you need me to get a nuke from across the world? We have our own nuclear weapons."

Freddie rocked on her heels, as if she was accepting a school prefect's award. "Well, yes and no. You see, each bomb has a signature, like a master's painting. It tells where the uranium was mined, its country of origin. So to keep it bulletproof, so to speak, one must use a Chinese bomb, so the Chinese take the blame."

Hand rushing to her mouth, Eva gulped. "You're going to do it? You're actually going to use a nuclear weapon on your own people?"

Freddie tilted her head, as if to say, *c'est la vie.* "We weren't even the first to come up with the idea. The top brass in the US military thought up Operation Northwoods in the 60s to drum up support to invade Cuba. The joint chiefs even signed off on faking a terrorist attack, but the civilian leadership lacked the moral fortitude. We're just the first to have the balls to do it."

Eva's hands shook. "Fucking fantastic, I just gave it to you on a platter." Eva couldn't seem to stop pacing. She was in fight or flight mode, and right now there was a lot of fight. "Why are you doing this, Freddie?"

"Britain has stumbled. We are no longer the power we once were. Do you know why?"

"Chavs?"

"No, it is because we have no great enemy. This nation achieves great things when spurred on by the threats of others. The Anglo–Spanish Wars? We dominated the seas for the next three hundred years. The Napoleonic Wars? We expanded the Empire like the world had never seen. Our country is fracturing, eating itself alive. We need to focus, we need to build on our history, become great once more."

"Right, this is a unique idea, never been tried before. Will your shirts be black or brown?" Before Freddie could answer, Eva asked, "And who would lead this great nation, I wonder?"

Freddie raised an eyebrow.

Eva shook her head. "Oh, I get it. I totally fucking get it now. You set it all up. Patriot Lady Kensington tried to warn the PM about China, but she wouldn't listen, so you publicly resigned. You'll manufacture events at the G8 so China gets knocked back, they leave, and boom goes your baby. Worldwide shock, anger. No more PM, deputy, or other viable candidates. You come screaming in on your white horse saying I told you so and save the day. Is that it?"

"You've always been the clever one, Eva."

"Jesus Christ, Freddie. You really expect to create a new world order by blowing up your own goddamn country? The Night of the Long Knives has nothing on you, darlin'."

"Oh, don't think for one moment this is an act of hubris or lunacy." Lifting her head proudly, Freddie launched into a monologue as if she'd been composing it for a lifetime. "America's time as a superpower is over, it's just that nobody has the heart to tell them. There's talk of the Asian century—please." She shook her head sadly. "Not so long ago, the sun never set on the British Empire. The world has not forgotten the great power we once wielded. It will only take strong leadership to regain our place once more. We may be small, but we are mighty, and with true leadership we will achieve—"

Eva's slow clap interrupted Freddie's flow. "Great work, Mistress Megalomania, but don't try and frame this as anything other than your lust for glory over a pile of innocent corpses. This is nothing but one huge cry-wank for attention."

"No, *no*. This is not about me, this is about our nation." Freddie's hands trembled. "Everyone will benefit, Eva. Everyone."

"I'm sure the smoking atoms at the G8 will be giving you high-fives left, right and centre."

Freddie forged on, ignoring Eva. "You'll go back to work at a revitalised MI6, with appropriate funding and the power to properly do its job. Do you know what our budget currently is? Three billion. I mean, it's pitiful. The rest of the government spends more on stationery supplies. There are real threats out there and we're expected to protect the free world for the price of staples. When the country sees this atrocity they will rise up, creating a new dawn for Britain."

"You want a bigger budget? That's your reasoning?"

Freddie sighed, sadness enveloping her. "Eva, my daughter died because of a lack of intelligence about a terrorist attack. I refuse to let that occur again. Don't you see? We will all benefit from this, the world will be safer."

There was no persuading her. Eva could spend the rest of the decade arguing reason, but this woman had drunk her own Kool-Aid and had a roll of quarters in her pocket. She was off to see the mothership and there was no point trying to bring logic or empathy into the discussion.

"One does not establish a dictatorship in order to safeguard a revolution," came a croaky voice. "One makes a revolution in order to establish a dictatorship."

Wait, who was quoting Orwell? The voice seemed to have come from the cell next to Eva's. It sounded awfully familiar.

Taking a step back, Freddie peered into the space next to Eva's cell. "We obviously didn't dose you up enough. We'll be sure to rectify that little mistake."

"I don't suppose I'll be subjected to a nice mind wipe?" Eva's cellmate rasped.

Freddie smiled, but it wasn't the sort Eva was used to. This was pure malice, malevolence of the highest order. She seemed to take pleasure in her own evil. Eva shivered.

"No, Mr Davenport, I'm afraid your fate will be far more permanent and, well, satisfactory than Miss Destruction's."

Loch is here? In a cell? But wasn't he on Freddie's side? Eva's mind churned with possibilities. Why would Lady Kensington lock up one of her own?

Freddie must have seen the confusion etched across Eva's face. "Grey offered me this worthless corpse of a man as some sort of peace offering." She shook her head. "They needn't have bothered. He's betrayed everyone. Grey, me, you. I honestly don't know how we're going to dispose of him. I'd strap him to the bomb if it wasn't so clichéd."

"How did he betray you?" Eva tensed, waiting for the answer.

A look of amusement crept across Freddie's dark features. "Well, he sided with you, of course." Freddie tilted her head. "You... you didn't know, did you? Oh, the irony! This gormless little berk tried to welch on our arrangement when he was in France. Said he'd developed *feelings*. I mean, what sort of secret agent is that? Feelings. I love you, my dear, but, my god, I'd never let that interfere with a mission. Not when the shape of the 21st century is at stake. That's simply unacceptable. He's completely useless."

Overcome with dizziness, Eva took an unsteady seat on her bunk.

"That's not entirely true," Loch said. "I was told that the nuclear bomb would only ever be discovered at G8, never detonated. What you're proposing is sheer madness. And for the record, my feelings for Eva didn't suddenly materialise in France. It was well before then. I told Grey I was out long ago, before Eva went to Macau the first time. I tried to warn her, but missed her before she boarded the plane. I'd realised you were using your relationship to make her do exactly what you ordered. But you forgot one important thing."

"Oh really, what did I forget?"

"No one ever tells Eva Destruction what to do."

A raucous laugh burst from Freddie. She shook her head. "That's priceless. What, you're cosying up to her for one last hand job through the bars before your execution? You're too much, Davenport."

Eva's head spun. Was it true? Was Loch really on her side? Did he truly have feelings for her? Had they been in love before the memory wipe? Was that why her gut told her to trust him—she did actually care for him?

"Is that why you came to Macau with me?" she asked the man she couldn't see.

"Of course, Chérie. I couldn't be certain you'd be safe if you discovered the truth."

It was too much to process. How many times had Eva reassessed her life in the past week as new information came to hand? What was real and what was assumed?

"You said at the castle you didn't call Grey. So who did you call?"

Freddie raised a hand. "The stupid boy called to tell me personally that I should—what were the words you used? Ah, that's right, go fuck myself with a hedgehog. It was then I knew he'd spent far too much time in your company, my dear."

"You told me it was a scrambled phone that couldn't be traced." Loch didn't sound happy.

"Oh, it was." Freddie was jovial. "For anyone other than us. Now, all this is becoming tiresome. Eva, my dear, I look forward to our lovely chats once you've been reset. And Davenport, I look forward to never encountering you ever again." She straightened her jacket. "If you'll excuse me, I'm off to become the Prime Minister of the soon-to-be Greater Britain, with a huge budget increase for the military and foreign services, and a mandate that has been lacking for thirty years due to middle-of-the-road policy appeasement. Then supper. Cheerio!"

Freddie turned on her heels and headed for the door.

"Wait, there's still one thing I don't understand." Eva waved her hand through the bars. "Why did you send Grey to kill me after you'd wiped my memory? That doesn't make any sense."

Freddie sighed. "I didn't. Grey didn't quite agree with my light-handed solution to your meddling."

"Right." Eva wasn't grasping the point. "He's a different faction. But I don't understand why there are factions."

A shrug. *There just are.* "We all have the same goal in mind, it's just that our methods differ somewhat."

"All? So there are more than just you and Grey?"

"A quorum of like-minded—I hate to say this, given your feminist leanings—fellows, who have been working on this for decades."

"There you go, pandering to your pet again."

All heads turned to the door.

The man casually leaned against the doorframe, arms folded. "I'm curious, Lady Kensington. Did you give them the whole plan or just the parts that will have us executed for treason?"

"Where the devil did you come from, Grey?"

"Oh, you know the depths of hell and so forth." Grey stepped forward. It was only then that Eva saw the submachine gun.

"What is the meaning of this? We had a pact. How on Earth did you get in?"

Grey jangled a set of keys and sneered darkly. He slipped the keys into his pocket. Freddie stepped backwards, bumping into the bars of Eva's cell.

"I knew you wouldn't execute the bitch so I thought I'd pop by."

Attempting to put on a brave face, Freddie puffed out her chest. It was pure bluster. The woman was rattled.

"As you can see," she motioned to the cells, "everything is contained."

"Yet you're divulging our entire plan?" Grey shook his head and tutted.

"It will be confined, Grey. He'll be taken care of," she gestured to Loch's cell, "and she'll have her memory wiped."

He frowned mockingly. "Right, because that worked so well last time." He shook his head. "I knew having a woman as part of this was a mistake. You're too soft, too sentimental. Christ, how many times does this piece of Australian trash have to ruin your plans before you get the hint? Just fucking kill the daft cow already."

"That's not your call to make, Grey." Freddie seemed to have recovered from the shock. Her words were measured, foreboding.

"Oh, but it is. I'm glad you talked me out of killing her back in France. We can use her far better now." He held up the submachine gun to show Eva. "Do you recognise the gun? It's yours. Your DNA is all over this baby." Eva suddenly noticed that Grey was wearing latex gloves. "We have footage of you carrying it, of you breaking in and trying to assassinate the Foreign Minister. Your relationship with Kensington is well known. Your fate is sealed, bitch," he sneered.

"Why," Eva's voice broke, "why would I kill Freddie?"

"Because you're working for the Chinese, obviously."

Eva stared at him blankly. She turned to Freddie, her face just as blank. So she was their patsy now. It wasn't difficult to see how Grey would play it. Eva had acted inconsistently on her first Macau mission. They would have evidence, manufactured or real, showing her buying the Chinese nuclear weapon. She had refused to report to the field office, headed back to London and claimed memory loss. They would probably frame the attack in her apartment to her detriment as well. The second mission to Macau, where she went rogue, was easy enough to spin—there were official SIS records. Then it was just a matter of making up some story about how she transported the nuke into the country. They had footage of her breaking into Freddie's place, and the testimony of the guard who found her. All they needed was some reason why she'd tried to kill the Foreign Secretary. Given a couple of hours Eva could work out the finer details. Though she doubted she had that long to live.

Freddie couldn't save her. Grey's strategy was the better one if their plan was to succeed.

Eva was going to die.

He waggled the gun at Eva and turned to Freddie. "You see, Kensington, you're driven by deluded patriotism. Myself? I'm driven by pure self-preservation; greed, if you will." He circled around Freddie, the two of them locked in a slow, deliberate dance. "I'm a professional, I see the larger picture. You want everyone to sit around a campfire and sing 'Kumbaya' once this is all over. That's why I have to make this call."

"Grey, stop. Listen to me—"

"No!" He turned the gun on Freddie. "Enough listening. You'll thank me one day. But right now, someone has to have the balls to do it, and that someone sure as shit isn't you, Lady Kensington. Stop talking and do what's needed. We need action."

Slowly, he swung his gun in Eva's direction and poked it through the bars, aiming directly between her eyes. She took a step back. Not that it did any good. The cell was tiny, she had nowhere to go.

"Grey, I'm warning you." Freddie's voice was cold.

Freddie had a pistol in her hand. It was aimed at Grey's head. He didn't see it; he was too busy sneering at Eva. He seemed to be enjoying himself so much he probably had a hard-on.

"It's time you listened, Kensington. What we need is action, no more words. No more—"

Grey's speech was cut short as his head exploded, fragments of brain splattering all over Eva's face.

Freddie sighed. "How's that for action?"

CHAPTER SIXTEEN

Eva was certain her scream should have carried all the way to Whitechapel. The silence that followed was far more deafening. Wiping her face only seemed to smear Grey's remains over her hands. Every part of Eva shook.

Breathing deeply seemed to help, though that was probably just the shock kicking in. Eva forced herself to stare at Grey's lifeless corpse. It lay sprawled across the floor before her. She hated the guy, but wouldn't have killed him. And she never would have thought her former friend would have been capable of such an act.

She looked at Freddie, whose lips were moving but Eva couldn't process a word. Eva thought she'd found a mentor, a like-minded advisor who could guide her career and life choices. Instead she'd found a complete twat.

"… and he just hastened his own demise." Finally, Eva tuned in to the words being spoken. Freddie shook her head. "There's no way a man like that could be left to roam the country once this terrible business is done. He was a psychopath. No, it's better this way. The plan can proceed without him."

Eva was too emotionally wrought to utter a word.

"Are you going to kill us too?" Loch asked.

"You? Oh, most definitely." She paused. "I don't mean to sound callous, but I don't want to provide you with false hope, Davenport. For what it's worth, I am sorry you became embroiled in all this, but certain sacrifices must be made. I'm sure you understand, at least from an academic perspective."

"Freddie," Eva said weakly. "Please don't do this. There has to be another way."

Freddie frowned in . "If you will both excuse me, I have to find out what Grey's done." She turned to face Eva directly. "I can't promise you will be fine, my dear, but I shall try my best."

She pivoted on the spot, picked up Eva's submachine gun and walked out, leaving the three of them: Eva, Loch and the partially decapitated corpse of Grey.

With great effort, Eva found the bunk and sat. All she could do was concentrate on staying upright. Every time she closed her eyes there was the faintest hope that when they opened, the room would miraculously transform into something less grotesque.

"Chérie, you still with me?" came the voice from the adjacent cell.

"I'm not sure…"

"We can get through this. All we need—"

"No. You didn't let me finish." Eva inhaled deeply. "I'm not sure I'm talking to you."

"Oh, right." Loch had the good sense to leave it. Or perhaps he knew her that well. It only added to Eva's frustration.

Anxious to fix on something other than Grey's body, she addressed the man next door. "I need you to tell me something straight. And Loch, if I find you lied about it I will hunt you down and kill you, twice. To be clear, that's not an exaggeration or a euphemism. Were we lovers? I mean, before?"

"Yes. One hundred per cent we were, Chérie. And not because of a mission, because I loved you. I loved you then and I do now. And you know what? I'd want you to hunt me down and kill me if it wasn't true because I need you in my life."

"I might have to anyway, because that was cheesy as fuck."

"You're always the romantic."

"Loch, we're imprisoned in a basement with the dead body of a complete douchepoodle, all thanks to my former mentor. Romance can go suck elephant balls right now."

"Point taken." A rustling came from his cell. "So what's the plan? You always have a plan."

Eva didn't have a plan. Right now, she probably couldn't even spell plan. Was there a seven in it?

She had to refocus. Escaping was the priority. She could spend the next three hours trying to understand what Freddie had done, but what use would that be if it all ended with a bullet in Eva's brain? No. She had to escape and take down Freddie and her malevolent scheme.

First step, get out of the cell. She reached into the side of her pants and pulled out her trusty bobby pin.

More to herself than anyone else, she said, "I might not know everything that's going on, but I know locks." She got to work.

"I'm glad you think so. I know you don't remember us, before, but I assure you—"

"Dude. Locks with a k. You, as my mum used to say, I don't know from Adam."

"You know some. Like the thing I do when you're on your back and I get your legs—"

"Don't try and charm your way out of this. You lied to me the entire time I can remember you. That's not easily forgiven."

"I didn't lie when I told you not to trust anyone, including me."

"Lying by omission is still a lie." Eva continued to work on the lock.

"We're spies. That's in our make-up. The truth doesn't come easy."

Eva had to wonder if he left the last line hanging intentionally. If he knew her like he said he did, it was bait.

"Neither do I." Eva's tone was even.

"Liar."

Despite herself, Eva almost laughed. She glanced at the body of Grey and had no trouble wiping the urge away. Poking her tongue to the side of her mouth, she concentrated on the lock. She didn't have the right tools for the job. Her lock-picking tools usually travelled with her wherever she went, but her lucky set was back in France. She'd have to work with what she had.

It took a good five minutes to crack—far longer than usual. Many inventive swears were created in the interim. When the final tumbler clicked into place, Eva said, "Wazzocking jab-end arsebadger."

To exit the cell, Eva had to walk past Grey's body. His lifeless husk was slumped against the wall dividing the cells. Without looking, Eva left her prison.

For the first time, Eva was able to see Loch. He wasn't in a good way. His left eye was turning purple. Crusted blood covered several parts of his head. His clothing was dirty and ripped in places. When he saw her, he smiled. He was still very pretty.

"You going to let me out now?"

Eva shook her head and walked away.

"Chérie!"

It was only a few strides, but it seemed like miles. Loch desperately called to her, begging her not to abandon him. She could have, possibly even should have, but that wasn't why she walked away.

Eva could have spent another five minutes unlocking the other cell, or thirty uncomfortable seconds rummaging through Grey's pockets to see if he had the key. She chose the latter.

It didn't take thirty seconds. She tried the front right pocket of his jacket and found the set of keys he'd jangled in front of Freddie when he'd entered. As distasteful as it was, Eva had what she sought. She approached Loch's cell, found the right key and opened the door.

"Can you walk?"

He grinned. "I'll do anything you ask me to."

"Let's start with walking."

It was probable there were armed guards on the other side of the door. There were no weapons to be found in the basement. Their options were to stay put or brave whatever awaited them outside. There really was no choice.

Eva gripped the door handle and braced herself. In a whisper, she asked, "You ready?"

Loch gave her a determined nod. "And, Chérie, before we face whatever is out there, I want you to know I am sorry. I will live to make it up to you, I promise."

"Let's just get through this first, yeah?"

Another nod. She blew all the air from her lungs then ripped the door open. Fists raised, she burst into the hallway. The only things facing them were a small landing and some steps leading up to the main house. There was no one to fight. They were unguarded. *When will people stop underestimating me?*

In retrospect, Freddie's men were most likely spread thin. Either they were off ensuring the nuclear weapon at the G8 wasn't discovered, or they were real government employees guarding the house against another breach. Guarding a beaten CIA agent and an unarmed Australian were probably low on the priorities list. Eva would see to it that was the last mistake they made.

Foremost among the myriad of things Eva didn't understand was why Freddie had killed Grey. There had to be more to it than just protecting Eva. Wasn't Freddie in charge? Was this a way to shore up her leadership? Eliminate probable future challengers?

"Who was Grey?" Eva asked.

Loch's features became hard. "Assistant to the Chief of the General Staff."

"The assistant to the head of the British military? Jesus. This isn't rebellion, this is a coup d'état." Eva's eyes narrowed. "How did you get involved?"

"Quite by accident." Loch winced as he followed her. He wasn't as fine as he was trying to make out. "My immediate superior in London, who assigned me the liaison role, brought me into a think tank. At first I believed it was a thought experiment. You know, let's think of all the permutations and devise defensive strategies, that kind of thing. But as I got into it further I could see they were heading down one path only. When I raised my concerns with Evan, he simply pushed me further into it. By then I knew something was up."

"So the CIA are in on this too?"

"I doubt it, but some key people definitely know. I only stayed quiet because I wasn't sure if it was real. I had my suspicions, but nothing concrete."

"And me?"

He smiled his girl slayer smile. "You and I hooked up totally independently of this. I saw you in Lady Kensington's office one day and we got to talking. We went on a few dates, and, well, things really took off from there. Evan asked me to keep an eye on you, ask some indirect questions. I refused. I didn't know you had been sent to Macau until it was too late."

"Why didn't you warn me after the memory wipe?"

"I did, remember?"

"Not specifically." Eva frowned. "And why didn't you tell me when we were headed to Macau the second time?"

"I didn't know who to trust. I thought it was odd that Bishop had been assigned with you."

"He's a sexist pig, but he's my sexist pig. I would trust Bishop with my life. I have, many times."

"Well, I didn't know him, or Yuji for that matter."

"But what about after? You could have told me everything in Hong Kong."

Loch's face went blank, and he remained silent for a long time, as if he were embarrassed. That was a first. "Yes, well, it would have been all over then, wouldn't it?"

Eva was incredulous. "So you could have saved the world but you'd rather keep shagging me?"

He lowered his head slightly. "Something like that."

"Wow."

Loch frowned. "I don't know if it's that's a good wow or a bad wow."

"Me either." Eva shook her head. "I'm going to have to unpack this later. We have more important things to worry about."

Their first step was to alert MI6. That meant getting upstairs. They took the stairs deliberately, careful to step on the outer edges to avoid making any noise. It was slow going, but they were as silent as a librarian wearing hush puppies.

At the top of the stairs the door opened with a slight *creak*, which to Eva sounded like a brass band. Peering through the crack in the door, the long corridor seemed empty. No noise at all in the house. Without waiting for approval from Loch, she stepped into the hall. Nothing happened. No alarms, no gunfire, not even a Bronx cheer. The house was silent as a tomb. Loch lifted a quizzical eyebrow. Eva had to agree. Something wasn't right.

Eva led the way to Freddie's office, hoping Freddie was otherwise occupied. Carefully Eva pried open the door. The room was empty. *This isn't right*, she thought to herself.

Racing to the phone, she picked it up to dial SIS, but there was no dial tone. She even clicked the receiver like they do in the movies, despite knowing it did nothing to help. Tracing back the phone cable, she saw it was plugged into the right socket. She moved the mouse on the computer and the screen came to life. The desktop was open. Silently chastising the former Foreign Secretary for poor desktop security, she brought up a browser. A message appeared advising her to check the internet connection.

"We're cut off," she said to Loch.

He gestured towards the window, only half listening. "Check this out. All these security guys, they're all facing outward. If the phones have been cut, they could be expecting something."

Eva joined him and peered out. He was right. Half a dozen security men were spread out a hundred feet apart, halfway between the house and the perimeter fence.

"Who cut them, do you think?" Eva asked.

"If I was a betting man, I'd say Grey. What better way to clear everyone from the house, away from us, than by creating a fake security alert?"

"Too bad he underestimated her," Eva said.

"Was there a hint of pride in that statement, Chérie? She's a sociopath. No normal human being would be planning what she's doing. Don't confuse former friendship for—"

"You're right." Eva cut him off. "I know."

Eva heard a car driving along the gravel driveway. Carefully peering out, she saw a guard open the car door and Freddie get in. She held a stack of files, and seemed unperturbed by having taken a man's life just minutes earlier.

Eva watched the car leave the estate. "We need to go through this PC." She regarded it with trepidation. Computers weren't her thing. It was dreadful for a spy in the 21st century to be a techno-phobe, but Eva had spent the better part of her life avoiding them. Her café had a shoebox instead of a point of sale.

"Mmmm," Loch said absently, and moved the mouse. "How about I take this one for the team, Miss The-Files-Are-in-The-Computer?" He grinned and went to work.

So Loch knew about her technophobia. Maybe he really did know her. Maybe he'd read it in her dossier. It frustrated Eva that she didn't know. Was he genuine? Was he someone she should tie up and run away from, or someone to tie up for fun? Would she ever know? Could she ever really trust him?

Just then, the memory from Sussex came flooding back. It couldn't have been a dream, it was so vivid. Was it a fragment of her memory fighting through? Was it a side effect of the drug Freddie had given her?

"Our time together." Eva gazed at the floor.

"Hmmm?" Loch replied, concentrating on the screen.

"Where was your favourite destination when we went away?"

He turned to her, giving his full attention. "Is now the best time for this?"

Loch was right. Now definitely wasn't the time. Not at all. Still…

That smile. *Hot damn*, that smile. "Let's worry about it once we get through this, okay?"

Eva dipped her head in acknowledgement, though her sense of disappointment was overwhelming. The question was selfish, and poorly timed. She was an agent for MI6, her personal feelings were irrelevant right now. Survival first. Save the world second. Her love life came way down the end of the list, somewhere near "arrest bad guys" and "have a nice bath".

"And Chérie?"

"Yeah?"

"Sussex." He kept his eyes on the computer. "We hired a cabin. It was the best weekend of my life." Loch looked up. "Now go check the house."

Her legs felt weak. What had just happened? Was that confirmation? Did it mean he really loved her, or had he merely been playing the part at the time?

Oh darlin, you're in for years of therapy, she told herself.

She had to focus on the mission at hand. She scanned the grounds. The guards seemed unmoved, but their attention was aimed in only one direction. A figure at the front gate caught her eye. It wasn't one of the security staff. The man leaned against a black Audi parked at the gate, as if expecting to drive it through. He was talking to a guard through the main gate. Even from this distance, the stance was unmistakably arrogant and condescending.

She pointed Freddie's old navy telescope in that direction. It was him alright. Eva needed to get his attention, but how? Then a sardonic expression crossed her features. She picked up a cigarette lighter that lay next to an ashtray on the desk.

"Stay here." Eva was already halfway out the door.

It took longer than she wanted to find the attic. Longer still to find a window to the roof. When Eva finally managed to scramble onto the rooftop, she half expected him gone. Luckily his stubborn streak was too strong. He stood, fists on hips, arguing with the security guards, occasionally pointing at the house.

She reached under her t-shirt. Balancing high on the old tile roof, Eva wriggled out of her bra and held it aloft. Using the cigarette lighter, she set it on fire. It took some patience, given the light breeze, but once it was alight, that baby burned.

What better way to grab the attention of the patriarchy than by burning your bra?

The flames spread and the smoke stung her eyes, but Eva continued to hold it up as long as she could. Eventually the flames grew too high, and she flung it away. She watched the entrance. He glanced her way and gave the slightest of nods. He'd seen her. He finished his conversation, got in his car and backed out of the driveway.

Eva's hand stung, she'd inhaled toxic fumes and had to find a way down from the roof. But none of that mattered.

Bishop was coming.

CHAPTER SEVENTEEN

"When is he coming?" Loch asked.

"I don't know," Eva replied with a smile.

"How's he getting in?"

"No idea."

"Does he have anyone with him?"

Eva shrugged.

"Then why are you so damn happy?"

The grin spread across her entire face. "Because a Bishop rampage is a beautiful thing."

The two of them were hunkered down in a seemingly abandoned wing of the mansion. Sheets were draped over furniture and a thin layer of dust covered bare surfaces. No children living with the Foreign Secretary and no longer having a husband, Eva assumed Freddie didn't require all the rooms Chevening House had to offer.

They had chosen a corner room, which offered the best possible view of the grounds. Eva had to wonder how Bishop would handle the situation. He might wait until nightfall, sneak in and utilise his years of training to infiltrate a high-security installation on high alert. Or he could come in all guns blazing, though she doubted he would.

Bishop was no blunt instrument. A stickler for the rules, the MI6 agent had no authority to use force within his own country. Plus, as Eva had reminded herself when breaking in, the men on security detail were merely performing their duty. They weren't the bad guys. No, Bishop would be subtle, he would probably take his time and follow the rules.

Eva's thoughts were interrupted by a noise. She glanced up. The roar from the road could be heard all the way to the mansion. The black Audi sped recklessly around the edge of the compound, racing towards the front gate. It wasn't slowing down. If anything, it was speeding up.

The men at the front gate raised their guns and fired. The car kept coming. Bodywork punctured, cracks appeared in the wind-screen. The car kept coming. Another volley of shots. The car kept coming.

The guards at the gate dove out of the way just before the gates splintered apart and Bishop's car ploughed through. The bonnet crumpled but the car sped on, up the gravel path towards the mansion.

"Our ride's here." Eva sprinted towards the door.

It seemed Bishop was capable of bending the rules. Who was Eva kidding? He'd taken a sledgehammer to them and was laughing maniacally as he did so. It seemed Eva wasn't the only one who could be reckless.

Tearing down the stairs they discovered the mansion was thankfully still deserted. The two of them burst through the front door as Bishop came tearing up the driveway. The car went into a controlled skid on the gravel and spun to a halt as Eva and Loch arrived. The door flew open and Bishop beamed.

"Someone call an Uber?"

The two agents leapt in; Loch in the back, Eva in the front. Before the doors shut, Bishop threw the car in gear and floored it. As he sped down the long driveway the security personnel ran towards the house, forming a blockade directly across their path, guns raised.

"Is this car bulletproof?" Eva asked.

"No, but it does have extra cup holders."

"That'll have to do," Eva replied. "Punch it."

Bishop gave her a sideways glance. "Seatbelts, people."

They complied. Eva looked up. They were approaching the guards at speed. Before she could express her alarm Bishop yanked the wheel, snaking the car off the driveway and onto the open lush lawn. He took a wide arc around the security staff.

"Heads down!"

The car was peppered with gunfire. When the first volley was done, Eva yelled, "All clear!" Bishop and Loch confirmed they hadn't been hit either. Eva doubted they'd be so lucky again.

The car's long sweep around the guards came back towards the driveway. It was a good strategy. Bishop had lured the security staff away from the main gate, driven around them and now had fewer combatants to contend with at the exit. The only trouble was he had to approach the gate from the grass at incredible speed and on completely the wrong angle. It was like trying to kick a goal from the penalty corner while the opposition were shooting at you. Even Eva didn't think he could do it.

"Down!" Bishop screamed.

With turf flying from the back of the car he hunkered down as the first bullets from the guards at the gate hit the engine block. The car didn't slow down. More bullets pummelled the vehicle, but Bishop kept his foot to the floor.

Eva raised her head. The gate loomed large, but the angle was so acute, she couldn't see through it. All she could glimpse was either side of the wall, no blue sky between. They weren't going to make it.

With a deafening war cry Bishop gripped the steering wheel and the car became airborne.

Time stopped.

The next few milliseconds seemed to stretch out to eternity. Eva saw everything. Bishop's hands were anchored to the wheel. Loch in the back held his seatbelt, seemingly ready to release it should they need to fight, his face grim but determined.

The red brick wall loomed larger and larger until it enveloped the shattered windscreen. They were going to crash, physics demanded it. Then, amazingly, there was a splinter of blue. With the passing of another fragment in time it grew infinitesimally larger. They'd passed the side of the gate.

Bishop had miraculously threaded the needle.

The car landed with a thump and Eva was back in real time. Bishop oversteered beautifully to stay on the road and didn't careen into the embankment. He maintained the momentum and raced down the country road.

Eva was thankful Loch wasn't driving. She doubted he could have started the car without stalling it.

Amazed they had made it, Eva let out a breath she'd been holding since leaving the house. They were alive. As her amazement began to fade, the practicality of it dawned on her. She ran her hand over the dash. The impact should have set off the airbags.

Bishop glanced her way and must have read her mind. "I pulled the fuse for the safety features, airbags, traction control and the like. Thought they might have gotten in the way."

She whistled, impressed. "That was some driving, Tex."

Bishop's eyes twinkled. "I do like penetrating tight spots."

Eva let that one go. He deserved one after the rescue. "Thank you. How did you know I was in danger?"

He checked the mirrors. "As much as it pains me to say so, you don't show me your bra unless you're in trouble."

From the back seat, Loch said, "There are so many things wrong with that statement I don't know where to start."

Bishop glanced in the rear-view mirror, regarding Loch and his injured features. "You've never looked lovelier."

Loch replied with an extended middle finger.

Bishop sped through small towns, checking for any tailing vehicles, but thankfully there were none. Bishop's rescue must have occurred too quickly for them to have a pursuit vehicle ready. The pranged Audi attracted odd gazes as they drove through picturesque townships. They would have to ditch it as soon as they could.

Using a secure line, they phoned Paul. Eventually they were put through.

"Hey, Paul," Eva was cut off by Bishop's raised hand.

"Wait". Into the phone, he said, "Croquembouche."

"Spatchcock," came the answer.

Bishop displayed his palm, as if saying, *continue*.

"What the living Christ was that?"

"Just a private little code Paul and I have to ensure neither of us is compromised."

Eva gave them a brief rundown of how Freddie drugged her and locked her up, and the appearance of Grey. In return, Paul explained that something hadn't rung true in his conversation with Kensington, and that's why he had dispatched Bishop. As succinctly as she could, Eva repeated what Lady Kensington had told her about the switching of the G8 venue and the plan to blow them all to hell.

Paul exhaled slowly. "We won't be able to move it again. Once was a security nightmare. Twice would cause an international furore."

"So would a nuclear explosion up the arse," replied Eva.

Bishop shook his head. "To move it the first time required doubt. To cancel it altogether would require proof."

"What about the dead body of the Assistant to the Chief of the General Staff?"

Simultaneously, Bishop and Paul said, "What?"

Steam poured from the radiator. The engine chugged. They didn't have long. Alternative transport would soon be required.

"Freddie shot him." Emotion crept into the statement. Until recently, Eva's mentor had meant so much to her, it was hard to let go. "In the head. At some stage I'm sure they'll frame me for it."

"They already have, Evie." Paul's voice was grave. "I'm looking at an All Points here and it has your ugly mug all over it. There's grainy CCTV footage of you leaping over the wall of Chevening House. You've been royally stitched up, love. Use of force has been authorised. You lot be careful. Someone has put a lot of effort into ensuring you get taken out." He paused and Eva heard a slurping sound that she assumed was Paul drinking tea. "There's no way your word would move the G8. Not now. I don't have the authority to shut it down."

So Grey had already begun framing Eva before he stepped into the cell with her and Freddie. He must have expected that, one way or another, Eva wouldn't live to have her memory erased for a second time. That must have been why he was at Freddie's in the first place: to get the footage of her breaking in.

The mood in the car deflated. Had they busted out only to face another brick wall?

"This probably wouldn't help, would it?" Loch asked from the back seat.

Bishop turned down a smaller lane. "I can't see what he's holding. Is it his penis? He's holding his penis, isn't he?"

"It's a USB stick." Eva was unimpressed by Bishop's sarcasm.

"It holds the contents of Lady Kensington's computer." A smile appeared on Loch's face, so wide it appeared to have been applied using a paint roller. "I stole it while you were making your feminist statement on the roof."

"Clever boy." Eva gave him an impressed frown. "Anything useful?"

"Enough. There was a file called 'Burn it to The Ground', which seemed to be email files, I'm guessing of the incriminating kind. They were encrypted, but as she left her computer unlocked I'll go out on a limb and say they shouldn't be too hard to decipher."

Eva poked Bishop in the arm. "That's good work, isn't it, Bishop? That Loch did. Good work. Wouldn't you say? That Loch did good work, Bishop? Hey? Wouldn't you say? Bishop?"

Gripping the wheel tighter, Bishop remained transfixed on the road ahead. His knuckles turned white.

Paul spoke up. "Then whatever you do, don't bring it to Vauxhall Cross. We have no idea who to trust here. You're likely to be shot on sight. Have no doubt you'll be framed for the death of Grey once it comes to light. You'll be public enemy number one."

"Paul," Eva said quietly, "what the fuck is Halcyon?"

There was a long pause.

"Paul? You already told me you knew what it was when you told me I was never to repeat the word outside of your office. I think it's time you shared with the group."

"You make it sound like an AA meeting."

"As I've gotten drunk with everyone present, there may be something in that. Paul, spill."

With what Eva deemed to be reluctance, Paul explained that Halcyon was devised in the 70s at the height of the cold war, when the threat of war between the superpowers seemed inevitable, when schoolchildren were taught to protect themselves from nuclear Armageddon by hiding under desks. Everyone was afraid of Brezhnev's eyebrows.

Halcyon was never meant to be enacted, or at least, that was Paul's understanding. It had a simple enough premise, but would take someone with all the balls in the world to execute. The idea was to explode a tactical nuclear device somewhere within a NATO country and blame the USSR. The theory was that every NATO military and espionage agency would be given enough funding to win the cold war once and for all.

The lunacy of the idea terrified Eva. Back then the world was on a knife edge, the threat of mutually assured destruction hanging over every country. To deliberately provoke a nuclear war seemed absurd. There were variations on the methodology, such as "finding proof" prior in strategically important locations. This would allow diplomatic confrontations rather than interconti-nental missile ones. Suddenly the image of Colin Powell telling the UN Security Council about WMDs that never existed jumped into Eva's mind.

"What sort of idiot would come up with this stuff?"

"A subset of MI6, the so-called high-end thinkers. They called themselves the Cambridge Elite."

"Oh, right. Because Philby was a high-end thinker."

"It was after his time, but yes, that's the sort of environment Halcyon came from. Inbreeding of the privileged. Back then MI6 was very much a posh boys' club, hence why this sort of thing was allowed to flourish for a time."

Steam emanated from the engine, along with a great deal of metallic hammering. The car shuddered violently.

"I just had the ruddy thing serviced," Bishop spat.

He jerked the wheel and steered the vehicle into the car park of an empty football club. The car spluttered to a halt. All was quiet except for the heat knocking and the faint sound of steam escaping from the engine. They weren't going any further in the Audi.

Breaking the silence, Eva said, "Kensington went to Cambridge."

"Yes she did, and the timeline would fit, too. But we have no proof."

"What do you mean, no proof? You're telling us about it, so it was obviously a thing. Let's find out who came up with it, who knew about it and who's still in government that we can convince she's the one behind it. It's a start, at least."

There was a pause at Paul's end. Eva imagined he was formulating a diplomatic answer. "There are no longer any official records of it ever having existed. I've looked, but they've all been erased."

"Then how do you know about it?"

A longer pause this time.

"Paul, you still there?"

"Yes." A sigh. "I know about Halcyon because I know the person who came up with it."

"Oh, Paul…"

"My father."

The car was silent for a time. Even the engine stopped making noise, seeming to pay deference to the moment.

"I tried searching a few times," Paul continued, "but the records had been deliberately erased. No doubt by Kensington or her cronies."

"What records?"

"The digitised computer files, scans of the original documents, reports and such. I even tried to retrieve them from old backups. The headings were there, but the actual files had been deleted."

"Digitised," Eva said, more to herself than anyone else.

"What?" Loch asked. "I know that look. What are you thinking, Eva?"

"You said digitised. If this was back in the 70s…"

"There may still be paper records of it!" Bishop was suddenly animated.

"I doubt it." Loch sounded less convinced. "Any competent bureaucracy would have junked the paper files years ago."

Eva and Bishop grinned at each other.

"Fuck!" Eva exclaimed. "That's it!"

"It's a long shot." Paul's doubt came through clearly.

"English bureaucracy, the most inefficient in the world." Eva laughed. "It's worth a shot at least."

The idea of delving into old MI6 archives appealed to her. Eva loved paper far more than ones and zeroes. She could trust paper; she could hold it in her hand. Given current circumstances, she wouldn't be able to do any of the research herself. But she knew just the person for the job.

Through the phone they heard a knock at Paul's door, and the sound of shouting. The ruckus became louder, as did the shuffling, as though a number of people were present.

"What's the meaning of this?" Paul demanded.

"Sorry sir, I tried to tell them you were on a call."

"That's fine. Thank you, Nathan."

"Luke Vincent, IA. Please terminate your call. We're here to ask you some questions, Mr Cavendish."

It wasn't a request.

"Then why are you all armed?"

"Terminate the call, now!"

"To Nancy's friend," Paul said quickly into the phone. "Do what you do so well. Go and be reckless."

There was a beep and the line went dead.

The car was silent for the longest time. Eva's workmate, one of her most treasured friends, had seemingly just been arrested. They were truly on their own.

"What would Internal Affairs want with Paul?" she asked, knowing the answer.

"Eva, you're one of his best friends in the world and you've had an All Points pulled on you. To be honest, I'm floored they waited this long. Kensington is making her move."

Sitting up in her seat, Eva stared forward, steeling herself for the battle that was sure to come. They were no longer fighting a couple of unknown warring factions. They were up against their own organisation, their own country.

"What do we do now?" Loch asked.

"You heard the man. Time to be reckless."

CHAPTER EIGHTEEN

Eva was surprised there were payphones left in England. It had taken some time to find one, even longer to find a local kid to call the number for them.

Half an hour earlier, they had rolled the car under an awning near the football field to shield it from aircraft and satellites. They ditched all phones in the nearest rubbish bin. Only a few select items were salvaged from the car, everything else was abandoned. Thankfully, there was a charity bin nearby. Given their bloody and worn clothes, Eva and Loch dove in, looking for anything remotely suitable. Bishop refused to help, reluctant to get his pressed Savile Row suit creased.

The three spies had walked until they reached the next major town. From there they zeroed in on the most troublesome-looking teen they could find and convinced him to call MI6 and ask for a specific person. The clandestine nature appealed to the shaggy redhead. The twenty pounds helped, too.

When she was finally connected with the MI6 employee, Eva had to verify he hadn't been alerted to her current status. Trevor, the lovesick young junior officer, was as fawning as ever. She laid out her plan, appealing to his patriotism, and in no small measure to his crush on Eva.

Eva felt a measure of trepidation in embroiling him in all this. The kid could go to jail if they didn't play it right. He would be risking his career, or worse. Eva had weighed all this up, but in the end, he was their only way in. She would lay it all out for him, including the risks. He had to know the dangers, for there were many.

In her best *Mission: Impossible* voice, she advised him that his mission, should he choose to accept it, was twofold. First, she was going to send him some encrypted files that she wanted him to decode. It would need to be done off the books, and without using MI6 networks or equipment. There was no way to be sure that unlocking the files wouldn't trigger some alert that could see Trevor locked up quicker than you could say "just comittin' treason, yo'".

Luckily, Trevor had his own tools and offsite location to crack open the files. He didn't even seem surprised that Eva had asked him. Having him bend the system for her to submit timesheets after the deadline was one thing, but Eva had assumed he'd at least question where the files came from. There were no queries, just an unwavering acquiescence.

The second task was a little more analogue. She gave him the assignment of finding any paper reference to Halcyon, if one even existed. Eva could feel his disappointment bleed through the phone.

Eva repeatedly gave him an out, a way to politely decline their requests. What they were asking was in direct contravention of MI6 regulations. She begged him to take every precaution neces-sary, because one slip-up could mean he would be hauled away and unceremoniously thrown in the stockade for sedition.

When it was clear he was on board, despite the risks, Eva promised to make it up to him by taking him out to see the next decent Aussie band to tour the UK. It wasn't a date, she stressed, just a show of gratitude. His squeal of delight was higher-pitched than he'd have liked, Eva was sure. She rang off and promised to send him the files as soon as she could.

Bishop folded his arms as he scanned the street for threats. "I've never known a spy to have groupies before."

"Trevor's not a groupie," she replied.

Loch and Bishop exchanged smirks. It was the first time they had been civil to one another. And it was at Eva's expense.

She chose to ignore them. "We need to email these files to Trevor."

"They're too large to email." Loch tilted his head, as if suggesting that Eva should have known that. "We'll upload them to a secure commercial cloud server and email him the link."

Eva grimaced at the tech speak.

The task was harder than anticipated. They had Bishop's private tablet computer, but there was no way to connect the USB to it. They were told there were no internet cafés for miles around. Loch eventually used his extensive charm to talk a local florist into lending him her office computer for half an hour. Eva felt a pang of jealousy when she saw him flash his million-dollar smile and touch her arm playfully.

Which was odd. Eva didn't do jealous. She couldn't pick jealousy out of a line-up of one. Loch's flirting was for their mission, but Eva felt an element of possessiveness that was completely foreign to her. *What was it with Loch?*

With the files uploaded, they left the slutty florist and headed to a nearby café for a debrief and a watered-down substance that vaguely resembled coffee. Eva told Bishop everything she knew, including her take on the situation with Loch, which she conceded may not be completely accurate. The insinuation was that he could still be part of the conspiracy, out to get them.

To his credit, Loch remained silent while Eva described his actions, only occasionally rising from his chair when he appeared to take umbrage. Once Eva was done, he offered to tell them his side of the story. Bishop thanked him for the offer but invited Loch to insert his genitalia in a woodchipper instead.

The duality was killing Eva. Did she love Loch or was he a

double agent? Or—worst-case scenario—both. She wanted black-and-white answers in a profession where everything was grey.

Given the short time they had, the group turned their attention to the mission at hand. Part one was in play. None of them were comfortable with their dependence on a near-foetus with a crush on Eva, but given the circumstances, they didn't have much choice. The passivity frustrated them all. Eva had an idea about how to change that.

"You guys ever see *The Italian Job*?"

Loch shook his head. "I've never been much of a Mark Wahlberg fan."

"What? No. Look, I will start going out with you just so I can break up with you over that. I mean the original Michael Caine version—the only version." Steadying herself, she went on. "So in the movie they steal gold right out from under the noses of all this security and nick off with it. A smash and grab, if you will."

Bishop sat up. "There's a bus in it!" He pointed. "On the side of the mountain. I've seen this."

A wry smile crossed Eva's lips. "Only the best movie ending of all time. Ambiguous endings are the best, life doesn't stop just before the credits." Eva tilted her head at Bishop. "Maybe you're not a total loss after all, Bishop."

Loch lifted an eyebrow. "Now let's not get ahead of ourselves." He sighed. "I really hope you're not thinking what I think you're thinking." He paused. "Because it's unthinkable—I think."

She leaned forward, a grin spreading across her face. "We're going to sneak into the G8 and steal a nuclear weapon."

"This is quite possibly the stupidest idea I've ever had." Eva gazed through the binoculars.

The three of them were positioned on a hill overlooking the valley of Royal Tunbridge Wells, where the G8 meeting was to be relocated. The area was a flurry of activity. Marquees were being set up, a helipad was being constructed, dozens of important-looking people in suits hurried about holding computer tablets and doing a lot of pointing. No one appeared particularly happy.

Most of the activity was centred around the main Salomons Estate mansion. The outer perimeter was surrounded by hastily erected chain-link fences, topped with razor wire. Security at the event was significant. This was to be a meeting of the leaders of the most important countries in the world. As Eva said, security would be tighter than a platypus' arse. There were new-model Scout armoured vehicles positioned at strategic intervals, as well as rotating legions of exceptionally well-armed Royal Marines. There also a myriad of listening and detection devices designed to hold back even an ant that lacked the required credentials. In short, they were screwed.

"What about white chocolate milk?" Loch asked quietly beside her.

"What?" Eva asked, not taking her eyes off the scene.

"Your idea for selling white chocolate milk. That was far stupider than stealing a nuke."

Eva turned and frowned at him. "There is no way that was worse than—"

"Or helium-filled furniture?" Bishop chimed in.

"Oh yeah, good point," Loch replied. "Helium-filled furniture was kind of crazy. And what about that time you wanted to hire two private investigators to follow one another?"

"And who could forget the taco hammock," said Bishop. "Which I still don't get."

"Alright, you two," Eva growled. "First of all, helium-filled furniture is genius. Imagine all the extra space. Secondly, I blew your mind with white chocolate milk, admit it."

"How about we focus on the subject at hand, folks?" Bishop motioned to the impossible scene before them.

"Fine." Loch folded his arms. "We have no weapons, no intel, we are facing extensively trained and, let's face it, snazzily dressed armed forces. We're hamstrung by the force we can use because they're not the bad guys here. We have no communications, no backup, nobody on the inside—or, let's be honest, on the outside—and as far as I can tell, absolutely no plan whatsoever."

Bishop snorted. "I know you're a traitor, but do you have to be a negative nelly too?"

Eva ignored the obvious bait and hoped Loch would too. "We know they've already delivered the bomb, so it has to be somewhere it won't be easily stumbled upon. We just have to find out where. Plus, we have to, you know, get in."

"I think I might be able to help on that front." Bishop switched on his tablet and started typing. "Yes! Luckily for us Paul's access hasn't been shut down yet."

Eva cocked her head. "Ah, how did you get Paul's credentials?"

Bishop pursed his lips and became intensely interested in the screen in front of him.

"Bishop?"

He rolled his eyes. "Let's just say I have a lot of expenses that need to be approved from time to time and I don't want to hassle Paul about every little detail, so…"

"So you slept with a woman in IT to give you access."

"So I slept with a woman in IT to give me access." He tilted his head in acknowledgement. "And let me tell you, those IT boffins really go off when they finally get a chance to—"

"Bishop."

"Yes, Eva?"

"If you could stop being a misogynistic prick for five minutes, that would be great."

"I can't promise anything, but I'll try."

"That's all I ask."

Loch glanced between them. "I'm stunned the two of you haven't boned yet."

Bishop continued to type on his tablet. "It's one of the mysteries of the ages. Like Stonehenge, or the Bermuda Triangle, or the enduring appeal of Coldplay."

"It's not that difficult, actually. It comes down to two words: con and sent," Eva replied.

Bishop squinted at the screen and didn't seem to be listening. "Alright, Paul had access to all the G8 protocols, so I'm guessing..." There was a pause as an optimistic expression spread across his handsome face. "It's here. All the files he was reviewing are still here. We... we have information."

Perhaps Paul hadn't been arrested after all. Either that or the IT department were lax in shutting down his access. Whatever the reason, Eva wasn't going to complain. They were long overdue for a break.

For the first time in what seemed like forever, Eva felt hope. "Can you add us to a list of staff? Generate us badges? Get a list of delivery vehicles that have arrived in the last forty-eight hours?"

"Woah, slow down Myrtle. One thing at a time. I'm going to have to go through this pretty thoroughly. It will take a while."

Loch sighed. "I'm not doing much here." He observed Eva holding the binoculars and Bishop studying the tablet. "How about I go and forage for some food. We'll need to keep our strength up."

"We don't have any money," Eva said. "We gave our last twenty to the pimply kid at the phone booth."

"Ah, yes, but I have this." Loch pointed to his face and wiggled his eyebrows.

Despite his facial injuries, he was still a very handsome man. Pushing himself off the grass, he bent down to kiss Eva as if it were the most natural thing in the world. Eva pulled away and he looked shattered. Eva wasn't sure which one of them was more shocked.

"Sorry, force of... sorry." He backed away and proceeded down the hill, away from Royal Tunbridge Wells.

Once Loch was out of earshot, Bishop casually asked, "So what's going on with you and Traitor Boy?"

Eva resumed her surveillance. "I honestly don't know."

"Right."

Her eyes flicked to Bishop. "What does that mean?"

"You're obviously into the guy, and he seems to worship the ground you walk on. Have you seen his long loving glances? He's positively made out of puppy dog eyes. Apart from the whole betraying his country and potentially plunging the world into nuclear war, he seems to love you."

"Well, as for the traitor stuff, we'll have to see. His version of events may be true. Or it might not be. That one will have to wait."

"And the feelings side? How does the real Eva feel about him?" Not for the first time, there was a hint of something else in Bishop's question.

Eva gripped the binoculars tighter. "It's like he's a best-of album with half the tracks missing, most of them the really great songs. What's left is okay, but there's nothing I can sing along to."

"You know that analogy makes no sense whatsoever, right?"

"Then it's very apt."

Bishop's gaze followed Loch down the hill. "If he is the bad guy, you just let him go alert his compatriots."

"You think I don't know that?"

Bishop grunted. "So it was a test?"

Eva tried her best innocent look.

"I know Paul told us to be reckless, but even so, Eva…"

She pointed at the tablet in his hands. "If he's not a traitor you'd better get cracking before he comes back with a picnic basket and a bucket of Dom Perignon. If he is, well, we could be expecting a phalanx of one-armed angry paramilitary types. Either way, get typing."

Loch returned, but it wasn't with Dom Perignon. Nor was it with a paramilitary force. He had three chicken sandwiches, two bags of crisps and a bottle of soda water. At first he claimed to have charmed a farmer's daughter, but then admitted he'd actually knocked on the door of a nearby house and told the elderly woman who'd answered that his car had broken down. He'd pretended to call a tow truck while claiming his friends would be hungry. She'd gladly put together a care package and sent him on his way. He seemed awfully pleased with himself.

In the interim, their mission had started to take shape. Through Bishop's access to Paul's files, they had determined a way to infiltrate the compound. Their friend still had access to the central archive for the G8 documents. There weren't lists of flights or attendees—Eva assumed they would be held somewhere more secure—but what they had was enough. Support staff were listed, along with their rosters and police checks. There were proposed maps of the area, identifying security, HR and staff dining areas. They'd need some luck, but Eva believed the universe owed her.

Where was Paul right now, Eva wondered? Was he in danger because of her? This whole thing was so much larger than the two of them, but Eva was so worried about her mate she found it hard to concentrate. The thought of him being held in a cell, accused of treachery or subversion, was unbearable. He had been nothing but doggedly loyal to King and Country. For him to be treated so harshly because of Kensington and her Machiavellian scheme made Eva livid. She used her anger to regain her focus. Revenge has a way of centring one's attention.

She wished she could call Nancy to see if she knew why Paul wouldn't be coming home. But she couldn't. The mission could be compromised. And even if she could, Eva wasn't even sure Nancy would answer the phone. Eva slipped further into a funk.

As they munched on the sandwiches, Bishop outlined the mission. With Paul's access they'd been able to add fake identities to the list of authorised staff. Bishop was to be on the civilian security force, as was Loch. Eva wasn't surprised that Bishop would want Loch close by so he could keep an eye on him. Eva's role was to be a familiar one. Bishop had used existing file photos to create fake IDs for each of them. Eva was glad her identity didn't sound like a dive bar stripper.

So now they had a way to get in, but that was nowhere near the end of it. Salomons Estate was vast, which meant so was their search area.

"What do we do when we get in, just wander around?" Eva was overcome with dread. "Wait, do we even know if it's in the estate?"

Bishop scratched the back of his head. "Well, the DF-4 is a three point three megaton warhead, so you'd expect the fireball to be around two thousand feet, and the immediate radiation blast to be around two point four miles. Now, given the undulating landscape and the goal of eliminating all life within the vicinity, I would place the device no more than one mile from the main building to ensure maximum devastation."

Eva and Loch gaped. Bishop shrugged as if to say, *doesn't everyone know that?* Eva hoped her shake of the head in return conveyed, *no, they fucking well don't.*

They had access, that was a start. But there were a few potential snags to the plan besides their IDs not working, or failing to find the nuke. One was plain to them all: Eva hadn't showered since Hong Kong. Neither had Loch. They smelled like a hobo's jock-strap. Loch and Eva had endured much, beatings included. Despite her smart Kmart ensemble, courtesy of their charity bin drive, she probably looked like she'd slept with a bag over her head… because she had. She'd kill for a bath and a hairbrush. She might have to.

Thankfully, they were in luck. The staff entered a portable building in jeans and t-shirt and came out in standard white shirt and black slacks. It appeared that certain staff were being issued with uniforms. Bishop jumped online and added them to the list.

As he was typing away, he asked, "Eva, what size top are you?"

"Six."

He nodded and typed in the answer. "Pants?"

Eva frowned. "Same."

"Bra size?" he asked with the innocence of an altar boy.

"Bishop, they're not asking for bra size."

"They could be."

She shook her head. "Anyway, you know my bra size."

Loch, who had remained silent during the exchange, lifted his head. "Uh, excuse me?"

Eva shrugged. "Nothing insidious. He only knows because he was fondling my bra in my apartment a few days ago."

Loch scowled. "Oh, that makes it way better."

Bishop turned off his tablet. "As much as I enjoy talking about Eva's chest, we'd best get a wriggle on. Time is not on our side. We ready?"

"No," replied Eva.

"No," echoed Loch.

"That's the spirit." Bishop clapped his hands together. "Let's go."

They cleaned themselves up as best they could then headed towards the staff entrance down in the valley. Bishop had to go first, as he was the only one with photo ID to get through the first checkpoint. He waited in line with a bunch of casually dressed people. When he reached the front of the line he presented his licence and was ushered through. Fifteen minutes later he emerged, dressed less formally than he had been before.

Flashing his new pass, he gave security a lazy salute, then moved out of their line of sight and motioned for Eva and Loch. He handed them their new IDs from inside with their photos on them. Without another word, he headed back inside.

Loch and Eva waited in silence until a bus arrived and unloaded. Merging into the group, they waited in line until it was their turn to show their IDs. Eva's blood was liquid nitrogen for a good five minutes. Despite her fears, they both had their badges scanned without incident, and were granted access. No blaring sirens, no fanfare; it was automatic, quite perfunctory. They were through.

Within minutes, Eva was frisked twice, as was every other member of staff. It seemed the threat of a nuclear bomb really put the wind up security. Too bad the bomb was already inside the grounds. Loch and Eva made their way to an area designated "New Arrivals".

Their security clearance didn't give them access to the inner perimeter of the G8, only the outer one, but it was enough.

They split up, sticking to the plan. Eva had her character memorised. Her role wasn't an unfamiliar one, but it was critical. If she screwed up, the whole thing would fall apart. She had to maintain focus and stick to the plan. She approached a friendly looking staff member sitting at a desk.

The woman glanced up from her laptop. "Name and assignment?"

"Hi, I'm Gwen. I'm a barista."

CHAPTER NINETEEN

"Was it the expression, 'gives a golden shower of bat piss a bad name'?"

"No."

"Tastes like boiled arse hair left out in the sun?" Eva asked. "Was it that one?"

Her supervisor shook his head.

"Was it when I told you I would prefer to drink Starbucks poured into a wank sock than taste your coffee again?"

With barely controlled anger, he nodded.

"Okay. Good to know."

Between clenched teeth, he replied, "I've made coffee for heads of state."

"Did any of them survive?"

Eva had been at her station for less than half an hour. Her role was listed as "barista", but when she arrived at the staff coffee tent her supervisor, a pasty middle-aged white man with a receding hairline and a face like crumbling concrete, told her she wouldn't be making coffee. Her role, she was informed, was to take orders, not screw up, and stand there and look pretty. It had taken a grand total of thirty-seven seconds before her hackles were up.

Eva had tried to convince him of her coffee-making skills, but he'd protected the coffee machine like a misogynist defended pay inequality. For the sake of the operation, she sucked it up. Well, tried to. It was when her supervisor had told her to smile more and suggested, ever so politely, that perhaps she should "show a bit of tit" for the boys, that she'd decided to share her opinion on his coffee-making abilities.

And now she was fired.

She'd been sacked in shorter amounts of time. The two other female staff members at the coffee tent stared at her in equal measures of shock and admiration.

Not one to give in, especially to the likes of him, Eva strode past her supervisor to the coffee machine. It wasn't her beloved La Marzocco, but the La Pavoni was fine. Ignoring the supervisor's wrathful howls, she prepared three long blacks in quick succession, ensuring the crema was extracted ristretto.

With a defiant look, she handed two to her fellow staff members and held the third cup out to the supervisor. He glared at it as if she'd taken a dump in the cup. She waggled it at him. He shook his head.

"You're fired," he said emotionlessly.

"I know. I'll go straight to HR to sign out and won't say a word about you being a sexist pig if you drink this." His face was like stone. "Or are you afraid I'll show you up in front of the skirts?" she added.

With lips stretched thin as rubber bands, he snatched the cup and drank. The metamorphosis on his face was astonishing. In mere seconds he went from anger, to shock, to surprise, to enjoyment, to appreciation then all the way back to anger again.

Her fellow staff members took a sip. "Holy crap," the blonde one exclaimed.

The brunette with pink highlights stared at the cup in awe. "I think I just came a little."

"This doesn't change the fact that you're fired for insubordination." The supervisor's anger was subdued.

"And?" Eva raised as many eyebrows as she could muster.

He mumbled something incomprehensible.

Cupping her hand to her ear, Eva said, "I'm sorry, I didn't catch that."

"The coffee's good."

The women behind him did their best to stifle giggles.

"Now that wasn't so hard, was it?" Eva gestured towards some portable rooms behind her. "So, HR's this way?"

An expression of trepidation crossed his features. "You're not... you're not going to report me, are you?"

Eva tilted her head as if considering it. "Look, I'll tell you what, you give them a call to tell them you're overstaffed *and* you promise not to be a sleaze around these bright, intelligent women, and no, I won't report you."

The pasty man pulled out his phone. Eva left, giving each of her co-workers a high five. "Don't take any shit from The Man."

They beamed and seemed to stand several inches taller. Eva made her way to the portable building marked "Human Resources". She was behind schedule.

She knocked on the door and a pleasant-looking middle-aged woman greeted her with a smile as weak as her supervisor's coffee. She had a phone to her ear but seemed to only be half listening to the person on the other end. "Sorry," she mouthed, and ushered Eva into a reception area.

After a minute, she ended the call, saying, "Thank you Justin, I'll keep you in the loop," and hung up. She turned to Eva. "Sorry, that was the boss."

"Hi, I've been sent for reassignment," Eva said brightly.

"Ah, yes, Gwen, come into the office."

It was only a few minutes before the conversation went downhill. In the tiny prefabricated office Eva saw the writing on the cheaply painted walls. The HR manager, Amanda, was going through the motions with little interest. It became increasingly clear that she was reluctant to assign Eva another role. Eva had no time for this.

Amanda seemed nice, in an officious, overbearing way, but Eva needed to leave her office as soon as possible.

"So, Gwen." Amanda folded her hands together. "Mr Lenton said he was overstaffed, but I have to ask, just us girls, did he reassign you due to the—ah, how can I put this delicately? Did he reassign you due to your smell?"

"Smell?"

"Yes, dear. I should probably be more tactful, but, to be frank, you stink."

"I don't stink, I have an adorable feminine musk." Eva shifted uncomfortably in her chair. "He was overstaffed, that's why I'm here."

The woman made a cat bum face, clearly not believing a word of it. "Be that as it may, I don't appear to have another job for someone of your, ah, qualifications."

Eva did her best to appear heartbroken. "I understand, but I've come all this way. Can I just wait in reception for a bit, in case something comes up?"

Amanda's features creased, appearing reluctant.

Eva quickly added, "I'll wait for an hour and if nothing pops up I'll get out of your hair. That's fair, is that cool?"

Amanda did her best to maintain her pleasant façade. "That's fine, dear, but I'm almost certain nothing will materialise."

"Not a worry, I appreciate the opportunity."

Eva went to shake her hand but Amanda baulked, as if taken aback by the move. As Eva retracted her hand she bumped Amanda's purse, knocking it off the desk. Eva quickly picked it up and apologised. The manager plastered on a fake smile and wished her the best. Eva returned to reception and took a seat. A young man was positioned behind a desk, staring directly ahead, his back rigidly straight. He moved so infrequently Eva began to wonder if he was a mannequin of some description. She sat and waited.

Eva was never going to find a nuclear bomb making coffee. Her mission was to infiltrate the building. There were limits to the information Paul had access to. The vital material was contained within the HR building—in fact, just through the door behind the reception desk.

Eva was disappointed she couldn't go straight into the HR building on arrival. She had quickly determined that the only way in was to be sacked. Not a hard assignment, given the circumstances. The only trouble was, obtaining the information meant Eva would have to use a computer, her least favourite thing after leg waxing, pap smears and acid jazz.

The HR building also contained a security office. Not the main one, which was located within the central perimeter, but a backup, in case that one was compromised. It would have security computers with access to the current security logs. All she had to do was get past Mr Mannequin.

As a precaution, all secondary G8 locations were locked down in case they were needed. It was far easier than tossing out a conference of accountants halfway through their annual junket about standardised taxation mediation. Before the Switchback protocol had been initiated security would have been lax, but it did exist. All visitors would have been required to sign in and out, kind of like signing in to the office for a school visit. Nothing too strenuous.

Eva hoped to access these security logs, the ones from before Switchback had been triggered. She wanted to find an entry for a large vehicle that had arrived between the time Eva had jumped out of the truck and when Freddie had mentioned it was already in place. Hopefully something would turn up. With any luck it would tell them where to start looking.

While Eva performed this role, Bishop and Loch would be part of the security team sweeping the grounds, actively searching for somewhere you could hide a nuclear bomb. If they didn't kill each other first. It was becoming increasingly evident that Bishop had feelings for Eva. It was just as plain that Loch's puppy dog eyes were unlikely to be an act. What would she do with all that? She was an independent woman; she didn't have to choose either if she didn't want to. And yet, Eva felt an unexpected pull that she hadn't anticipated, which complicated matters.

Mr Mannequin abruptly stood and left without a word. Toilet break, possibly? Or perhaps he'd gone to change his oil. Either way, Eva had a tiny window to do her thing. She leapt into action. She had been surreptitiously eying the keypad next to the security door the entire time she'd been in reception. It was a Sentex. When she'd seen this, Eva had performed a silent and hopefully not obvious little happy dance. The Sentex keypad was at least ten years old. In that time, its security had been proven to have more holes than a porcupine's condom. Holes Eva knew how to exploit.

She was taking a chance that, because it had been hired for the event, they probably hadn't changed the administrative password. Three stars to enter the admin code, six zeroes, which was the factory-default password, and then three more keystrokes to open the door. She hit enter.

The light pinged green and there was a small click. It was way too easy. Eva had at least thought she might have to try the most common PIN numbers, but no, the default still worked. If she hadn't known it off by heart due to a former, more nefarious, life, a quick internet search would have uncovered the code. She'd send the head of security an email if she ever got out of this alive.

Eva opened the door and went in. Clearly the security team didn't expect they'd need to use the backup room. Mismatched chairs, half-constructed desks and visible network cables criss-crossed the floor. That was all fine as far as Eva was concerned. There were three powered-up computers. All she needed to do was hack into one. Not exactly her forte.

Pulling out a mobile from her pocket, Eva dialled a number. It was Amanda's phone. Eva had pilfered it from her brightly coloured purse when she'd "accidentally" knocked it off the table. She would delete the call history and leave it on the floor of reception on her way out. No use ruining Amanda's day; she hadn't done anything wrong.

When the voice on the other end answered, Eva was overwhelmed with a sense of relief. She wouldn't have succeeded without him. She definitely owed him a night out in London. But that was all. She didn't want to ruin him for life.

She explained the situation. Trevor was more than eager to help her out. She imagined him bouncing on his chair in excitement.

"Okay," he said slowly, probably anticipating his frustration to come, "what operating system are they using?"

"Ah, I don't know."

"That's fine, just click on the system icon and tell me the build and the patch versions."

Silence was Trevor's answer.

"Eva, have you turned the monitor on?"

She scoffed. "Don't be ridiculous." Eva turned the monitor on. "What was the first question again?"

Fifteen minutes later Trevor had patiently and miraculously helped her hack into a "level five security" computer. It was all due to his perseverance and nothing to do with Eva's computing skills. She would definitely take him out and help him get laid.

"How are you going with decrypting the files?"

"Good. Knocked over three of the four protocols. I should have something within the hour—maybe all four, depending if they're using hexadecimal for the last layer." There was a pause. Eva suspected he realised he'd gone too hardcore nerd. "Um, Eva, there's a video file here that's not encrypted that you really need to know about."

"Is it about the bomb?"

"No, it's not, but you probably want to look at it—"

"Trev, if we get through this I will, but right now we can only have a single priority."

"Okay." He was reluctant. "But you should really…"

"I will, promise, but for now I have to go. Thanks again, you're ace. Oh, and if we don't make it, find Paul Cavendish, wherever he is, and give him everything."

Trevor rang off, sounding fairly confused, and Eva got to work finding what she needed. Thankfully the file structure was logical, so navigating was relatively easy. Within minutes she had a list of the vehicles that had entered the grounds during the timeframe she was interested in. It was a start. Two were small staff transport buses, unlikely to carry something that went boom. One was the owner's car—the annotation beside it stated "Porsche Cayenne (wanker)". Eva dismissed it as too small. That left only two viable candidates. One was so garish she initially dismissed it out of hand. The other seemed far more likely.

The gate security staff had noted one vehicle down as a "crypt maintenance van". An hour and a half later it had been signed out. Something about it struck Eva as odd. It had arrived at the same moment as the other garish van, but had only stayed for a short amount of time. The other van had never been signed out—it must still be in the grounds. Satisfied that she had what she needed, Eva shut down the computer.

Opening the door of the secondary security room she found herself staring straight into the startled eyes of Mr Mannequin. Eva gave him a friendly wave.

"Everything's in order here," she said, putting on her best officious voice. Eva leaned towards him conspiratorially. "Just between you and me, there's going to be a fire drill in about an hour. I'd recommend grabbing a coffee beforehand." She paused. "Actually, a tea. I'd recommend getting a tea. Just a heads-up."

He blinked at her several times. "Don't I need to see some sort of ID for you to…" he pointed at the security door.

"Oh no, you're good. Your security clearance is fine for you to sit there." Eva opened the front door, hoping he'd be discombobulated by her confusing replies.

"No, I meant, ah—"

"Don't sweat it. I'll let Justin know you're doing a bang-up job. We're looking for some extra help over in the main building. I'll put in a good word." She tilted her head at the security door. "Is that shut properly?"

As Mr Mannequin turned, Eva deposited Amanda's phone out of sight on the floor. Before he'd turned back she was out the door. Lurking around secure areas followed the same principle as faking your way into VIP areas of nightclubs. Walk around acting like you belong and no one ever questions you. Eva strode towards the outer gate.

The temporary chain-link fence surrounding the outer

boundary of the rolling grassy hills wove between beautifully manicured gardens. The harsh fence sat at odds with the natural surroundings. Further into the complex, closer to the mansion, everything took on a more regal appearance; even the fencing was fancier.

It didn't take Eva long to find Loch and Bishop. All she had to do was follow the plumes of steam coming from their ears. They were at the main commercial vehicle checkpoint; neither was armed. Not that they needed to be with Royal Marines nearby.

Loch was using an under-car mirror to sweep a newly-arrived bus for explosives. Bishop held a clipboard; Eva assumed he was ticking off vehicles as they entered. Even from a distance, Eva could see the two of them squaring off.

There were two lines of vehicles and many staff. When Eva approached, both men broke into broad grins, then scowled at each other. Eva felt like she was in high school, although these days she didn't have braces, had a lot more tattoos and could give a definitive critique of every position in the *Kama Sutra*.

"What's up, gents?"

Before Bishop could utter a syllable she held up a finger to silence him. No time for innuendo. She flicked her head, gesturing for them to follow her. It took several minutes before they could extricate themselves from their duties; Eva distinctly heard the words "irritable bowel syndrome" before they managed to get away.

They huddled together under a large oak tree overlooking the lush valley below. She quickly gave them a rundown of her findings.

"So, the crypt, you reckon?"

"It would be out of the way, it's big enough, and it's not something you'd generally inspect too closely."

"Let's check it out," Loch said.

They found a hilltop position where they could look down on the crypt without being seen. It was a large stone edifice with carved gargoyles and crosses. Not exactly welcoming. Just as unwelcoming were the three guards stationed around it. Unlike Loch and Bishop, these civilian guards had rifles.

"Why would you guard a crypt?" Bishop asked.

"To stop zombies getting out?" Loch offered.

Eva playfully nudged him.

Bishop observed the move and scowled. "My supervisor was complaining about being stretched too thin, so I doubt they would waste resources, unless…"

"… these guys aren't part of the normal security force," Eva finished for him. "They're the only blokes I've seen with guns, apart from the Marines. So, either the crypt is of critical cultural significance, or…"

She didn't finish her thought. She didn't need to. The other two nodded. Eva seemed to have found what they were looking for.

Bishop whispered. "I hate to be Debbie Downer, but how do you plan on getting the nuke out of here?"

"It's over there."

She pointed to the van parked 20 metres away from the crypt. Its plates matched those of the garish vehicle that had arrived at the same time as the "crypt maintenance van" but, unlike that vehicle, it never left. It had a hand-scrawled "Out of Service" sign on the side window.

"Where?" Bishop asked, his eyes darting around for targets.

Eva pointed at the out-of-service van and he baulked.

"That?"

Eva nodded.

"Seriously?"

Eva nodded again.

"*That?*" he asked in disbelief.

Eva's lips pursed and she rolled her eyes, irritated. "Yes," she hissed. "It came with the bomb; I don't think it's what it appears to be. I think it's their support vehicle. The one they're going to use to get the hell out of dodge when the shit goes down." An evil smirk crossed her lips. "It's also what we're using to get the bomb out of here."

Bishop went to argue, then his shoulders slumped as he realised there was no arguing with Eva. Loch stared at her blankly.

"Okay, so in order for us to save the world, we have to defeat those guys, break into the crypt and then," she paused, realising how ridiculous it was going to sound, "we have to steal that ice-cream truck."

"I take it all back," Loch said.

"Take what back?"

"Helium-filled furniture is no longer the most ridiculous idea you've ever had."

CHAPTER TWENTY

Eva, Loch and Bishop approached slowly from the north. The closer she got, the faster her heart pounded. The guards hadn't moved an inch. That meant they were well trained, not given to petty distractions or boredom.

The ice-cream van looked the part. White, with stencils of multi-coloured confectionery adorning the sides and an absurdly large plastic ice-cream cone on the roof. The more she scrutinised the van, the less its occupants seemed the ice-cream vendor type. Clean shaven, military issued haircuts, thick necks and muscles bulging beneath their white coats. If that wasn't enough to pique Eva's interest, the next sight clinched it.

The two men in the van were far more casual than the guards outside it. Relaxed, they chatted, using animated gestures. As one was midway through a seemingly tawdry tale that seemed to involve someone with large breasts, the other man pointed. Well, he would have, if he'd had a left hand to point with.

Lefty.

She had to ignore their history together and Lekan's death back at the castle. Eva had to stick to the plan. She was to take out the guards with Bishop. She couldn't let Lefty's presence distract her, despite really, really wanting to shoot him. A lot.

"We're going to need weapons," Eva said quietly.

"Already ahead of you," Loch replied.

He opened his jacket and handed Eva a Glock 17s; the standard semi-automatic pistol of the British Army. He handed another to Bishop, who checked the clip, then the sight, and then cocked it. Each had a silencer attached. Bishop nodded. Loch did the same. Both had their game faces on. In an instant, petty rivalries were dispensed with. They had each other's backs.

"Do I want to know where you got these from?"

"There was a vending machine in the gents', right next to the pheromone spray." Loch winked.

Eva assessed the gun in her hand. "Is this going to be enough?"

Bishop tilted his head. "It's going to have to be."

Eva was a crack shot. She had been ever since she'd dated a useless, emotionally abusive boyfriend who worked at a shooting range. Bishop was just shy of expert marksmanship qualification. Loch was an unknown force, but as long as his shooting was better than his driving, they could hold their own.

They fanned out in an L formation, careful to use trees and manicured hedges for cover. Loch and Bishop were dressed in security shirts, so could generate at least several seconds of doubt. Eva, dressed in her barista garb, had no such luxury.

Without needing a signal, they took their positions. A shift in stance told Eva the guards were aware of their approach. These men were heavily armed. The SA80 service rifles strapped to their backs told her they weren't there for a soft serve.

Bishop walked towards them with an airy disposition. "Hey, guys!"

The guard nearest the entry to the crypt unslung his weapon; his two compatriots did the same. Bishop continued to walk towards them as if greeting an old friend. All three men leaned into a slight crouch, tension visible in their necks.

The doors of the ice-cream van opened. Lefty and his companion alighted.

It was now five against three and Eva's side weren't the ones with the heavy artillery.

She took position behind a large oak where she had unobstructed views of the van and the crypt. Eva fought to keep her adrenaline high from engulfing her. She had to make every second count, her aim had to be true, her every move unquestioningly the right one. They had one shot at this, and there was no second team if they screwed up.

Bishop was on point, being the least recognisable of them. He approached casually, his features friendly, his pistol tucked under a sheet of paper on his clipboard. He stopped his advance three metres from the lead fake guard.

"Hi fellas, everything in order?"

Over Bishop's shoulder, Lefty's eyes narrowed. His hand twitched and his right arm moved ever so slightly to his left shoulder. The move was subtle, but enough to tell Eva he had a shoulder holster.

The guard painted on a thin veneer of a smile, as genuine as a Chinese market-stall Rolex. "All good here, cheers."

"Good-oh." Bishop rocked on his heels pleasantly. He didn't move from his spot.

As all five men glared at him, Bishop did his best village idiot impression. None of the men had unnatural bulges under their clothing, so it was unlikely they wore bulletproof vests. Or at least, Eva hoped that was the case.

Loch had finished his long trek around the back of the crypt and was in position. One of their number noticed and took a step back, conscious they were being boxed in by unknowns.

"You right, mate?" Lefty asked, the sneer visible to all.

Bishop turned to him and evaluated the fake ice-cream salesman from bootstrap to hair gel. "Me? I'm all good, thank you."

One of the guards flicked the safety off his SA80 and dug in his back foot, in readiness to fire. His offsider did the same. These were no amateurs. These were trained soldiers. They would be Eva's first targets.

A Mexican standoff ensued, with neither side willing to show their hand. Eva kept reminding herself that these were not good men who'd just been misinformed, like the other security guards. These guys knew their mission. They had smuggled in a device with the express purpose of pushing the world to the brink of nuclear annihilation, if not over it.

Jaws clenched. Fingers twitched. Sets of eyes from both forces swept for more targets. Lefty's found one.

"It's her!" he screamed, pointing his stump directly at Eva.

Fucksies.

She didn't hesitate. Eva drew her weapon and fired directly at the scapula of the lead guard. He fell back, his crisp white shirt erupting in a sea of red. With the suppressor attached, her shot was no louder than clicking her fingers.

One down.

A split second later Eva replicated the shot on his compatriot. She double-tapped the round, as he had greater reaction time. She needn't have bothered. Her second and third shots were as true as her first.

Two down.

Having position and most of the element of surprise, Loch and Bishop downed their designated targets with equal efficiency, if more lethally. Bishop blew out the back of the skull of the white-coated driver, then added two shots to the heart for good measure. It was a technique he'd taught Eva, and used very effectively on a previous mission to Prague.

Loch was just as clinical. His three bullets hit the chest of the last fake guard. Centre mass, classic clustered formation. The target was dead before he hit the ground.

Only Lefty remained standing.

He fumbled for the weapon in his holster. Before his fingers even wrapped around the pistol his teammates were all lying on the ground, either dead or incapacitated. Three guns aimed at his head. He raised his hands. Hand.

The whole thing had gone down in seconds, making no more

sound than a couple of breaking twigs. The three of them were a lethal combination.

Bishop stepped towards Lefty, gun pointed, unwavering, at his forehead. Loch stripped the wounded of their weapons and threw them through the open window of the van. Eva swept the area for additional threats. Bishop placed his pistol on Lefty's temple.

"Don't." Eva cut in. "He's coming with us."

Three voices simultaneously said, "What?"

Eva was already on the move, conscious of how little time they had. Anyone could have heard the commotion. She grabbed Lefty by the collar and pushed him towards the rear of the ice-cream van.

"We have a distinct lack of witnesses and this cock-smoking chunder monkey is the closest we've got. He was in my apartment, he was at the castle and he knows about the bomb." She opened the door. "He's coming too."

"I won't talk."

"Darlin', as I've said to other skeezy 3 am pick-ups before you, you're coming with me and I don't want you to talk."

Nobody had an answer for that. She went to guide Lefty into the van but he pivoted and pushed her away. He drew back his right arm and took a swing at Eva. Her Krav Maga instinct kicked in and she ducked low and shouldered him into the van. Enraged, he roared and took another swing, this time with his left arm. Eva had more time to anticipate the move this time, and countered it with a punch of her own. Right in the stump. The stupid bastard had forgotten he no longer had a hand there.

The scream would have been heard all the way to Inverness. Another reason to get a move on. Lefty crumpled in a heap on the ground, a snivelling mass of pain and regret. The wound was only a few days old. It would have hurt like a bitch. Eva wanted to do it again.

"That was for Lekan, you piece of filth," she spat.

She bundled him up into the back of the van. The interior wasn't what Eva had anticipated. It was far wider than expected, with lots of hatches lining the walls. This wasn't decked out like an ice-cream van, this was more like a military support vehicle. Eva opened a hatch and gas masks spilled out. No wonder they were out of ice cream.

They tied Lefty up securely, gagged him and got to the task at hand. The three of them stared at the crypt doors. The heavy brass doors towered in front of them imposingly.

"Anyone have a key?" Eva asked.

"Why would a crypt need a key?" Bishop replied.

Eva scowled at him, "We mentioned zombies, right?"

Yanking at the crypt doors, Bishop grunted. They didn't move. He leaned down and ran his hand over the large keyhole, then turned and frowned at Eva. Loch held out a bulky metal key. Bishop tilted his head at it, then at Loch.

"It was in his pocket." Loch pointed to the lead guard. "I figured seeing as he was standing closest to the—"

"Yes, yes, fine." Bishop snatched the key and unlocked the door.

With a groan the great doors parted. Mottled light obscured the contents of the crypt. It took several seconds for Eva's eyes to adjust to the dark. There it was, smack bang in the middle of the crypt, Illuminated by tiny shards of light. Eva's bomb.

The first thing they did was drag in the dead or moaning. Those Eva had injured seemed to have lapsed into shock; they offered no protests other than cries of pain when they were deposited in the corner of the crypt.

The bomb was the same as she remembered: triangular, with the uppermost section removed. There had been some modifications, however. It sat on a low metal platform with solid castors, like she'd seen in warehouses. She assumed that was to aid with transporting it off the truck. There'd also been an addition to the side of the warhead; a prominent metal box had been fastened to it. That must be the trigger mechanism. There was no longer a big button Eva had hit when in the truck. It had been replaced by a black box with five smooth sides and no indication as to its purpose. Why make it easy?

Eva harrumphed. "Where's the big red readout?"

"The what?" Bishop asked.

"The big LED countdown clock."

"There's no… this isn't a movie, Eva."

"Yeah, but I still want a readout, so when we disarm the bomb with seven seconds left we get to exchange sardonic smiles then go off for cocktails and a shag."

"Now you're talking." Bishop waggled his eyebrows.

"I'll just stand here silently, shall I?" Loch asked.

"Settle down, Bishop," Eva said. "I didn't say it would be you."

Bishop gave a lopsided grin. "You didn't say it wouldn't be either." Then an expression of confusion crossed his features. "Why seven seconds?"

"Because it reads zero zero seven on the readout." Eva shrugged as if it should be completely obvious.

Bishop shook his head, not comprehending.

Eva sighed. "We have a lot more Bond movies to get through, dude."

"I just had a nasty thought," Loch said.

"Hmmm?"

"What if this thing is remotely detonated? We're assuming it's on a timer, but there's no obvious timing mechanism here. It might be internal, but what if it's detonated remotely, and as soon as they know we took it they press the big red button?"

"Oh, sure, there's a big red button, but my countdown clock is unrealistic."

Loch smirked. "Metaphorical big red button. It's probably just sending a text message or something."

"Can it be a big red phone?" Eva asked.

"Can we please focus?" Bishop said, annoyed. "We don't know how this thing is triggered, but we do know we need to get it the hell out of here. That's our first priority."

For the next ten minutes that's exactly what they worked on. They carefully rolled the warhead out into the sunlight and over to the van. The grassy terrain made the going slow. Eva didn't fancy chasing a nuclear weapon rolling down the hill.

It took all three of them to hoist the bomb into the back of the van. Anchor points and discarded fastening straps told Eva that the nuke was actually transported in the van, and not in the truck like she'd supposed. The truck must have been for troop transport, to ensure there were no issues getting the nuke in position. Once in place, only a few guards were needed.

By the time they'd finally managed to get the bomb in place, Eva was sweating. She turned to Lefty, who was tied to the back of the van with zip ties. He glowered at them. Eva undid the gag and asked if he had anything to say. He looked at the three of them, scowling, and said he didn't. His rage was barely contained behind clenched teeth and a shaking fist. The expression on his hard face made it plain he would love nothing more than to kill Eva very slowly, bury her deep, then dig her up and start all over again.

Clicking the last strap into place, Eva pointed at Lefty. "Thanks for the hand."

Lefty sneered. "I suppose you think you're funny."

"Pretty much."

The three spies exited the van and took a moment to steady themselves.

Bishop handed Eva the keys. "Drive slow, this thing will attract enough attention as it is."

Eva glanced at the van. "By the looks of it, I don't think I'll have much of a choice."

Loch's attention bounced between them. He ended up on Bishop. "You're not driving? After your effort leaving Kensington's estate I would have thought…"

Bishop smiled at Loch. It was the first genuine smile she'd seen Bishop give him. He tilted his head at Eva. "As much as it pains my male ego to say it, you haven't seen her drive."

"Sure I have, we drove through France."

"No, you haven't seen her *drive*."

She shrugged. "I used to steal cars for a living. Well, briefly. Clichéd teenage rebel." Eva tossed the keys in the air, then caught them. "I gots mad skills. Let's hope we don't need 'em. Come on."

The van started with a roar, not the whimper Eva expected. Bishop was in the back, Loch in the passenger seat. Dropping the van into gear, she put her foot lightly on the accelerator. The van leapt forward with a jerk, causing her to take her foot off the pedal immediately.

Loch smirked. "I thought you could drive."

Eva curled her lip. "Smartarse. That wasn't me. I think this thing is supercharged. This baby was never an ice-cream van."

Eva drove gingerly towards the exit. In retrospect, she wasn't surprised the van was high powered. If you're leaving the site of a soon-to-be-detonated nuclear bomb you don't want to fuck around. You want a vehicle with grunt.

There were no issues passing through security. Their main focus was vehicles entering the G8, not those leaving it. The only obstacle was a rotund guard asking for a mint Cornetto. Eva politely declined. And, just like that, they were out and heading for the A26.

There were no sighs of relief. There could be no celebrations. Freddie was still out there scheming and moving into position. Paul was under arrest. Senior government officials and probably military leaders were conspiring to take thousands of innocent lives, and if they succeeded, millions more would likely perish. Every branch of law enforcement was after them, not to mention Freddie's sycophants. No, there could be no let-up until Freddie's mad scheme was shut down and the bomb had been disarmed.

On the road, Eva felt exposed and an easy target. She repeatedly checked the rear-view mirror for tails, but so far they remained clear. The sooner they left the motorway, the better. The plan was to use the back roads and park the van at nice little cottage with a large barn where Eva had spent a pleasant weekend years before. She didn't tell the boys she'd had exceptional sex in the cottage. And the barn. And the gardens. Ignorance was bliss.

She hoped the cottage was secluded enough that if the bomb went off it would kill as few people as possible. Unfortunately that didn't do her, Bishop or Loch any favours. Trading their lives for those of world leaders and the security of global peace wasn't a hard decision to make. But it didn't make driving down the A26 any more comfortable.

Breaking her out of her maudlin thoughts, Loch said, "How you doing with all this?"

"We're driving an ice-cream truck with a three point three megaton warhead in the back. I don't see how I could be anything but relaxed."

Loch smiled his patented girl-slayer smile, which would have made Eva swoon if she were given to such things. "We'll be fine. I'm pretty sure the worst is over."

Eva checked her rear-view mirror again. It wasn't as clear as it had been previously. In fact, it was downright congested.

"The three white SUVs that just sped up behind us beg to differ." Eva pressed down on the accelerator. "Buckle up, boys, things are about to get bumpy."

CHAPTER TWENTY-ONE

"Okay, we have three SA80s, four Glock 17 semi-autos." Loch checked over the weaponry. "And that's it. No spare rounds."

Eva frowned. Her eyes darted to the rear-view mirror and the three encroaching SUVs. "We'd have a hard time fighting off a Fiat Punto with that."

Bishop poked his head through the small gap leading to the rear of the van. "I don't think armaments will be an issue."

Eva glanced beyond Bishop and saw open lockers. Dozens of guns and boxes of ammunition lined the shelves. She spotted SIG Sauer MPXs, Magpul FMGs and endless clips. There was enough to stage a comprehensive invasion of the Falkland Islands.

"Shit on my tits," Eva gasped. She leaned over to Lefty, who was seething in a vapour of resentment. "What the hell is this thing? And why the fuck is it an ice-cream van?"

Lefty glared back. He probably would have given her the finger if he'd had a hand free. Or a hand.

"Dude, it's not like you're divulging state secrets. I just want to know why we're driving around in a souped-up munitions van with a novelty ice cream on top."

More to himself than anyone else, Lefty mumbled, "Wasn't my idea."

"What wasn't your idea?" Loch asked.

"The van," he spat. "It was the only one available. Army Intelligence had used it for a previous operation. The cone? It's a sophisticated surveillance array. It was either that or a regular troop transport, which would attract more attention than a supposed ice-cream van with an 'Out of Service' sign. Happy now?"

Eva wondered why Lefty had become so talkative all of a sudden. Then she realised what he was doing. While he'd been talking, the lead SUVs had leapfrogged two more cars on the motorway. The time for talk was over.

"Bishop, use up the SA80s first, they're better for long range. Save the MPXs until they're close enough for us to key the car."

Bishop was busy loading weapons in the back. "Gee, thanks Captain Obvious for the suggestion. Should I breathe in and out as well?"

Eva wrinkled her nose at him. "Sarcasm, useful."

She checked the SUVs. Two occupied a lane on either side of the dual carriageway. The third seemed to be deliberately lagging behind.

Loch took the weapons Bishop handed him and flicked the first into automatic fire mode. "I've got the left covered. Bishop, I'd suggest opening the right back door only; use the other to obscure your movements."

"Roger." Bishop went back to the rear of the van. "Waiting for your signal, Eva."

Behind them the vans were manoeuvring into position. The rear one held back, doing its best to remain obscured behind lorries and campervans. The two lead vehicles kept pace with Eva, always remaining one car behind. Until now. In a well-orchestrated manoeuvre they each passed the vehicle in front. They were making their move.

Eva put her foot down. "Let's see what this baby has under her hood."

The van lurched forward momentarily, leaving the two SUVs in their wake. That didn't last long. They surged ahead, catching up with the van in no time. Without indicating, Eva took the exit onto the A21 at speed, cutting off a less-than-pleased Citroën driver. The new road was wider and straighter. With only two lanes on the A26, Eva had been limited with how fast she could go. The A21 wasn't exactly built for high-speed pursuits, but it was better than the A26.

Planting her foot, Eva overtook a family sedan on the left hard shoulder of the road just before it abruptly ended at an overpass. That bought them a few moments, until the road straightened out again.

"Bishop, get ready to open the back door and fire on the lead vehicle."

"Affirmative."

"Loch, when I say go you fire everything you have on the second one."

He wound down the window. "Anything you say, boss." He placed a hand on her knee. "And Eva, I want you to know—"

"Not now, Loch." She spared a second to gaze into his eyes. "But soon. But right now…"

She swerved around a slow-moving tractor.

"We have to mess up some bad guys first?" Loch asked.

Eva nodded. "Yep." The lead vehicle matched her move and sped towards them. "Here we go, folks. In three, two, one—go!"

The rear door flew open and Eva heard the heavy metallic twang of Bishop firing successive rounds from the SA80. Loch leaned out the window and fired controlled MPX bursts into the second vehicle.

Bishop gave a cry of frustration. "The bastards are armoured."

Eva grunted. "Of course they are."

Despite the gunfire, the SUVs maintained their position. At the same time, the windows of the pursuit vehicles lowered.

"Incoming!"

The ice-cream van was peppered with gunfire. It sounded like sledgehammers were being used to attack the body of the car.

Nothing fell off, there were no cries of pain and no broken glass. So far, so good.

In quick succession, Eva, Loch and Bishop yelled, "Clear!", confirming there were no injuries.

"I'm fine too," Lefty said. "Thanks for asking."

Tiny specks of sunlight shone through the left side of the van. They weren't as bulletproof as the SUVs. Loch went to fire, but before he could pull the trigger he ducked back inside as another volley of bullets sprayed the van. The left side mirror shattered.

Eva picked up the microphone on the centre of the console. The loudspeaker on the roof burst into life.

Eva pressed the button and yelled, "Stop firing at the nuclear bomb, you cockwombles!"

Her request prompted another spray of gunfire. Loch and Bishop responded in kind. Whatever button Eva had pushed for the loudspeaker had turned on the ice-cream van's music. The soothing tones of "Greensleeves" filled their ears.

From the back, Bishop yelled, "Can you turn that off? It's distracting me from firing assault weapons, being aggressive and so forth."

Eva hit every button she could find, but nothing would silence the amplified rendition of "Greensleeves". As more bullets showered the van, the melodic tune continued unabated. There was a loud *clang* and Eva saw one of the van's back doors bounce along the road behind them. She was going to die in an ice-cream truck, listening to muzak.

Not on my watch. One of the SUVs sped forward, drawing level with the van. Its partner was rapidly approaching the rear. They were trying to box her in.

"I'm going to try something really stupid."

Loch grinned. "I'd be disappointed if you didn't."

Eva shifted down one gear. "Bishop, heads up, I'm going to try a PIT."

"Do it."

The Precision Immobilisation Technique was used by police forces around the world. It was risky at the best of times, downright irresponsible when facing more than one hostile vehicle, but they were running out of options. Traffic had greatly reduced since the gunfire started. However, they were still overtaking slow-moving vehicles who had no idea what was coming up from behind. Eva had to time it right to ensure she didn't take out anyone she shouldn't.

"Hold the fuck onto something, people."

Eva tapped the brakes, allowing the lead vehicle on her left to pull ahead a little. As the van's front wheels aligned with the SUV's back ones, Eva turned the wheel and gently tapped the SUV's side, steering sharply into it. She hit the accelerator to make sure the van's bumper didn't slide off the target. The SUV's rear tyres lost traction and skidded wildly. Eva gritted her teeth and floored it, moving past the out-of-control vehicle.

The driver of the SUV was skilful. He tried valiantly to recover from the skid, but it was too late. The SUV careened over the road shoulder and completely lost its grip of the road. It spun repeatedly, smashed violently into an embankment and flipped onto its roof. A wheel flew off into the treeline.

One vehicle down. There was no time to celebrate.

Eva yelled, "Hit the second vehicle with everything you've got!"

Over the dulcet tones of "Greensleeves", Loch and Bishop pummelled the second SUV with gunfire. When one weapon was spent, they simply picked up the next and continued shooting. And the next and the next. There was no time for the SUV to return fire.

Bishop called out, "I'm seeing steam from the grille!"

"Hit it!"

Loch and Bishop did exactly as they were told, firing relentlessly at the pursuing vehicle's engine. Sparks flew, steam intensified. It wasn't long before the car shuddered. The gap between vehicles widened. In spite of the relentless fire, a dark-clad soldier leaned out of the rear passenger window. Bishop fired on him before he could shoot. His chest exploded in rapid pops of red and he slumped across the car door. Someone dragged him back in, blood smearing across the crisp white exterior of the SUV.

A metallic knocking from the engine turned into a constant din and the SUV fell back. It skidded to halt ingloriously in the middle of the dual lanes. Two down. Cars behind weren't keen to overtake it, effectively stopping all traffic behind. The third SUV, which had seemed reluctant to enter the fray, was stuck in the traffic jam.

Loch whistled. "Damn, you can drive, woman."

Eva tilted her head. "I'm a woman of many talents."

Loch's eyebrows danced. "Many many talents."

From the van's cabin, Lefty said, "I think I'm going to be sick."

Bishop frowned at him. "The ride's not that rough."

"No, the two lovebirds up the front. I'm going to lose my lunch."

Bishop growled, "You vomit on my Berlutis I will personally kill you regardless of how valuable you are as a witness, understand?" Moving toward the front, Bishop asked Eva, "How are we doing, position-wise?"

"We overshot our exit point miles ago; we shouldn't be on the A26 at all. I don't fancy doubling back with the SUV behind us, it's too risky. Can we find another isolated location between here and London?"

Loch pulled a map from the glove compartment. "Going to be tricky, we're hitting larger population centres the further we go. Let's hope we don't go boom before then."

A snort came from the back of the van. Eva heard the words, "Stupid fuckers."

"Do you have something to contribute to the discussion, Lefty?"

Silence was her answer.

"Look, you're going to be blown up just as much as we are if we fuck this up, so you've got nothing to lose by helping us out, yeah?"

Baring his teeth, Eva could see the inner turmoil bubbling below Lefty's surface. He'd love nothing more than to skin her alive.

"It's not going to get triggered remotely!" he blurted, kicking the bomb. "It's on a timer. The thing's set to blow tomorrow afternoon. Just get me clear before then. There, that's my deal."

"Wait," Eva overtook a tourist bus, "your deal is we have to unstrap you from this van before tomorrow? But you just told us what we needed to know. How is that a deal? You're rubbish at negotiation." Eva shook her head.

The realisation swamped Lefty's flat features. He'd screwed himself over in a fit of anger. He began kicking again.

Bishop tapped him lightly on the head with the barrel of his machine gun. "Please stop kicking the nuclear device."

If the bomb was on a timer, that changed the game slightly. Now they had more time. If a nuke went off in the countryside, even if they managed to find a remote location, it would still be an international incident. Disarming it was the priority now. They had to find someone to disarm the bomb, but they couldn't trust MI6, the army or anyone else without knowing who was in on the conspiracy. Their options had become both easier and harder at the same time.

Static crackled and interrupted their discussion. "..va… are you… epeat, Eva… there?"

All three spies traded confused expressions. Bishop was the first to twig. "Radio."

He leapt up and rummaged around the back of the van until he found a compact black radio in a jacket. He handed it to Eva.

There was probably some radio protocol she was meant to use, saying words like "foxtrot" or "over" or whatnot. Instead she pressed the button and simply said, "Hello?"

"Eva, what are you doing, my love?"

She knew the voice. She'd never wanted to hear that voice again.

"Where are you, Freddie?"

"I'm safe, tucked up here in London. They're patching me through the car behind you, we'll probably be out of range soon, so we don't have much time."

"There's nothing I want to say to you."

"Now, don't be like that. You've caused quite the fracas, haven't you, my dear? But I still love you. I'm sure we can come to some sort of arrangement with all this, we have time."

"I want no part of your mental scheme, Freddie. I will do everything I can to take you and your co-traitors down."

Freddie tutted. "I did nothing but protect you, Eva. When others wanted you dead I was the one who saved your life. This is how you repay me?" There was a pause. "Is that 'Greensleeves' I can hear?"

"I owe you nothing, Freddie. I never asked for my memory to be wiped, and you only did it because you knew I would have no part of your evil scheme. I'm coming for you, you crazy bitch. I'm coming after you and all your Cambridge elite megalomaniac bastards. And you know me well enough to understand that you can't hide. I won't stop until each and every last one of you is locked up. You'll all pay for the murders you've committed and were about to commit in the name of displaced patriotism. There is no rock you'll be able to hide under. I will find you, you filthy shit-splattered clunge-munching dildo-fingered cum-rag."

Static was Eva's answer.

Bishop turned off the radio. "She probably dropped out a minute or so ago. Good speech, though. Almost Churchill-like. I, for one, was inspired."

Loch tilted his head. "Dildo-fingered?"

"I will admit it got away from me a bit at the end there."

They took the next exit and saw no sign of a tail. Eva drove in circles, ensuring no one was following, then found the nearest petrol station. They were thankful to find that when the engine shut off, so did "Greensleeves". Using money from Lefty, they bought high-fat, high-sugar snacks for all. Eva was starving. She reluctantly fed Lefty a microwaved cheeseburger, then went back into the station with Bishop while Loch stayed with Lefty in the van. With the small change she had, she used the public telephone.

The voice at the other end was eager to hear from her. As usual. Bishop rolled his eyes.

"How goes it, Trev?"

Again, the pang of guilt hit her. Was she using Trev because he had a crush on her? Was she exploiting his feelings? As much as she tried to justify her actions, he was risking so much, most likely because of Eva. It was hard to be a clinical heartless spy when you actually had a heart.

"Good, Eva, really good! I've cracked it."

"The code, you've decrypted it?"

"Done and done. Ah, I'm pretty sure most of this stuff is way over my paygrade."

"Let's not worry about that right now. Trev, we owe you big time, fuck, the planet owes you big time. You need to find Paul Cavendish and give him everything."

"Yeah, on that, um, there's a rumour going around he's, like, been arrested and stuff."

Eva wasn't surprised that word had gotten out. Freddie would have found a way to implicate Paul once the bomb went off. After all, he was the bureaucrat who had instigated the Switchback protocol, placing the world leaders directly in harm's way.

"You need to find him anyway; he'll know what to do. If he really has been arrested and you can't get to him, give it all to the media. Every bit of it."

"There's some pretty saucy stuff here, Eva."

"I'm aware, Trev. We don't know who to trust, so we'll have to give it to the free press to sort out for us. That's what they're there for, to protect us from tyranny." Eva took a breath. "Trev, are you protecting yourself? If any of this could expose you, or put you in danger—"

"It's all good, Eva. I wrote most of the protective protocols myself, it's untraceable."

"That's good, but I don't want you taking any unnecessary risks, you hear?"

"Loud and clear." There was a hesitant pause. "I also found the other stuff, the paper stuff on—"

"Don't say the word, Trev. It could trigger listening devices."

"Oh, right, yeah. Okay, so I went through all the paper files for… that word. Man, I've got, like, a million paper cuts and I smell like old paper."

"I love the smell of old paper." Eva instantly regretted saying it.

"Oh really?" Trev said, as if committing the detail to memory. "It, um took some doing. I had to crawl through three warehouses to find what you wanted."

"Did you find it, Trev? The missing documents, were they there?"

"It was there, Eva, it was all there. It hadn't been junked at all."

"Brilliant! I need to know, is Lady Kensington on the list?"

"Yes, she is."

"And the Chief of the General Staff?"

"Yes, him too. It was a long time ago, though."

"That's enough for me." More to Bishop than to Trevor, she said, "That's enough to establish they're engineering a putsch and seizing the state for their own ends."

Bishop nodded. The Halcyon files would be compelling in their own right; combined with the decrypted files, Freddie and her cohorts were going to be locked up in maximum security for the rest of their lives.

"Listen, Eva." Trev sounded uneasy. "Like I said last time, you need to see this recording…"

"I will, Trev, we've got a bit on at the moment. Thank you, you really don't understand how amazing you've been in all this. You're going to get a medal of some description, that's for sure."

"And a night out?"

Eva grinned. "Yes, and a night out rocking out to the best tunes we can find."

"Outstanding!"

"Trev, you need to find Paul. He has to be your priority now. Get a message to him if you can." She eyed the counter selling cheap mobile phones and SIM cards. "Trev, we're going to hit the road. I'll call you from a different number. We need to know if Paul is contactable. We're coming to London. I can't tell you how—hell, even if I did you wouldn't believe me, but we're coming. Keep safe, we're almost there."

Eva rang off. She used what money they had left to buy a mobile, then tucked the box under her arm and marched towards the exit.

Bishop glared at her. "What do you mean, we're coming to London? If we turn up to Vauxhall Cross, they'll kill us. You know that, right?"

Eva walked back to the van. Her mind was racing. A plan was forming. There were a lot of ifs in it—probably too many—but it was a plan. Sort of.

"I didn't say that's where we're going," Eva replied.

"So where are we going?"

She opened the door to the van and started the engine. "We're going to give the Chinese their bomb back."

CHAPTER TWENTY-TWO

Driving down the motorway at a pace that wouldn't cause any undue attention, the fact that they were driving an ice-cream truck with multiple bullet holes, a lost rear door and a missing side mirror notwithstanding, Eva went through what she knew. They now had paper files linking Lady Kensington and the head of the army with previous knowledge of the Halcyon strategy. They had Freddie's computer files and email correspondence. They had a witness, albeit a reluctant one, in Lefty. Oh yeah, and they had a big-arse nuclear bomb with their fingerprints all over it. Would it be enough to get every law enforcement agency off their backs long enough for them to state their case? There was only one way to find out.

"Can I please state for the record that I object to this course of action?" Bishop said from the back of the van.

"There's no record, Bishop." Eva kept her eyes on the road.

"Then I want to state that your plan sucks balls," Bishop replied. "Like, old wrinkly ones with suspicious spots."

"Got it." Loch put the mobile phone together and activated it.

Eva gave him the number to call. They waited for what seemed like hours until it connected. When Trev answered and found out it was Eva again he almost squeed. Almost. He must have been practising controlling his elation. Maybe they'd make a field agent out of him yet. He got down to business.

"I've found him. Paul, I mean. I know where he is."

"And?" Eva asked, knowing she wasn't going to like the answer.

"He's here, at SIS headquarters, although…"

"Although what, Trev?"

"It says here he's not under arrest, yet. The note I saw said that he's being held pending official charges under the *Official Secrets Act*. That's heavy, Eva. He's not in the commissary eating a sandwich. I don't know how to get to him."

"I do," Bishop piped in. "Here's what you need to do, Trevor."

Bishop went through his idea. It was risky, with the potential to expose their entire operation, but they had a fallback. Trev would set up an automated email that, if they failed, would release all they knew to the media. Everything. If none of them got out alive, at least the truth would. The best part was that it didn't expose Trevor. He still had a job and a head connected to his shoulders; the others were doing their best to keep it that way.

Eva told him the other part of the plan, the part where she explained why they were headed to London. Trev's reaction could best be summed up as stunned silence. After the shock had worn off, he said he was ready to go, but not before one last thing.

"I can clear the way for you," he said.

"Clear what way?" Eva asked. "What do you mean?"

"I mean I can clear the traffic on the motorway. I've got software for that. I just jump on and swarm the GPS data collection for Android, Apple and a few others and make them believe there are huge traffic snarls. They'll direct traffic off the main routes and you'll have a clearer run."

"Is there anything you can't do, Trev?"

"Get a woman to let me feel her boobs."

All was quiet in the van except for the faint sound of sniggering in the back from Lefty.

Eva gave a slight smile. "Oversharing, Trev."

"Right. So I'll get on the…"

"Yes, please."

"I can probably part the waters when you get to the city. There's this hush hush thing on the traffic system called the Queen's Covenant. Never hacked into that one. Basically, it would give you a green light to wherever you want to go. Uh, where do you want to go?"

Eva told him.

There was a pause. "I think I'm re-evaluating our night out. I think you might be too crazy for me, Eva."

"You have no idea, Trev. Can you do it?"

"I'll see. You start getting green lights along the way, you know who to thank."

They rang off and Eva focused on the road. For ten minutes, not a word was spoken. What was there to say? Their course of action was, to use a phrase Eva had heard so many times recently, reckless. Then again, so were the deeds of those they fought against.

As they got closer to London, the motorway traffic did seem to be thinning out. At this time of day Eva would have expected the traffic to be bumper to bumper, with most drivers engaging in the polite, silent rage the English do so well. But no. The volume of cars was reducing, not increasing. It reminded Eva of a post-apocalyptic movie. She expected bands of Mad Max types to leap out at any moment to steal her fuel. Trev was definitely going to get laid, even if she had to lock him in a room with a group of available females until one of them caved and at least gave him a sympathetic handy.

When they entered the city proper, true to his word, Trev managed to supply them with green lights at every intersection. Eva even gave a couple of pedestrians a queen-like wave. It seemed too good to be true.

It was.

"Heads up," Bishop said from the back. "We've got company."

She checked her remaining side mirror. The familiar outline of a white SUV hurtled towards them. It had used the slipstream they'd created to catch up.

Eva was about to chastise Bishop for the use of such a clichéd saying, but decided to focus on her driving instead. The labyrinth streets of London afforded no chance to lose concentration, even for a second. Thousands of Londoners and tourists lined the streets. This was no high-speed chase. It was faster than Eva had ever driven in the city, but by no means did she have her foot to the floor. The SUV behind them had no such reservations. It hurtled through the streets, gaining on them every second.

Landmarks flitted past. The Imperial War Museum. The Old Vic. She drove over Waterloo Bridge to the Victorian Embankment. This was her stomping ground. She didn't need green lights any more. She knew the rat traps better than anyone. Eva yanked the wheel and took a sharp left. This was her turf. A few more hard turns had the SUV lagging behind.

Almost before she realised it, they were on her street. Her café came up fast. A tall blonde hulk of a man carried a garbage bag out the front of Kanga Brew.

Eva honked the horn and stuck her head out the window. "Hey Anchor!"

The big Swede lifted his head, utter confusion splashed across his face. She could understand that. Eva had been MIA for days, and now she was speeding past him in a shot-up ice-cream van with a SUV in pursuit. She wasn't a normal boss.

A shot rang out and everyone ducked. Perhaps she shouldn't have stuck her head out. Successive gunshots echoed around the hallowed streets. The idiots were firing in the middle of London on a weekday afternoon. Eva dropped a gear and hunkered down. Nobody shoots up her adopted town.

Trev must have been tracking them, because lights were still changing in their favour. With every turn they managed to put some distance between them and the SUV, but on every straight piece of road they lost ground.

A spray of bullets peppered the side and splintered the

contents of the van. A loud *thunk* reverberated. Eva had the uneasy feeling the nuclear bomb had just been hit.

With all the twists and turns, the shooters had to keep retracting into the SUV and changing positions. It was hard to get a direct shot, but they took every opportunity. Eva's van was getting pummelled.

"Do we return fire?" Bishop bellowed.

"We can't," Eva yelled back at him. "There are way too many people around. There's no way an innocent person isn't going to get caught in the crossfire. It's far too risky."

"Well, won't this be fun," Bishop grumbled.

"Eva." Loch said as she mounted a footpath to speed through an intersection. "We have to fight back."

He was right, of course. They couldn't keep taking bullets with no reprisals. They had to take out the SUV.

"Loch," she said, inhaling deeply, "take the wheel."

"What?" Loch and Bishop said simultaneously.

"What what?" Lefty asked, even more confused than the others.

"Keep on this road, yell when we pass Duchess Street. Don't slow down for anything. No need for a gear change, just stay on this street. Got it?"

His look of fear was almost adorable. "Okay." There was no conviction in Loch's voice whatsoever.

Eva held onto the wheel, her foot barely on the accelerator while Loch manoeuvred into place. When he slid into the driver's seat Eva didn't waste any time heading to the back of the van. She picked up the nearest pistol.

"Enough of this bullshit." She cocked the weapon. "Time to end this."

"You know they're armoured, right?" Bishop asked with a smirk.

"Doesn't mean I can't piss them off."

"We all have our talents." Bishop gestured towards the encroaching SUV, as if saying *all yours*.

The driver of a black Mini between the van and the SUV saw

Eva's pistol and made a hasty illegal turn to get out of the way. Eva aimed the gun and fired directly at the SUV driver's head. The bullet bounced off the armoured glass. She fired again. And again. And again. She fired an entire clip. She dropped the spent pistol and held her hand back. Bishop slapped another weapon into it. She didn't bother cocking it, knowing Bishop would have it ready for her. He did.

Another clip and still no fractures in the glass. Not that Eva expected otherwise. It was about distracting the driver. It's hard to stay fully focused when someone's firing bullets at your face.

"Loch, hard left, now!"

"You said…"

"Now!"

The van took the corner way too fast. Eva slipped across the van's floor as the vehicle leaned onto two wheels. Loch struggled to keep it from toppling over. They were so close to their target, it would be tragic to end it all mere blocks away. With a jerk of the wheel the van righted itself and landed with a *thump*. The SUV overshot the intersection and skidded to a halt. Vehicles behind it did the same, making backing up problematic. It hit reverse anyway, smashing into the cars behind that didn't get out of the way.

It gave Eva the time they needed. "Take the next two rights, Loch." After a moment she added, "A bit slower this time."

Loch did as he was instructed, grinding the gears as he did so. Bishop and Eva picked up the closest SIG Sauer MPXs and readied them for the final stand. The white SUV screeched around the last corner in angry pursuit. It wouldn't make the same mistake again.

Loch took the second right then called out, "Okay, now what?"

"The large brown brick building on the left corner?" Eva yelled. "See it?"

"Yes."

"That's the Embassy of the People's Republic of China." Eva blew out a breath. "I want you to smash through the front door."

"You what?"

"Drive this fucker right through the front doors. It's extraterritorial sovereign territory. Nobody can enter it, even if they're under attack or on fire. We'll be safe there."

"Except for the armed guards, peeved we attacked them with a van containing a nuclear weapon," he called back. "Apart from that, right?"

"I'm not a fan of this plan," Lefty called out. "I don't want to die with you people."

Eva ignored him. "Do it! It's the only way we'll be on Chinese national soil. You have to breach the front door. Crash it, Loch!"

Loch planted his foot and the van jerked forward. Eva hoped the Chinese didn't have a protocol for an ice-cream van smashing through their front entrance. The SUV behind them seemed to have determined their course of action and fired everything they had. Bullets ripped through the van, tearing holes throughout the van's body. She and Bishop returned fire, purchasing precious seconds.

Loch planted his palm on the horn, clearing the way of pedestrians. The van gained speed. The front wheels hit the kerb hard and the van launched into the air. For what seemed like hours, it hung there.

The SUV kept firing, as did Eva and Bishop, who were also airborne. When it came, the crash was horrific. Grinding metal thundered into shattering brick and wood. It was like a sonic boom.

Eva and Bishop were thrown like ragdolls across the interior of the van. Eva's back slammed into the bomb, then she bounced off it and smashed into the wall. Everything went black.

Eva must have only blacked out for a moment. When her vision returned, she saw seven fancily dressed Chinese soldiers running towards the van, guns up. The elaborate entranceway they had crashed into was filled with smoke and detritus. Screams and sirens assaulted her ears.

In a hoarse voice, Eva called, "Clear."

Beside her, under a pile of gas masks, Bishop grunted, "Clear."

"You people are fucking nuts," Lefty spat, still tied to the internal wall.

There was no reply from Loch in the front of the van.

The soldiers screamed at them in Chinese, probably unsure if they were under attack by an ice-cream van or if they had just encountered London's worst driver. Eva pushed herself up. Every piece of her body ached. Ignoring the rabid orders being shrieked at her, Eva staggered towards the front of the crashed van. There wasn't much of it left. The windscreen had splintered into a million pieces and the entire front of the van had crumpled into itself. There was no way anyone could have survived.

A cough came from the front seat. Loch was bloodied, with the steering wheel pinned to his chest. He had gashes all over his face and was coughing blood. But he was alive.

He grimaced. "Not a word about my driving, okay?"

She kissed his cheek. "I would never stoop so low."

"Uh-huh."

Chinese soldiers reached the rear of the van and saw the abundant weaponry strewn across the cabin's floor. They aimed submachine guns at them and tensed, waiting for any excuse to fire.

Eva stepped into the back of the van and raised her hands. "I wish to speak to Li Wei, Cultural Attaché Sub-Supervisor Office of Cultural Affairs."

Her only reply was seven blank expressions and the barrels of numerous weapons being pointed at her. Eva smiled. That shocked them even more.

"Li Wei, please," she said, as politely as she could. She sat on the tailgate of the van. "I'll wait."

Eva just hoped he'd recognise her outside of Kanga Brew, and that he'd be willing to go along with her scheme. She'd know in a few minutes.

"Eva? Is that… what is this?"

Li looked exactly as she remembered him. Why wouldn't he? It was only a week ago—or possibly a lifetime. Eva couldn't remember. Cheap suit, matching haircut, kind face. At least they wouldn't be trading USBs this time.

He cleared the security barricades and walked briskly towards her.

"Hey, got a question for you," Eva said, rubbing her rib.

"Ah, yes?"

"Want the biggest promotion of all time?" Eva asked, seeing the confusion cross his features. "Do you want to be the guy who brings down the UK government and pretty much guarantees China's entry into the G8?"

Li tilted his head, and she detected the slightest hint of an amused smirk. Eva had just launched his career into the stratosphere.

Eva gestured towards the armed guards. "Call off the soldiers and we'll talk. I'll warn you now, I've got a wild story for you."

Li nodded to the soldiers, who lowered their weapons.

Eva said, "There's a man at the front who needs urgent medical attention, could you see to it that he's looked after?"

Li issued a sharp set of instructions and someone ran back into the building.

"Thanks." Eva stood, then groaned and grabbed her side. Li raced to keep her from toppling over and she inhaled, trying to manage the pain. "Oh, by the way, there's a nuclear bomb in the van."

The soldiers immediately raised their guns, looking panicked.

"Sorry, should have mentioned that before."

CHAPTER TWENTY-THREE

It took an hour before things settled down. There was a lot of shouting, pointing and people rushing about. Loch was seen to by the in-house physician, rather than the ambulance Eva had requested. The Chinese weren't letting them out of their sight. Which was understandable. Eva had crashed a nuclear bomb through their front door, after all.

Emergency services had cordoned off the street with barricade tape, but had not been allowed inside. They would have asked too many questions, especially about the large item in the back of the van.

Li was officious and never once gave the slightest indication that he knew Eva well. Whatever his reasons for betraying his country, she'd just given the guy a massive promotion, which meant he'd be privy to far more sensitive intelligence. SIS would be so pleased when she told them. If they didn't execute her first.

Technicians were examining the bomb but hadn't yet started to pull it apart. At first Eva found it odd that the building hadn't been evacuated, but on reflection, she saw the logic. This wasn't a fire drill. You couldn't just pop over to the park across the road and hope for the best. If things went wrong, the building, the road and the park would be vaporised within seconds. From her position across the foyer she could see the bullet-hole-riddled van. It was utterly destroyed. In an odd way, Eva felt sad. The ice-cream van had weathered much, and had got them exactly where they needed to be. It was a feisty little thing. She wondered if the people who had witnessed the trail of destruction would ever know what that van represented. That the odd ice-cream van and its occupants had staved off World War Three. Maybe. Eva wasn't in it for recognition or glory. She was in it for the coffee.

As she sipped the insipid coffee she'd been given she understood why Li walked blocks to get coffee at her café. It was almost as bad as the coffee her supervisor had made back at Salomons Estate, though nothing could be quite *that* bad. At least it was warm. Eva shivered, then realised it was probably the shock kicking in, rather than the cold. She had subjected her body to so much. Little sleep, constant trauma, unbelievable adrenaline highs. There was only so much it could take. As soon as she laid her head down, she'd sleep for a week. It could be a five-star hotel or a prison cell, at this stage she didn't care.

Bishop lay on the hard floor, arm over his face, sleeping off his post-saving-the-world buzz. Lefty was handcuffed—by his good hand—to Bishop. He'd tried unsuccessfully to get someone to uncuff him from "this madman", but had eventually given up and was now stewing in a surly, sullen miasma.

The doctors moved away from Loch and he unsteadily sat up. He was bruised and battered, which on him somehow looked rugged and suave. He smiled at Eva. *Oh boy.* He hobbled over and sat down next to her on the hard marble floor with a grunt. She kissed his forehead.

Eva shook her head. "Dude, I give you the wheel and what's the first thing you do? Crash the bloody thing."

"You told me to!"

"I'm not interested in your facts." She held his hand. "I'll need to teach you how to drive properly one day."

"That mean we have a future?" There was flinty hope in the question. "You and me?"

Eva didn't immediately answer, instead staring out at the chaos they had created. The skid marks across the white marble floor, the demolished front entrance. Her actions had caused so much devastation. Eva just hoped she'd saved more than she'd wrought.

"When I said be reckless, this isn't exactly what I had in mind."

Eva's head shot up to see the lumbering hulk of one of her best friends in the world. She ran at him, her exhaustion forgotten, wrapping him in a bear hug. Her arms squeezed him tight and she was determined to never let go. Paul hugged her back and winced.

"I saw on the news that some idiot had crashed into the Chinese embassy, and somehow I knew exactly who that idiot would be."

He extracted himself from her embrace and looked Eva in the eye. "Are you okay?"

Overcome with emotion, Eva simply nodded.

Unmoved from his reclining position on the floor, Bishop replied, "I'm fine, too."

"I thought you were asleep?" Eva said.

"Spies don't sleep, they wait," he said, unmoved.

She ignored him and began interrogating Paul about how he had managed to extricate himself from MI6 custody. Trevor had done exactly as instructed. He'd followed Bishop's plan and managed to pass messages to Paul via Bishop's trusted allies. Paul had presented certain printed documents from Freddie's archives. That made MI6 officials literally sit up and listen. Within minutes, the tables had turned, and the interrogation room had become a war room. Paul was no longer being questioned, he was the leader of the charge.

Trevor was in line for a promotion, and probably a medal of valour. The kid had single-handedly saved MI6 from the biggest blunder ever experienced by any intelligence service on the planet. Eva hoped they'd shower him with hookers and cocaine, but doubted that was the MI6 way. He'd probably get a stiff handshake and a low-carb bagel.

As they spoke, Internal Affairs were going through MI6 floor by floor, ripping everything apart and pursuing co-conspirators. The place was in lockdown. No information was coming in or out.

"The hammer's coming down, Evie. We got them."

"And Freddie?" Eva asked, an edge in her voice.

"She's still at large." A wry grin crossed Paul's lips.

Eva tilted her head. "Then why are you smiling?"

"Because we know exactly where she is." He paused—for dramatic effect, Eva was sure. "Want to go for a drive?"

"Where to?"

He smiled again.

"Are you shitting me?"

In the back of the plush government car, Paul pursed his lips. "Please mind your language. Remember where you are."

It was hard not to. Everyone in the Western world knew this place. Despite having lived in London for years, she'd never been inside. That was about to change. Eva was almost certain she wasn't ready.

Paul had worked his magic back at the embassy. Using his position, and no small amount of cajoling and bluster, he had convinced the Chinese to allow outsiders into the embassy. The UN office for Disarmament Affairs helped the Chinese dismantle the bomb. UNODA were far better equipped to safely deactivate it. The last thing anyone wanted was a nuclear explosion in the middle of London. Li had farewelled Eva with a promise of further discussions.

Loch and Bishop were escorting Lefty to MI6, where Eva was certain much unpleasantness awaited the vile little slug of a man. She was disappointed she'd miss it, but she was equally sure she didn't want to miss what Paul had lined up for her.

As they drove through the gates of Buckingham Palace Eva sucked in a deep breath. She was smeared with blood, she hadn't brushed her hair in days and, as Amanda the officious HR Manager had pointed out, she stunk. Not exactly how she had envisioned her first visit to the residence and administrative head-quarters of the reigning monarch of the United Kingdom. She'd always thought it would involve a gown of some description, not a blood-splattered barista's uniform.

But there was no way she was going to miss it. Freddie was inside, getting ready to officially resign her position as Foreign Secretary. She was to stay overnight for a special thank-you function and would formally resign the next day. Eva had to hand it to her. The woman was smart. What better place to be when the shit went down? If Freddie had timed it right, the bomb would explode and the king would simply refuse her resignation. She'd step in to save the government from chaos. It was just a pity Freddie had chosen the wrong side. That side would always be the side Eva wasn't on.

The best part was that Freddie didn't know they were coming. As far as she knew, her plan was still in motion. Police had appre-hended the final SUV before they'd had a chance to contact her. Freddie hadn't received word, so she most likely believed there was still a chance her side possessed the nuclear weapon. She was following the scheme through to the end, and that included being at the Palace when the bomb went off. Except it wouldn't.

Eva was going to enjoy this.

The car rolled up to the red-carpeted side entrance. A top-hatted doorman opened the car door and greeted Paul by name. The doorman must have been exceptionally well trained, as his face showed no sign of surprise when Eva alighted from the car.

Two hard-looking men in dark suits were there to greet them. Paul introduced them. One was an MI5 agent, the other a senior detective from Scotland Yard. The latter was the one who would do the actual arresting, as this was a domestic threat. The others were there so all agencies were present and nobody got their noses out of joint.

Paul excused himself and went to talk to a protocol steward. The MI5 agent and detective stood with hands clasped in front of their crotches, scanning the area unemotionally, like Terminators.

As she stood at the entrance to the world's most famous palace,

Eva did her best to ignore the sour looks from the guards and staff. *Screw you guys.* She wasn't here for them. She was here to ruin the day of the woman who had brought the world to the precipice of nuclear annihilation. The woman who had almost caused the deaths of tens of thousands of her own people, as well as the leaders of the most powerful nations on Earth. Eva could handle a few sideways glances. She had vengeance to dispense.

Paul clicked his fingers at her, and like that, they were in. The steward led the way, the MI5 agent and Scotland Yard detective followed. They entered a cavernous entrance, replete with lush red carpet, ornate gold-leaf filigree and chandeliers bigger than Eva's apartment. The opulence was staggering. She might ask who their decorator was, in case she ever needed to update her castle.

The steward wove through the various corridors effortlessly. Hands behind his back, Paul seemed overcome with quiet veneration. This was the guy Eva had once seen chug a can of Newcastle Brown to the tune of "Anarchy in the UK" while wearing a pink tutu. Eva chose not to mention that.

The steward glided to a halt at a set of huge baroque double doors. Wringing his hands together, he nervously advised that they'd arrived. The MI5 agent and detective visibly tensed.

Paul leaned over to Eva. "Wait here, Evie. We'll officially arrest her then bring her out here." He pouted, as if stifling a grin. "Unless you don't have anything to say to her?"

Eva cast an incredulous look. Paul held up his hands in surrender and gave her a wink.

"Give us a few minutes." He pulled at the base of his vest. "I will relish this."

Before Eva could say another word, the men disappeared behind the massive entrance, leaving her alone in the vast, over-elaborate hallway. If she were honest, Eva was pissed at not witnessing the moment Freddie's world came crumbling down around her ears. She'd just have to settle for seeing her face in the grim aftermath. Eva felt a warm tingle just thinking about it.

For a fleeting second she thought about how dead on her feet she was, but that was all she allowed herself. If she mused on it for too long she would collapse in a shattered heap on the floor, and some poor member of staff would have to sweep her up and throw her in the bin. The thought of the king putting out the bins in his dressing gown made Eva giggle, proof in itself that she was beyond exhausted. She hadn't slept properly since she'd left London for Macau, which seemed years ago. She needed rest. Eva needed to just stop the world for a moment. She closed her eyes and lapsed into a tiny micro-sleep while still standing.

When her eyes jolted open, she saw that further down the hall two people had emerged from a doorway and were deep in conversation. One was a middle-aged, balding white man in a blue suit. The other person Eva knew - well. Without a second thought, Eva stormed down the hallway. She was suddenly very awake.

Stabbing an accusatory finger in the air, Eva shouted, "Excuse me, may I have a fucking word, you festering puke-riddled dickpigeon?"

Freddie spun around in shock. Eva was the last person she'd expect to see in the stately surrounds of the palace. Her astonishment was so complete, Freddie's mouth flapped open as she stood there, dumbfounded.

Eva got up in her face. "Your little coup d'état is over," she spat. "Your false flag operation has fallen apart and you're going to be put away for the rest of your life you twatwaffle shit-eating cock-taco."

"Winifred, why is there an Australian swearing at you?"

For the first time Eva looked at the man. Up until that point she had completely ignored him. He was just another man in a suit. Except, he wasn't. He really should have been more familiar to Eva. After all, his face adorned all the coins in the land, and quite a few bank notes.

"Oh holy shitkittens."

Paul and his cohorts ran up to them in the hallway. The detective and MI5 agent hurriedly flashed their badges. Freddie gaped at Paul—he should have been locked up within the walls of MI6. Her eyes betrayed the fact that she knew the jig was up.

Freddie regained her composure and replicated the bombast of an offended senior government official. "Gentlemen, escort this woman out of here. She is a wanted criminal who has been disavowed by her former employer. There is an All Points on her person. Ensure she is arrested at once!"

The senior detective ignored her order. "Lady Kensington, you are charged with high treason under the Treason Act of 1351, as well as misprision of treason and compounding treason under the common law. You do not have to say anything but it may harm your defence if you do not mention—"

Freddie scoffed. "This is absurd!"

The detective pressed on, "—when questioned, something which you later rely on in court. Anything you do say may be given in evidence."

He presented handcuffs and proceeded to manacle the former Foreign Secretary.

Freddie wasn't giving up that easily. "Your Majesty, this is a farce. Please, I implore you, remove these people, they are obviously deluded. I can explain everything."

The king stepped back, curious as to what was happening, but on receiving a nod from his protocol steward, remained silent. A shake of his head sealed Freddie's fate. She would receive no aid from the Crown.

"Explain?" Eva clenched her fists. "What are you going to explain, Freddie? That you planned to kill the world leaders and start a nuclear war, you pissflap stained munter-loving shitnoodle?"

Paul leaned over and dipped his head towards his majesty. In a quiet voice, he said, "Evie, you should probably stop swearing now."

Eva looked over at the amused king and said, "I can't fucking seem to knobbing-well stop."

The king thankfully changed the subject without embarrassing Eva. He graciously introduced himself to Paul, the MI5 agent and the detective. He acted as though law enforcement entering his residence to arrest one of the most senior government officials was an everyday occurrence. Eva got the impression nothing could faze the monarch. He was the epitome of grace under pressure. Once the pleasantries were done, he turned to Eva.

"And to whom do I owe the pleasure?"

"Eva Destruction, your majesty." She wasn't sure if she should curtsey or offer a handshake. In the end, she gave an awkward version of both.

The king baulked slightly. "I'm sorry, I don't think one heard that correctly. Is that... is that really your name?"

"Yes, your majesty."

"Well," a genuine smile crossed the king's lips, "that's fucking fantastic."

CHAPTER TWENTY-FOUR

Eva slept for a full day. Paul had to walk her up to her apartment and let her in. The place was immaculate. Everything had been cleaned and put away. Eva asked if he'd hired a cleaning company. He told her he hadn't, he'd simply let his wife in to clean up. So, Nancy didn't hate her as much as she thought. When Eva was able to form a sentence she'd seek out her best friend and find out what the hell she'd done to piss her off so much. Later. First, sleep.

Eva hadn't even bothered to undress. She simply fell on her bed and slept. It wasn't until midday the next day that she was awoken by the sound of her phone ringing. She'd actually forgotten she had a landline. When she managed to clear the fug in her mind she found her answering machine. The red flashing display said she had twenty-seven messages. She listened to them all. Apart from a couple from Microsoft telling her she had a virus on a computer she didn't own, the rest were from Loch.

She didn't call him back straight away. First, she stepped into the shower and scrubbed herself clean. She could have remained there for another day. But she didn't. Partly because the hot water gave out, but mostly because she knew she had to talk to Loch. It wasn't going to be a fun talk.

The decision had been made long ago. Back in Salomons Estate. Since then, she'd done her best to filter it out. But now that Freddie had been taken into custody, reality was beginning to set in. She picked up the phone and dialled.

"Loch, we need to talk."

"I thought you said nothing good came of that phrase?" he said with a hint of trepidation.

"Yeah," she said, looking about her tidy apartment. "I know."

Twenty minutes later Loch sat opposite her on her couch, cradling a coffee she'd insisted he have. His apprehension was obvious. The fact that they were still clothed may have been a give-away of what was to come.

"So, you and me," she began. He didn't interrupt, letting her say what she had to say. "I've been playing catch up all this time, trying to be where you are with the relationship, and to be honest I don't know if I'll ever get there. Or should, for that matter."

That made him flinch. "What does that mean, or should?"

"Loch, you were lying to me for the majority of the time we were together. I don't know if I can reconcile that with how I feel about you. Trust is super important to me. You weren't truthful, you weren't honest when I needed you to be. I was flying blind, dude, and you lied to me. I need better than that. I deserve better. I've had deceit."

Her thoughts turned, as they often did, to Harry Lancing, her ex, the man who had blackmailed governments of the world to bend to his will. He had lied to her, repeatedly. She had promised herself she could do better than a deceitful megalomaniac. She was fussy like that.

"Loch, I've had someone not be who they said they were. It always seems to end with gun battles and explosions. I can't do that anymore. I need someone who tells me exactly what they're thinking, and is candid about what they're feeling from one moment to the next."

Loch gave a nervous chuckle. "Sounds like you should be dating Bishop."

Eva didn't answer straight away.

"To be honest, given my record, I'm pretty sure I should never date again. I'm sorry, Loch. I am. My heart is screaming at me right now."

"I'd say listen to your heart if it wasn't a Roxette song." He gave a weak smile.

"But it's high time I listened to my head. I've ignored it for too long. There's too much history here, between us, that I can't reconcile, and probably never will. I know it's not what you want to hear, and I know I'm going to regret it as soon as you walk out that door, but I have to take ownership of my life. I have to be able to trust the person I'm with. It's taken me a long time to get here, but I need what's best for me for the long haul, not what my heart wants right now. I'm sorry, Loch."

To his credit, there were no flung cups. No tantrums. No accusatory looks. Loch simply placed the coffee on the side table. He nodded and pulled his lips into a sad frown. In the quietest voice she'd ever heard him use, he said, "Okay, Chérie, okay."

Emotions playing out under the surface of his skin, it was obvious he was conflicted. He wanted to fight for her, to convince her this was wrong, that he wasn't the man she thought he was. But he didn't. Perhaps because he knew it was a fight he couldn't win. Her mind was made up. Eva Destruction was many things; stubborn was most definitely one of them.

He stood and kissed her forehead. "I will miss you, Chérie, always. There is no one like you in the universe, but I'll spend the rest of my days trying to find her."

With that he turned and headed for the door. His stoicism and respect almost made her waver, but she held strong.

"Loch, can you tell me one thing?" she said before he reached the door. "Why do you call me Chérie?"

Loch paused for a very long time. Eventually, he gave a slight shake of his head. "No, I don't think so. That was between me and Chérie. My Chérie, my Eva. I'd like to keep it that way if it's alright with you."

Eva bowed her head and said nothing further. She noticed Loch's hand shake as he reached for the door handle. The man was barely holding it together. But he was, for her. The familiar lump in the back of her throat made its presence felt. She swallowed it down.

The door closed quietly with a *click*. Eva stared at it for a long time, and all the while her heart screamed, *what have you done, you stupid bitch?* But she ignored it. She had to.

She collapsed into her couch, fighting off tears, but in the end they won the battle and burst forth. She cried for Loch. She cried for Yuji. She cried for Lekan. Eva didn't even try to stop. She needed to mourn those who had passed, those who had died because of her, those that she would never see again. As she sat alone in her apartment, the sound of a busy and oblivious London flowing around her, Eva cried for the first time in... well, she couldn't remember the last time she cried.

With a clean outfit and a splash of make-up, Eva felt like a million dollars. Australian dollars, but still.

SIS Headquarters was certainly more receptive to her arrival than it would have been a day earlier. She wasn't shot on sight, for one. There were a lot more high fives than she honestly thought was necessary. She wasn't really the high five type, but you never leave a brother hanging.

Vengeance had been swift for Freddie and her cohorts. So far, the former Foreign Secretary, the Chief of the General Staff, three of his assistants, two cabinet ministers, six senior members of MI6 and two from MI5 had all been arrested. The wrath had spread across the pond and three members of the CIA's senior staff had also been rounded up. One had tried to smuggle himself into Mexico, but had been apprehended at the border. Eva was sure there was more to come, but the tide had turned. The good guys had won.

She'd tracked down Bishop in his office. He sat at his desk with his back to the door, well-dressed and groomed once again. Only

Bishop could make sitting at a desk look sexy. He gazed out the window and must have caught her reflection in the glass.

"You know, when women sneak into my room, they're usually wearing sexy lingerie."

Eva smirked. "Who says I'm not?"

He turned and raised an eyebrow. "Touché."

It was good to have the old Bishop back. Not that she'd tell him that.

Bishop brought her up to speed. Loch had been given a leave of absence until his involvement in the whole affair could be clarified. Bishop, no friend of Loch's, was certain he would be acquitted, given his actions in extracting the bomb.

Bishop was in the midst of writing up the report on Lefty's interrogation. Grey's offsider had apparently sung like an inebriated accountant at a work karaoke function. He would turn king's evidence in exchange for leniency.

"Once the guy started talking he wouldn't stop. I think he realised after a while that he'd said too much, but by then it was too late."

"Like trying to put wine back into a bottle."

Bishop tilted his head. "You can get wine back in a bottle. You could use a funnel, or—"

"Wine does not go back in the bottle, Bishop!"

Bishop chuckled. "Of course."

They spoke for a few minutes until Eva told him she had an important task to carry out. Before she left, she said, "You and I will have a chat soon, Mister."

"Sounds ominous." He tilted his head. "It's rare to see you like this."

"Like what?"

"Vulnerable."

Could he see what was going on in her head? She hoped not. Nobody should be subjected to that. About to leave, Eva had one more question she urgently needed an answer to.

"Do you still have 'Greensleeves' in your head too?"

Bishop frowned. "Constantly."

She bid him farewell. Bypassing her own desk, Eva had another destination in mind. A very important one. It was tucked away in a tiny, unpopular corner of the Vauxhall Cross. Not all of the lights worked, either by design or neglect. She found him in an alcove, huddled over a computer. Of course he was.

"Hey, Trev."

He jumped out of his chair as if it was spring loaded. "Eva!" His voice broke, it was endearing. "I thought they'd give you the month off."

"They tried to, but there are a lot of loose ends that need clipping."

Trevor bobbed his head as if he had nothing else to say. His puppy dog eyes would be plain to anyone within a two-mile radius.

"And Trev?" Eva said. Before he could answer, she scooped him up in a huge hug. He let out a tiny sigh. "Thank you for saving the world. The country owes you a big one—huge." She released him. His face was practically glowing. "I've spoken to Paul, you're getting a promotion. A big one. But more importantly, MI6 are going to pick up the tab for the biggest blast out on the town next time a cool Aussie band is in London. I think Violent Soho are coming next month."

"That," he said, keeping his excitement in check, "would be amazing."

"No hanky panky, though, right?" Eva said sternly, but with enough humour as to not offend.

He nodded, most likely hoping she didn't mean it. She'd do her best to hook him up with someone who would blow his geeky little mind. The kid had earned it. Without him they wouldn't have succeeded. He had single-handedly saved tens of thousands of lives. Regardless of what had motivated him, he deserved recognition and reward. And at least a couple of lap dances.

Eva stayed with him for over an hour, regaling him with her side of the story. For much of it his mouth was agape, having had no idea that while he delved into computer code and old dusty files, firefights and explosions were happening around the world.

As she finished up, Trev pointed at the PC.

"It's a computer, Trev. I've seen them before."

For the first time, Trev's face turned grave. "Like I kept telling you, there's something you need to see."

He clicked on a file and handed her a pair of headphones. Trevor gave her his seat. In return, Eva gave him a curious look.

"It's from Lady Kensington's files. It was one that wasn't encrypted. Best I can tell it was swiped from your phone before your..." he tapped the side of his head. "Looks like they erased it before you knew it was there. I—" he hesitated. "I think you'd better sit down. I'll leave you alone."

He did just that. She tentatively clicked on the file he had high-lighted. It was a video file. She pressed play. A beaming face grinned back at her.

"Hey Eva," said the smiling face. "It's me... Eva."

She appeared to be in a toilet cubicle, or a very confined space. Her voice was hushed. She looked well, far better than Eva was currently. There was an urgency in her voice that Eva recognised. She was in danger, and she knew it.

"I don't have much time, you've just come back from Macau and shit is all kinds of messed up. There are things you need to know before they wipe your memory. Oh wait, yeah, they're going to wipe your memory." There was a pause. "But you probably know that if you're watching this. Shit. Sorry, this has all happened so quick. Okay." She blew out a breath. "Right. Newsflash, Freddie is a fucking lunatic. I don't know what she's got planned, but it's not good. She tried to convince me to give up where I sent the nuke, but the more she talked, the more I know I did the right thing. She's dodgy as, Eva, dodgy as fuck. Don't you dare give her the nuke. Shove it up your own arse if you have to, but do not trust Freddie, no matter what she says.

"If they do take months from us, there are other things you need to know. First, investigate Freddie. The way she was talking she's planning a goddamn new world order. She's talking about sacrificing lives for the greater good. That's not something we want a part of. Fight her, Eva, take her down."

Eva smiled at her doppelganger on the screen. She'd done exactly what past Eva had wanted. If only she'd had this video when she'd first woken up, life could have been a lot easier.

On screen, Eva continued. "I heard them talk about carving out a couple of months from your, our, brain. I could be a vegetable after all this, who fucking knows. Hence," she waved to the camera. "One hugely important thing," she sighed. Eva knew that forlorn look, it was a replica of the look Trev gave her. "You love Loch Davenport, oh my god how you love him." On-screen Eva almost shone. "And he loves you, you stupid messed-up bitch. Trust him with your life. I highly suspect he's been working for them, but he's doing it to protect you. He's risking his career and his life for you. Despite all your many many *many* faults and all the logical arguments against it, he loves you, his Chérie. Do everything you can to love him back, my god, the man is worth it."

On screen, Eva's face lit up like a fireworks factory fire. It was the real deal. Eva couldn't fake that level of contentment, of adoration, of joy. She had fallen for Loch, and hard. This was despite knowing he was working for Freddie. Despite all her flaws.

"I don't know if he can keep it to himself or not, but trust him, Eva, your life may depend on it. Knowing they will wipe my life away like this, wiping him away, is unbearable. I love him, *you* love him, but in a few minutes, it's going to be gone. Every experience you've forged together, every beautiful memory we've made will simply be deleted. Giving your life for a cause is one thing, we've almost done that so many times, but this—" she sniffed, emotion getting the better of her, "—this is harder, so much harder. They're stealing my happiness, your happiness. They're taking the reason I get out of bed in the morning, the man who can make me laugh at the mere thought of him. They're taking the best part of me, and you know what? It fucking sucks." She wiped away a tear and held it up to the camera. "We don't cry, do we? You and me, we're made of tougher stuff. No man's going to make us cry, right?" On screen, she contemplated the tear at the end of her finger. "Well, that's just further proof that you know bugger all, Eva Destruction."

Looking at the screen, Eva realised that her tears after Loch had left her apartment earlier weren't the only time she'd cried for him.

On the video Eva heard the rattle of a doorknob, then Freddie's voice came through clearly. "You alright in there, my love?" In a low voice, the Eva on screen said, "Got to go. Bye Eva, be kind to yourself, oh, and for god's sake, tell Nancy you're sorry about the fish!"

The screen went blank.

Glue-sniffing tit warblers.

She stared at the screen for a long time.

The Eva in the video wasn't Eva. It was some strange alternate reality Eva. A reality where Eva was happy and in love. A reality where she had met a man, and despite their collective flaws had fallen deeply in love with him. But that wasn't Eva's reality. Not her memories. Not her circus, not her monkeys.

It made Loch's noble departure even more honourable. She had truly loved him, and he her. And yet, he had wilfully walked away when she asked him to. He loved her that much. Did that change anything? Had she royally screwed up by telling Loch she couldn't be with him? The other Eva certainly seemed to think so.

Eva needed to take a walk.

The River Thames looked the same as always. So did Westminster. So did the London Eye. It was Eva that had changed. As she strode along the bank, a million thoughts bombarded her. The clear blue sky was in direct contrast to her clouded mind.

Did the video change anything? Everything? Should it? It certainly confirmed a lot of things. Complicated them, too. When she said goodbye to Loch, it was with the confidence that her logic was sound, despite the screams of protest from her heart. Now everything was muddled. Did Past Eva have all the facts, or just some of them? What should she do now?

Her thoughts were a jumble. Bishop was in there too. Of course he was. The man who was completely wrong for her loomed large in her mind, giving her a mischievous grin.

The further she walked, the clearer things became. In part, because she let her emotions have a vote—usually an unwise move for her.

After half an hour she'd reached Hyde Park. The beauty of the green surrounds had somehow cleared her head. She had her decision. Only time would tell if it was the right one.

She pulled out her new phone to call him. She knew he'd answer. But before she selected the contact, her phone rang. It was a blocked number. Reluctantly, she answered.

"Hello?"

"Hello, Eva."

She knew the voice. Intimately. She was too shocked to answer.

"Miss me?"

"No." Her voice was a block of ice.

The man who had put her through so much. The man who had tormented her dreams for years. The man who had bought her a castle.

"How can you be so calm when your pants are on fire?" he asked.

Eva ground her teeth. This man was the last person she wanted to speak to. He had used his technology empire to stick his digital fingers in everyone's pie. He had manipulated governments and corporations and tried to reshape the world as he saw fit.

"Aren't you meant to be in a deep hole somewhere, Harry?"

"Me? No, you must have me confused with someone else." The casualness grated on her.

"What do you want, Harry?"

"To hear you say you miss me too."

"Not going to happen."

"Then I'm upset."

"Diddums."

Eva stepped onto Bayswater Road, home to many embassies and upmarket eateries. She looked at the city of London, her city, and tried to calm herself.

Just as she managed a measured breath, the Russian embassy exploded, engulfed in a fireball. The orange and black of the explosion was in direct contrast to the stark blue sky. A second explosion blew out windows. Billowing black clouds belched from the huge building.

Eva staggered towards the chaos, phone pressed against her ear. Harry was still on the line. When he spoke, his voice was flat and emotionless.

"We need to talk."

The End

SPECIAL OFFERS

Want special offers, heads up on new Eva Destruction stories and free stuff (who doesn't like free stuff?), you can sign up for my VIP Book Club -
https://davesinclair.com.au/newsletter/

THE ROOKIE'S GUIDE TO ESPIONAGE

Did you wonder what happened to Eva in Vienna? Wonder no more!

Eva's next adventure – The Rookie's Guide to Espionage: An Eva Destruction Espresso Shot!

A rookie spy. Europe on a knife edge. A distinct lack of coffee.

Eva Destruction is back in her first ever assignment. Straight out of the MI6 academy, Eva is on the trail of a supposedly dead fellow agent. It's a nothing assignment given to a rookie, but when suicide bombers hit a NATO conference the mission is kicked into high gear.

Eva chases a carnage of gunfire and explosions across Europe in search of the mysterious shadowy organization, 'The Tempest'. *The Rookie's Guide to Espionage* is a high-octane thrill ride that will keep you guessing until the very last page.

Pick up your copy today!
https://davesinclair.com.au/books/the-rookies-guide-to-espionage/

ACKNOWLEDGMENTS

I've heard that writing a second book in a series is harder than the first. Don't believe them! I had an absolute blast bringing Eva back for her second adventure – I hope it translated to the page. Jumping back into the world of Eva Destruction was as comfortable as slipping on an old pair of jeans. There will be plenty more Eva adventures to come!

Despite some significant personal upheavals in the last twelve months I managed to get words on the page. That was largely due to a group of friends called the G-Mob, all great writers and completely crazy individuals. Craig, Justin, Luke, Nathan, Steve, Amanda and Amanda have provided support, guidance, wisdom and laughs when I needed them the most. Plus they know all the best bars. Also, I stole every word of Chapter Twelve from Luke Preston. Go read their stuff! genremob.com

Thanks goes to my sister Alli, a fantastic writer who has far more books out than I do and has now been translated into German and Klingon (one of those may not be 100% accurate). allisinclairauthor.wordpress.com

My editor Vanessa Lanaway has my deep gratitude for making my words gooder and making sure I had no spelling mistooks.

Big hugs to my two awesome and amazing daughters, Quinn and Esther. I'm doing my best to ensure they grow up as fearless as Eva, but maybe not as sweary.

And a big thank you goes to Kristi who inspires me every day, makes me laugh even more and supports me unconditionally in this peculiar writing life I've chosen. Monkey heart unicorn.

And finally (well done for hanging on this long!) a HUGE thanks to you, the reader. I'm constantly surprised that folks find my books and pleasantly amazed when they enjoy them. Feel free to say hi or drop a review (always welcome) and hope you'll keep reading about Eva Destruction and her penchant for really loud explosions.

Cheers!

ABOUT DAVE SINCLAIR

Dave Sinclair is a novelist, a screenwriter and a really excellent parallel parker.

He lives in Melbourne, Australia with his two crazy daughters. He's also an award-winning filmmaker, a title that sounds far more impressive than it really is. He won a best comedy screenplay and cinematography award for a short film he wrote and directed, though at the time he didn't really know what cinematography was. A completed screenplay is currently doing the rounds.

Dave's overflowing bookshelves include many works by Douglas Adams, P.G. Wodehouse, Dashiell Hammett, Raymond Chandler, Janet Evanovich, Ian Fleming, Zadie Smith and John le Carré.

The Eva Destruction books are stories Dave wanted to read, full of action, laughs and fascinating characters. Eva has many more adventures up her tattooed sleeves.

To find out more, you can stalk Dave at his semi-reputable website:
https://davesinclair.com.au